Looking FOR A Miracle

Looking FOR A Miracle

Brides of Lancaster County

2

Wanda E. Brunstetter

BARBOUR
PUBLISHING

For more information about Wanda E. Brunstetter, please access the author's Web site at the following Internet address: www.wandabrunstetter.com

Cover designed by Greg Jackson, Thinkpen Design LLC, www.thinkpendesign.com

Published by Barbour Publishing, Inc., P.O. Box 719, Uhrichsville, Ohio 44683, www.barbourbooks.com

Our mission is to publish and distribute inspirational products offering exceptional value and biblical encouragement to the masses.

Member of the
Evangelical Christian
Publishers Association

Printed in the United States of America.
5 4 3 2 1

ABOUT THE AUTHOR

Wanda E. Brunstetter enjoys writing about the Amish because they live a peaceful, simple life. Wanda's interest in the Amish and other Plain communities began when she married her husband, Richard, who grew up in a Mennonite church in Pennsylvania. Wanda has made numerous trips to Lancaster County and has several friends and family members living near that area. She and her husband have also traveled to other parts of the country, meeting various Amish families and getting to know them personally. She hopes her readers will learn to love the wonderful Amish people as much as she does.

Wanda and her husband, Richard, have been married forty-three years. They have two grown children and six grandchildren. In her spare time, Wanda enjoys reading, ventriloquism, gardening, stamping, and having fun with her family.

Wanda has written several novels, novellas, stories, articles, poems, and puppet scripts.

To learn more about Wanda, visit her Web site at www.wandabrunstetter.com and feel free to e-mail her at wanda@wandabrunstetter.com.

To my six wunderbaar *grandchildren,*
Jinell, Madolynne, Rebekah, Ric, Philip, and Richelle.
You are each one of God's special miracles.

Commit thy way unto the LORD; *trust also in him;*
and he shall bring it to pass.
PSALM 37:5

Rebekah Stoltzfus sat on the sidelines in her wheelchair, watching with envy as the others who had come to the young people's singing played a game of volleyball.

Sixteen-year-old Harold Beachy zipped past Rebekah, nearly bumping into her wheelchair. "Oops, sorry."

Rebekah opened her mouth to reply, but Harold had already raced to the other side of the volleyball net to join the game. She sighed. "What's the use? No one seems to know I'm here anyway."

Self-pity was a common occurrence for Rebekah these days, as she struggled to deal with her insecurities and envy of others who could do all the things she couldn't do. Take her cousin, Mary Ellen Hilty, for example. Mary Ellen had lots of suitors and could probably have her pick of any of the young men if she wanted.

Rebekah and Mary Ellen had become cousins by marriage when Mary Ellen's father, Amos, had married Rebekah's aunt Miriam. The young girls had been friends before that, but after the joining of their families, they had become even closer, despite the fact that they were nothing alike.

Mary Ellen had dark brown hair and hazel-colored eyes, while Rebekah had light brown hair and pale blue eyes.

Mary Ellen, who had been teaching at the Amish one-room schoolhouse for the last year, was fun loving, self-assured, and outgoing, which was probably why all the young men admired her. Rebekah, on the other hand, was quiet, self-conscious, and certain that no one except her family could possibly love her. She lacked the confidence seen in most young women her age.

Rebekah hadn't always been shy, however. In fact, when she was a little girl, she used to be as outgoing as Mary Ellen was now. But thirteen years ago, everything had changed when a freak accident left her crippled.

Rebekah still remembered the details of the accident as though it had happened yesterday. A storm had come up just as Aunt Mim, who'd been the schoolteacher back then, had dismissed the class to go home after school ended for the day. Aunt Mim had promised to give Rebekah a ride home, and Rebekah had gone outside to wait in the buggy while Aunt Mim finished cleaning the blackboard. Rebekah had just reached the buggy, which had been parked under a tree, when she heard a terrible snap and was knocked to the ground.

The next thing she knew, she was in the hospital with doctors and nurses standing over her bed, looking ever so serious. Her distraught parents stood nearby, and Mom was weeping for all she was worth. When Rebekah had asked what was wrong, she'd been informed that a branch had broken from the tree and fallen across her back, knocking her unconscious. The blow had injured part of her spinal cord, and she would probably never walk again.

The reality didn't truly sink in until one month later when Rebekah was allowed to go home. It was then that she'd come to realize exactly what her limitations would be. She would be confined to a wheelchair, unable to walk, run, and play the way other children could do. Her grandmother Anna Stoltzfus had moved into their house in order to help care for Rebekah. That gave Rebekah a clue that she would always be a burden to those she loved. She would never be able to live a normal life—never marry, never have children of her own.

"Are you havin' fun?"

Rebekah's thoughts came to a halt when Emma Troyer skidded to a stop in front of her wheelchair, red-faced and panting for breath.

How can I have fun while I sit here on the sidelines watching you and the others play games? Rebekah kept her thoughts to herself and nodded in reply. After so many years of being left out of things, she had come to realize that there was no use in complaining, as it would do nothing to change her condition. She'd learned to suffer in silence and put on a brave front as though her handicap didn't matter. Trouble was it did matter because it singled her out as being different from the rest of her family and friends.

"We should be eating soon," Emma said, nodding toward the refreshment table.

"*Jah*, I expect so."

"Well, guess I'll go see if I can get in on the next game of volleyball." Emma patted Rebekah's shoulder, offering her a sympathetic-looking smile; then she hurried away.

Rebekah hated to see pity on anyone's face. It wasn't

their sympathy or pity she wanted. What she needed was a miracle. Some said she'd already had one miracle. Leastways, that's what everyone had called it when, after several months of physical therapy, Rebekah had been able to stand and even take a few steps on her own. Of course, in order to do it, she needed leg braces and a pair of special crutches strapped to her arms. Some miracle that was! It took a lot of effort to walk that way, so Rebekah spent most of her time in her wheelchair. One of the few things she did that she would consider useful was the monthly column she wrote for *The Budget*, an Amish newspaper. As one of the scribes for the paper, she often wrote about some of the major happenings in their area of Lancaster County, but that was nothing compared to what other people her age got to do.

Rebekah caught sight of Mary Ellen running through the tall grass across the yard with several young fellows right on her heels. Mary Ellen lifted her hand in a wave, and Rebekah waved back, wishing that she, too, could run through the grass with even one suitor following her.

It was obvious by the smile on Mary Ellen's face that she enjoyed all the attention she'd received this evening. And why wouldn't she? Rebekah was sure that any woman who had so many men interested in her would take pleasure in it, too.

She swallowed past the lump in her throat and squeezed her eyes shut, willing herself not to give in to the threatening tears. Crying wouldn't do her a bit of good.

Rebekah opened her eyes and wheeled herself back to the barn. She spotted the refreshment table inside the door and headed over to get something cool to drink, hoping it might help wash away that awful, familiar lump.

"Want some punch?"

Rebekah jerked her head to the right. There stood Daniel Beachy, one of the young men she had seen talking to Mary Ellen earlier this evening. "*Danki*, but I can get it," she muttered. "It's one of the few things I can do by myself."

"It's no bother. I was about to get something for myself anyway." Daniel ladled some punch into a paper cup, then handed it to Rebekah in spite of her refusal. "So, are you enjoying the singing?"

Rebekah smiled as she took the offered punch. "It's all right, but I wish we could do more singing and less game playing."

"Volleyball's a lot of fun, though."

Rebekah wondered if she should explain that the reason she enjoyed singing was because it was all she could do well. Game playing, at least the kind that required running and jumping, was out of the question for someone like her. However, she never got the chance to express those thoughts because Mary Ellen showed up.

"Rebekah, you should have heard some of the silly jokes Johnny Yoder told me," Mary Ellen said breathlessly. "I've laughed so much tonight, I don't think I'll have to laugh again for the rest of the month."

Rebekah feigned a smile as Mary Ellen related a couple of the jokes Johnny had shared. Her cousin's cheeks were bright pink, and her eyes shone with obvious enthusiasm. No wonder so many of the young Amish men wanted to court her. Rebekah couldn't be mad at Mary Ellen, though. It wasn't her fault she was so cute and such fun to be around. If Rebekah had been able to join in the games, maybe others would like her more, too. Some of the boys might want to court her if she could run, jump, and laugh at their silly jokes.

Mary Ellen leaned over Rebekah's wheelchair and whispered in her ear, "Johnny's asked if he can give me a ride home in his courting buggy tonight. You don't care if I go with him, do you?"

"But you came with me and Simon."

"I know, but I'm sure your brother won't mind not having to drive me home." Mary Ellen smiled. "After all, he has to go to the same place as you're going, and if I go with Johnny, then Simon won't have to travel clear over to my house."

"Jah, sure. Go ahead and ride with Johnny." Rebekah wasn't about to make a fuss over Mary Ellen riding home with someone else. She might appear to be jealous.

She glanced over at Daniel. Was that a look of envy she saw as he shifted from one foot to the other and stared at the concrete floor? Maybe he'd been waiting for the chance to ask Mary Ellen if he could give her a ride home and was disappointed because now he wouldn't get that opportunity. If Daniel hadn't wasted so much time getting punch for Rebekah, he might have been able to seek Mary Ellen out. Then it would be his courting buggy she would be riding home in tonight, not Johnny Yoder's.

Why do I always feel so guilty about things? Rebekah fretted. After all, it wasn't as if she had asked Daniel to get her some punch or kept him here on purpose. She hadn't intentionally spoiled his chances with Mary Ellen. He should have realized he was missing out on his chance and gone looking for the girl he wanted to escort home.

Rebekah tried to shake aside her contrary feelings as she said in her most cheerful voice, "I'm getting kind of tired, so I think I'll go find Simon and see if he's ready to head for home."

"Johnny and I will be leaving soon, too, I expect," Mary Ellen said with a nod. "Probably after we've had something to eat."

"I'd better see when my sister, Sarah Jane, wants to go. My two brothers will probably have dates to take home." Daniel glanced down at Rebekah and smiled. It was the kind of smile she'd become used to seeing—one of pity, she was certain of it. "*Gut nacht*, Rebekah." He looked over at her cousin and nodded. "Gut nacht, Mary Ellen."

"Good night," Rebekah and Mary Ellen said in unison.

As Daniel walked away, Mary Ellen leaned close to Rebekah's ear again. "He's kind of *gutguckich*, don't you think?"

If you think he's so handsome, then why aren't you riding home with him instead of Johnny? "He seems to like you," Rebekah muttered.

Just then, Johnny rushed up to Mary Ellen and grabbed hold of her hand. "Come on. Let's play one more game of volleyball before we eat, and then we'll head for home."

"All right, Johnny." Mary Ellen gave Rebekah's arm a little pat. "See you in two weeks at preaching, if not before."

"Jah," Rebekah murmured as she wheeled away in search of Simon.

As Mary Ellen walked away with Johnny, she couldn't help

but feel sorry for her best friend. She could tell by the dejected look she had seen on Rebekah's face that her friend was upset—probably because Mary Ellen wouldn't be riding home with her and Simon. As much as Mary Ellen wanted to please her cousin, she didn't want to give up the chance to ride home with Johnny tonight, knowing it could be the beginning of their courting days. At least she hoped it would be because Johnny was a lot of fun, and she really enjoyed his company.

Johnny squeezed Mary Ellen's fingers. "What's with the sour expression? I thought you enjoyed playing volleyball."

"I—I do. I was just noticing how glum Rebekah looks tonight, and I'm concerned about her."

"Ah, she always looks that way. How does she ever expect to get a man if she goes around lookin' like she's been suckin' a bunch of sour grapes all the time?" Johnny offered Mary Ellen a wide grin. "Sure am glad my girl likes to laugh and smile."

My girl? Did Johnny really think of Mary Ellen as his girl? Or was he only flirting with her the way so many of the other fellows had done tonight?

Mary Ellen thought back to the days when she'd been a young girl attending the one-room schoolhouse. None of the boys had showed any interest in her then—except to tease and taunt. Her *mamm* had died when Mary Ellen was still quite young, and many students had teased her due to her unkempt appearance.

But all that had changed after Pappy married Mama Mim. From that time on, Mary Ellen's dresses were mended and her hair put neatly in place. She'd felt a new sense of confidence, having both a mother and a father. Mama Mim had always taken good care of her, and Mary Ellen felt as though Pappy's new wife loved her as much as if she were her own flesh-and-blood daughter.

Now, as a young woman, Mary Ellen not only had more confidence, but she also taught at the one-room school-house she had once attended. She had a host of male admirers like Johnny, who seemed determined to win her affections. She just wished that at least one of those fellows would notice Rebekah. It might help her smile more if she knew someone had an interest in her, and it would surely boost her confidence.

"Are you gonna stand there all night watchin' the back-side of Rebekah's wheelchair, or did you plan to play volley-ball with me?" Johnny asked, breaking into Mary Ellen's contemplations.

She forced her lips to form a smile, knowing she needed to put on a happy face if she was going to keep fun-loving Johnny's attention. "Jah. I'm ready to play."

Rebekah's sixteen-year-old brother, Simon, pushed her wheel-chair up the wooden ramp Dad had built soon after her accident, and they entered the house through the back door. Rebekah spotted her parents right away, sitting at the kitchen table, playing a game of Scrabble.

Dad didn't seem to notice them as he tugged on his beard and studied the wooden letters on the tray in front of him.

However, Mom looked up right away and smiled. Her

eyes, much bluer and brighter than Rebekah's, seemed to dance in the light of the gas lantern that hung above the table. "Sit yourselves down and talk awhile. Tell us about the singing. Did you two have a good time?"

"Jah, it was great!" Simon pushed a lock of sandy brown hair off his forehead. "Just about every Amish teen we know was there." He opened the door of their propane-operated refrigerator, obviously looking for something to eat.

"And you, daughter?" Mom asked. "Did you have a good time?"

Rebekah shrugged. "It was all right, I guess."

"Just all right? It's been a good many years for me now, but as I remember, singings were always a lot of fun." Mom glanced over at Dad, who was still studying the Scrabble board as if his life depended on the next move. "It was right after a singing when your *daed* asked me to marry him, you know."

"Jah, well, I expect our family might be in for another wedding soon," Simon said, as he helped himself to a thick slice of apple-crumb pie and took a seat at the table.

Mom's eyebrows lifted. "Is there something you've been keeping from us, Rebekah? *Kumme*—come now—tell us your news."

Rebekah wheeled her chair closer to the table. "It's not me. I think Simon's referring to Cousin Mary Ellen."

"I see. So who's her lucky fellow?" Mom prompted. "Or aren't we supposed to know that yet?"

"It could be anyone. Mary Ellen's popular with several young men in our community. She can probably take her pick of whomever she pleases." Rebekah drew in a quick breath and released it with a moan. "I think Daniel Beachy is the one most in love with her, but Johnny Yoder won't give him a chance."

"Hmm. . ." Mom gave a slight nod of her head. "It sounds as if Mary Ellen might have to make a choice then."

"She'll pick Johnny," Simon said with his mouth full of pie.

"Really, Simon, didn't you get enough food at the singing? Sometimes I think all you ever do is eat," Mom scolded, though she was smiling when she spoke.

"Aw, leave the boy alone, Sarah. He's growin' so fast these days and needs all the nourishment he can get." It was the first time Rebekah's father had spoken since their arrival. Suddenly, he slapped the table and hollered, "My word is *zealot*! The *z*, which is normally worth ten points, is on a double letter square. The other letters are worth one point apiece. The *l* lands on a double word square, so my entire score is fifty!" He gave Mom a playful nudge on the arm. "I have only one letter left, so beat that if you can!"

Mom laughed and tickled Dad beneath his full beard, which had recently become sprinkled with a few gray hairs. "All right, Andrew, you've won the game fair and square, so now you're deserving of a reward. How about a piece of pie? If your growing son hasn't eaten it all, that is," she added with a wink.

"You two act like a couple of *kinner*," Rebekah said with a mock frown. "Watch out now, or you'll end up waking Nadine and Grandma Stoltzfus."

Dad chuckled. "Well now, we wouldn't want to do that, would we? Grandma might eat all the pie before any of us could make it to the refrigerator."

"Dad," Rebekah said with a snicker. "You know Grandma doesn't eat so much."

Dad bent down and tapped her under the chin. "That's true, but if Simon or little sister Nadine should decide to help her, then I might have to take on a second job just to pay for the grocery bills."

"You're such a tease," Rebekah said, as she propelled her chair quickly away from him.

"You're right, I am. That's why your mamm agreed to marry me. She loves to be teased." He turned his attentions on Mom again, tickling her in the ribs and under the chin.

She tickled him right back, and soon the two of them were howling and tickling so much that Rebekah was sure they really would wake Grandma or Nadine.

As Mom and Dad chased each other around the table, a pang of jealousy washed over Rebekah like the rippling creek running across the back of their farm. She couldn't help wondering how it would feel to laugh and run around with a young man—someone she loved as much as her folks obviously loved each other. *But that would take a miracle, and miracles only happened back in the Bible days, didn't they?*

A silent prayer for an honest-to-goodness miracle floated through Rebekah's mind as she directed her wheelchair toward her downstairs bedroom. What she really needed was to quit thinking about miracles and be alone for a while.

"I wonder what's wrong with Rebekah tonight," Andrew said to Sarah as they started another game of Scrabble. He squinted at the board and reached for two letters from his pile. "She sure didn't act like she enjoyed that singing so much."

"She didn't enjoy it at all," Simon chimed in before Sarah could respond. "You should have seen the way she sat there in her wheelchair watching the others play games with a big old scowl on her face. Guess she felt left out because she couldn't join in the fun, but I don't think that's any excuse for being such a stick-in-the-mud."

Sarah glanced over at Andrew. "I hate to see our daughter hurting so. Maybe it would be best if we didn't allow her to go to any more singings or young people's functions."

Andrew's eyebrows lowered as he frowned, causing deep wrinkles to form on his forehead. "We can't shield Rebekah from everything, Sarah. She's not a little girl anymore, and she needs to mingle with others her age, don't you think?"

"I—I suppose so, but—"

"It's time for her to grow up and realize that even though she can't do everything others can do, she's still a capable person and can do many things quite well." He added two of his letters to a word already on the Scrabble board, which gave him another ten points.

Sarah took her turn, making a five-letter word and racking up fifteen more points.

Simon chuckled. "You'd better watch out, Dad, or Mom might skunk ya on this game."

"Not if I can help it."

"Back to the subject of my moody sister," Simon said. "I read in the paper the other day that there's going to be a convention in Ohio next month. It's for Amish folks who are handicapped, like Rebekah. Maybe the two of you could hire a driver and take her there. That would give her the chance to be with some people she could relate to better, and maybe she'd even learn a few new things about how to cope with her disability."

Sarah opened her mouth to comment, but Simon rushed on before she could get a word out. "If you're worried about Grandma, Nadine, and me, I'm sure we can get along fine by ourselves for the couple of days you'd be gone."

Andrew squinted as he continued to study the board. "I read about that handicap convention, too, but I'm not sure I could get away from the farm that long, so your mamm might have to be the one to take her." He glanced up from the board and looked over at Sarah. "How do you feel about it? Do you think Rebekah would agree to go?"

"I don't know. I suppose we could ask her."

"You want to bring it up, or should I?"

"I'll mention it tomorrow," Sarah replied. "In the meantime, I'll be praying that she will be open to the idea."

Andrew nodded. "I'll do the same."

All the way home from the singing, Daniel thought about Rebekah—how cute she was, how sad she had looked sitting in her wheelchair all alone.

"It must be hard for her not being able to run around and play games like the other young people do," he muttered as he guided his horse and open carriage up the long driveway that led to his father's house and dairy farm. He had enjoyed his brief conversation with Rebekah tonight, even though she hadn't said all that much. He wished he'd been able to get up the nerve to ask if he could give her a ride home from the singing in his courting buggy.

Daniel pulled up to the barn and climbed down from the buggy. " 'Course it ain't likely that she'd have agreed to go," he mumbled as he kicked a couple of small stones with the toe of his boot. After all, there had been a lot more interesting fellows at the singing tonight than him—some with fancy buggies they'd fixed up to impress the girls, some with fun-loving personalities like Johnny Yoder. "Wish I could be more like him instead of being afraid I'll say the wrong thing or do something stupid."

He quickly unhitched his horse and led him toward the barn as a feeling of regret threatened to weigh him down. "Even if I had found the nerve to ask if Rebekah would take a ride in my rig, it ain't likely she would have been interested in riding home in my simple courting buggy with an ordinary fellow like me."

When Rebekah awoke the following morning, she felt physically drained and out of sorts. She had lain awake for hours, thinking about her disability and all the restrictions she had to deal with. She wondered if there was some way she could possibly fit in with the other young people her age. Since she wasn't able to join most of their activities, she couldn't really blame them for ignoring her, but it hurt, nonetheless. She seemed to be more accepted by older people—especially Grandma. Maybe it was because Grandma couldn't do as much as the younger ones did. Most of her activities, though not as restricted as Rebekah's, were still a bit hampered.

Rebekah knew her parents and grandmother loved her and were dedicated to taking care of her needs, but she worried about what would become of her when they were gone. Would her younger brother or sister, or maybe a cousin or niece, be stuck caring for her? She didn't want to be a burden to anyone and wished there was some way she could provide for her own needs.

Rebekah pulled herself to an upright position, using the

wooden side rails on her bed to lend the needed support. *I know I'll never have a husband or children of my own, but if I could at least be financially independent, I would be less of a burden to everyone.*

Unbidden tears slipped out of Rebekah's eyes, rolling down her cheeks in little rivulets. What could one crippled young Amish woman do that would provide her with enough money to care for herself? Was it even possible, or was it just wishful thinking?

"I think what I need to do is commit this problem to prayer," she whispered. "Jah, that's what Grandma would say I should do."

Closing her eyes, Rebekah sent up a silent petition to God. *Heavenly Father, what I need is a miracle. If You still perform miracles, could You please give me some kind of a sign? I know I've done nothing to deserve a miracle, and I'm not asking You to heal my crippled body or give me a husband. I only want to support myself, so I'm not such a burden to my family. If You could show me how to do that, I'd be much obliged. Amen.*

Silence filled Rebekah's small, unadorned bedroom. Had she really expected God to answer her out loud? Hadn't the bishop and other ministers in their church shared some scripture verses proving that God talked to people's hearts? Sometimes He spoke through other believers or from His Holy Word. Rebekah had read herself how God had spoken out loud to some people in the Bible, but she figured they probably needed that type of thing back then. If there was any hope of her receiving a miracle, she felt it would only occur if she learned more patience, read her Bible regularly, and prayed every day.

As Rebekah wheeled into the kitchen, Sarah turned from the stove where she had been frying a slab of bacon. "*Guder mariye*, daughter," she said with a smile. She hoped after a good night's sleep Rebekah might be in a more cheerful mood.

"Good morning," Rebekah mumbled.

"Did you sleep well?"

"I slept okay."

Sarah could see by the solemn expression on her daughter's face that she still wasn't in the best of moods. Maybe now wasn't a good time to bring up the subject of the handicap convention. It might be better to wait until after they had eaten breakfast to talk about the possibility of the two of them going to Ohio. Maybe Rebekah would be in a better mood once her stomach was full of bacon and eggs.

Rebekah wheeled into the middle of the room and glanced around. "Where's Grandma? She's usually the first one to the kitchen every morning."

"Still in bed. When I came into the kitchen and realized she wasn't here, I went in to check on her."

"Is she all right?"

"Said she wasn't feeling well, so I told her we could manage and insisted that she stay in bed and rest awhile."

"She seemed to be feeling all right yesterday evening before Simon and I left for the singing." Rebekah's lips puckered as her forehead wrinkled with obvious concern. "Sure hope it's nothing serious."

Sarah flipped the bacon over in the frying pan. "She's

been a little tired the past few days, but other than that, she's made no complaints until this morning. I think sometimes she tries to do too much for a woman her age."

Rebekah nodded. "I know she does. Ever since Grandma came to live here, she's done the work of two women. It wonders me so how she can keep up like she does."

"Jah, but in the beginning, I think keeping busy helped her not miss Grandpa so much, and now she's just developed a habit of always being on the move."

"It was nice that Aunt Mim and Uncle Amos named their son Henry, after Grandpa Stoltzfus," Rebekah said, changing the subject.

"I know it meant a lot to Grandma at the time, and even now, whenever young Henry's around, I believe she thinks of your *grossdaddi*."

"Jah. She's often said that in many ways Henry reminds her of Grandpa." Rebekah glanced at Grandma's bedroom door, which was just across the hall and right next to her own room. "Do you think maybe she should see the doctor?"

"If she's not up and around and acting like her old self by this afternoon, I'll speak to your daed and see that he takes her to see Dr. Manney."

Rebekah nodded and wheeled toward the table. "What can I do to help with breakfast, and where's Nadine? She's not sick, too, I hope."

"No, she's feeling fine. I sent her out to gather some eggs a little while ago." Sarah piled the crispy bacon into a glass pan and popped it into the oven so it would stay warm until breakfast was served. "I'll be doing some baking later this morning, and since we're having eggs for breakfast, we might run short. I checked the refrigerator, and there aren't as many now as I remember."

"Simon probably ate them," Rebekah said. "Now that it's summertime and he has a lot more chores to do, he eats enough to feed ten boys his age."

Sarah was glad to see Rebekah relaxing a bit and making a joke—even if it had been at her brother's expense. "You're right. Simon can surely put away the food these days." She clicked her tongue. "I pity the poor woman my boy marries. She'll probably have to cook from sunup to sunset in order to keep his stomach satisfied."

"Maybe we should start alerting all the eligible women in our community right now. That way, if anyone should ever fall for my little *bruder*, she can't say she wasn't warned."

Sarah reached for a can of coffee from the cupboard. "Enough about Simon and his eating habits. How about if you scramble up some eggs while I get the coffee going?"

Rebekah frowned. "You know it's hard for me to reach the stove from my wheelchair."

Sarah turned to face her daughter and squinted. "I thought you might decide to wear your crutches and leg braces today. You can stand at the stove for a short time if you're using them."

"Jah, but it's so much trouble to put them on. Besides, the braces make my legs stiff like a doll's."

"I know they're awkward and uncomfortable, but they do allow you to stand and even walk a short ways. It's much more than we could have hoped for, since the doctors said you would probably never walk again."

"Okay, Mom, I'll go get the leg braces," Rebekah muttered

as she turned her wheelchair toward the door leading to the hallway.

"Better wait on that," Sarah called. "The menfolk will be in from their chores soon, and we need to get breakfast on as quickly as possible because I'm sure they'll be anxious to get out to the fields." She motioned to the table. "Why don't you set the dishes and silverware out? Nadine can cook up the eggs when she gets back. We'll have more eggs by then anyhow."

"Jah."

The back door opened with a *whoosh*, and Nadine burst into the room, all red-faced and wearing a smile that stretched ear to ear. Instead of her usual stiff white *kapp*, she wore a black kerchief over her pinned-up brown hair.

"How'd it go in the chicken coop?" Sarah asked.

"I got over a dozen eggs." Nadine lifted the basket she held in her hands and grinned. "I'm thinkin' those fat little hens must like summer nearly as much as I do." She placed the basket of eggs on the counter and went to wash up at the sink.

"I'm glad it went well, and it's a good thing they're laying so well," Sarah replied. "We're having scrambled eggs this morning, and I was afraid we might run out and I wouldn't have enough for the baking I want to do later." She stepped away from the stove. "Nadine, would you please scramble up the eggs?"

"Sure." Nadine moved over to the stove; then she glanced over at Rebekah, who had just placed some silverware on the table. "How was the singing last night, sister? Did you have a good time?"

"It was okay."

"Just okay?"

"Jah."

"Well, I can't wait until I'm allowed to go to one." Nadine cast a wistful look in Sarah's direction.

Sarah smiled. "You'll get there soon enough, like as not."

Rebekah wheeled over to the cupboard where the dishes were kept. "Going to a singing isn't that exciting."

"You must be joking. There are boys at those singings, right?"

Rebekah lifted her gaze to the ceiling. "Of course there are boys."

"Then I think it would be a lot of fun to go to one."

"Which is why you're not ready to go to any singings yet," Sarah said firmly. "In my opinion, a girl of fourteen shouldn't be so interested in the opposite sex, either."

"Oh, Mom," Nadine groaned. "I'll bet if you had your way, I'd grow up to be *en alt maedel* like Rebekah."

"Nadine Stoltzfus, that's an awful thing to say about your sister. Rebekah is not an old maid. She's only nineteen and still has plenty of time to get married. I think you should apologize to Rebekah for saying that, don't you?"

Nadine's youthful face reddened as she looked down at Rebekah with her eyebrows drawn together. "Well, I–I–"

"Go ahead," Sarah prompted. "Tell you sister you're sorry for what you said."

Rebekah held up her hand. "It's all right. Nadine spoke the truth. I am en alt maedel, and that's just the way of it."

"Such nonsense," Sarah said with a shake of her head. "When the right man comes along and captures your heart, you'll marry and start a family of your own."

Rebekah's gaze went immediately to her crippled legs. "Like this?" She touched one knee and then the other. "Would any man want a wife who looks like me?"

"There's nothing wrong with the way you look, Rebekah."

"But who would want someone who can't do all the things a normal wife should be able to do?" Tears slipped out from under Rebekah's dark lashes, and she blinked several times.

Sarah rushed to her daughter's side and dropped down beside her wheelchair. "Oh, Rebekah, please don't say things like that."

Rebekah leaned her head against Sarah's shoulder and wept. "It's true, and you know it. No one will ever want me. I'll never find a husband, and I'm nothing but a burden to my family."

"That's not so."

"Jah, it is, and no one understands how I feel about things."

Deciding that now might be a good time to bring up the handicap convention, Sarah patted Rebekah's back gently and said, "Simon mentioned last night that he'd read about a convention for Amish people who have handicaps like you. It's to be held next month in Ohio, and your daed and I thought maybe you and I could—"

"I don't want to go anywhere right now," Rebekah interrupted. "Especially not to some convention where I don't know anyone." She released a quiet moan. "I just want to be able to take care of myself."

"Oh, but you do. You've learned to dress and groom

yourself, and you can do so many other important things."

"What kind of important things?"

"The column you write for *The Budget* is one thing you do well." Sarah smiled. "If you went to the convention, you'd be able to write about it when you returned home. It might give someone else in your predicament the incentive to attend the next convention."

"I'm sure it's a good thing for some, but I'm really not interested, Mom."

"Won't you at least give it some thought?"

Rebekah's eyes filled with more tears. "Are you wanting to get rid of me for a while? Is that it?"

"Why, no. Of course not. I just thought you might benefit from going, and I had planned to go with you." Sarah sighed. "But if you're dead set against the idea, then I won't mention it again."

"Danki, I appreciate that."

Nadine stepped up to Rebekah and opened her mouth as if to comment, but her words were cut off when the back door flew open and Andrew and Simon rushed into the room. Their faces were as red as one of the heifers out in the pasture, and they huffed and puffed something awful.

"Your son is gettin' too good for me now, Sarah," Andrew panted. "We raced all the way from the barn, and Simon nearly beat me to the back door."

"Nearly?" Simon scrunched up his nose. "What do ya mean, nearly, Dad? My feet hit the porch steps at least six seconds before yours did."

Andrew's deep laughter bounced off the walls. "Well, what does it matter? I got to the kitchen first, and that's all that counts." He thumped Simon on the back a couple of times. "So now I get the first kiss!"

"The what?" Simon took two steps back and bumped into the table, clattering the silverware.

"Not you, boy. I was referring to your mamm." Andrew marched across the room, drew Sarah into his arms, and planted a noisy kiss right on her mouth.

"Andrew, really! What kind of example are you setting for the kinner?" Sarah bit back a chuckle as she shook her finger at him.

"I'm settin' a good example, I hope." With that, Sarah's playful husband bent down and kissed her soundly once more.

"Oh, yuk!" Simon shook his head and groaned.

"I think it's kind of romantic. Don't you, Rebekah?" Nadine asked with a girlish giggle.

Rebekah, who had been busy drying her tearstained cheeks with a napkin, gave only a quick nod in response.

"And I think it's time for all this silliness to end." Sarah motioned to the sink. "Breakfast is nearly ready, so if my men will get washed up, we can eat and get on with our day."

Get on with our day? Rebekah gripped the arms of her wheelchair. Today was just another day. Nothing to look forward to, that was for sure. When Rebekah was a child, her disability hadn't bothered her so much, but now that she'd become a young woman, things were different—she was different. *That must be why Mom wants me to go to the convention in Ohio—everyone there will be different, too.*

She glanced at the door leading to Grandma's room. *Maybe if I did something worthwhile today, I would feel better. As soon as breakfast is over, I think I'll fill a plate with eggs and bacon and take a tray into Grandma. Then maybe I can read to her for a while. Since she's not feeling well, it will give me a chance to minister to her for a change.*

After the men had washed up, everyone took their seats at the table. Following a short time of silent prayer, Mom passed the platter of scrambled eggs around the table, along with some biscuits and crispy bacon.

Rebekah only nibbled on her food, as her thoughts vacillated between Grandma not feeling well and Mom wanting her to attend the handicap convention in Ohio. Even if the convention did have some helpful things to offer, she didn't want to be away from home that long. She would miss her family too much—especially Grandma, who seemed to understand her needs more than anyone else.

"You've hardly touched your food, Rebekah," Dad said, breaking into her thoughts. "Has your appetite gone away this morning?"

She nodded. "I'm worried about Grandma."

"I'm sure she'll be fine after a few more hours of rest," Mom put in. "But as I said before, if she's not feeling better by this afternoon, we'll take her to see the doctor."

"That's right," Dad agreed. "Even if it means we have to tie her to the buggy seat in order to get her there."

"Now why would you have to do something like that to Grandma?" Nadine asked, tipping her head and looking at Dad as if he'd taken leave of his senses.

Simon, who sat next to Nadine, poked her arm and

snickered. "He's only kiddin', *dummkopp*."

"I am not a dunce," she shot back, giving him a jab to the ribs with her elbow.

Mom wagged her finger. "That will be enough, you two. Just eat your breakfast, and no more goading each other."

"I wasn't." Nadine's bottom lip jutted out. "Simon was the one who started it."

"It doesn't matter who's at fault," Dad said, his eyebrows drawing together in a frown. "Just do as your mamm says, or I'll give you both double chores to do for the next week or two."

Simon and Nadine fell silent, and Rebekah was glad for it grated on her nerves to have to listen to their senseless chatter.

When everyone had finished eating, the men excused themselves, saying they were headed out to the fields and would be back in time for lunch.

"Jah," Mom said as she pushed away from the table. "We'll be sure to have the noon meal ready on time."

"Do you want me to help with the dishes now, or should I take Grandma a tray with some breakfast first?" Rebekah asked her mother.

"You can go ahead and do up the tray while Nadine and I start the dishes."

Nadine looked over at Rebekah and scowled, but she grabbed a clean dish towel without a word of protest.

As soon as Rebekah had placed a plate of scrambled eggs with a biscuit and two strips of bacon on a tray, along with a cup of tea, she set it in her lap and wheeled out of the kitchen, being careful not to bump into anything along the way.

When she reached Grandma's door, she knocked softly. Hearing no response, she rapped a little louder. "Grandma, it's Rebekah. Can I come in?"

Still no reply.

Rebekah opened the door a crack and peered inside. She spotted Grandma lying in her bed with her long gray hair fanned out across her pillow. It was one of the few times Rebekah had seen her grandmother with her hair down. Of course, Grandma was usually up and dressed way before anyone else in the family, so her hair had always been done up in a bun with her kapp set in place by the time Rebekah came to the kitchen each morning.

"Grandma, are you awake?" Rebekah called softly. "We had scrambled eggs, bacon, and biscuits for breakfast this morning, and I have a tray for you." She pushed the door open more fully and wheeled into the room. Grandma Stoltzfus's eyes were shut, and her Bible lay open across her chest. She looked awfully still. A strange feeling crept over Rebekah. Why hadn't Grandma answered her call? Maybe she was sicker than she had let on. Maybe she was too weak to respond.

Rebekah wheeled closer to Grandma's bed, being careful not to jostle the tray. "Grandma, can you hear me?"

Grandma remained silent and unmoving.

Rebekah looked down at the open Bible and noticed a passage of scripture from Proverbs that had been underlined: "Trust in the LORD with all thine heart; and lean not unto thine own understanding. In all thy ways acknowledge him, and he shall direct thy paths."

One of Grandma's wrinkled hands lay across the open

page, so apparently she'd been reading her Bible sometime during the night or early this morning. Rebekah reached out to touch the dear woman's hand. Cold! It was ice cold!

"Grandma, wake up! Please open your eyes and look at me."

There was no response from Grandma Stoltzfus. None at all. Her body seemed lifeless like a sack of corn. She had obviously gone to her reward in heaven and wouldn't have to do another chore or suffer any of life's pains ever again.

Rebekah sat still for several seconds as she let the reality of the situation fully sink in. Then, with an anguished cry, she let her head fall forward and sobbed for all she was worth.

Mom stepped into the room a few seconds later. "Rebekah? What is it, daughter? I thought I heard you weeping in here."

Rebekah jerked her head up and gulped on a hiccup. "Sh-she's gone, Mom. I'm sure that Grandma is dead."

"What? *Ach*, that just can't be! I spoke to her but a few hours ago." Mom rushed over to the bed and picked up Grandma's hand, feeling for a pulse. Glancing at Rebekah, she slowly shook her head. Then she placed her hand in front of Grandma's mouth, and held it that way for several seconds. "Oh, Rebekah, I believe you're right. Grandma's gone home to heaven."

Good-bye, Rebekah. I'm leaving you now." Grandma held her hand out to Rebekah, but when Rebekah reached for it, Grandma shook her head, turned, and walked away.

"I need you, Grandma. Please don't leave me all alone." Rebekah tried to run after Grandma, but her legs wouldn't move. She glanced down at the ugly metal braces strapped to them and drew in a shuddering breath. "Come back, Grandma. Come back to me!"

Grandma was gone–vanished into some kind of a misty, thin air. Tears streamed down Rebekah's face, and she trembled. "Please, please. . .don't leave me. I need you!"

"Rebekah, what's wrong? Why are you crying?"

Rebekah turned and saw her mother moving slowly toward her. She extended her arms, but Mom kept walking right past Rebekah, heading in the same direction as Grandma had gone.

"Mom, don't go. Wait for me, please." Rebekah struggled to lift her right foot, but it wouldn't budge. She gritted her teeth and tried to move her left foot, but it seemed to be stuck like glue. "Don't leave me! Don't leave me!" she shouted as Mom disappeared into the eerie mist.

"Calm down," Dad said as he trudged past her. "You'll wake

the dead if you keep on hollering that way."

"Something terrible is happening, and I can't seem to stop it." Rebekah gulped in some air and almost choked on a sob. "Can't you make it stop, Dad? Can't you bring Grandma and Mom back to me?"

He shook his head and kept on walking as though he hadn't heard a word she'd said.

"I need you!" Rebekah shouted to her father's retreating form. "I can't make it on my own. I need someone to love me and care for my needs."

Dad lifted his hand in a backward wave; then he disappeared into the misty vapor.

"Come back! Come back! Come back to me!"

"Wake up, sister. Wake up. Do you hear me, Rebekah?"

Rebekah felt someone shaking her shoulder, and she struggled to open her eyes. Was it Grandma? Had the dear woman come back from the shadow of death to be with her?

She tossed her head from side to side and moaned. "Grandma. Grandma, don't leave me."

"Rebekah, calm down at once, and look at me."

It took great effort on Rebekah's part, but she forced her eyes open and squinted against the invading light. "Wh–where am I? What's happened to Grandma?" she asked as Nadine's face came into view.

"You're in your own bed. You must have been having a bad dream because I could hear you hollering all the way upstairs." Nadine's forehead wrinkled as she stared at Rebekah. "That must have been some nightmare you were havin'."

Rebekah nodded, noticing that her nightgown was sopping wet, and so were her sheets. "I—I dreamed that Grandma was with me, but she disappeared in a fog. Then Mom and Dad came along, and they vanished, too." Her voice caught on a sob, and she shuddered. "It—it was so real, and I—I was so scared."

Nadine patted Rebekah's shoulder. "You'll feel better once the funeral is over. Mom says it's easier to deal with the loss of a loved one once we see them buried and allow ourselves some time to grieve."

Grabbing the sides of her bed, Rebekah pulled herself to a sitting position. That's right. . .today was Grandma's funeral. No one could have foreseen that just three short days ago the dear woman would be taken from them, but she had slipped quietly away from her family, making her journey home to be with the Lord. It had been determined that she'd died of a stroke. As soon as the news of her death had gotten out, the entire Amish community had rallied to do whatever was necessary in order to help with the preparations for the funeral service and the meal afterward.

Rebekah supposed that was some comfort, but oh, how terribly she missed her dear grandma, and not just because the woman had taken care of Rebekah through so much of her childhood. Rebekah would miss everything about Grandma Stoltzfus—her kind, helpful ways; her soft-spoken words; and her sweet, tender spirit, which was a testimony of God's love in action.

As Rebekah rolled her wheelchair into the living room a

short time later, she caught sight of Grandma's coffin—a plain pine box with a split lid. The upper part of the lid was hinged so it could be opened for viewing the body. According to tradition among the Lancaster Amish, Grandma's dress had been covered with the same white cape and apron she had worn on her wedding day many years ago.

Grandma's funeral service would be held after breakfast, right here in the house, with a second service going on in the barn simultaneously if there were more people than the house could hold. For two days prior to the service, Grandma's body had been available for viewing, but after today, Rebekah would never look on the dear woman's face again—not until they met in heaven someday.

Rebekah gulped on a sob and guided her chair out of the room, knowing her help would be needed in the kitchen and hoping the action of doing something constructive would take her mind off the pain in her heart. She discovered Mom and Nadine scurrying around the kitchen as they made preparations for breakfast.

"Are you all right?" Mom asked, casting Rebekah a look of concern. "Nadine said you'd had a bad dream and seemed quite upset when she woke you."

Rebekah's only reply was a quick shrug. She didn't want to talk about the terrible nightmare that had left her nightgown and bed sheets drenched in sweat. Talking about it would do no good, and it certainly wouldn't bring Grandma back.

"Rebekah?" Mom persisted. "Are you okay?"

"I'm fine." Rebekah rolled her chair farther into the room. "Want me to set the table?"

"If you don't mind."

"I would have done it, but Mom's got me squeezing oranges for fresh juice," Nadine said from her place in front of the counter. "Simon says he's comin' down with a cold, and he seems to think the vitamin C he'll get from the oranges will lick it quicker than anything."

"Grandma used to drink a lot of orange juice whenever she had a cold," Rebekah said, swallowing hard in hopes of pushing down the awful lump that had lodged in her throat. She guided her chair quickly over to the silverware drawer, determined to keep her hands busy so her mind wouldn't dwell on the funeral service that would be starting in just a few hours.

Rebekah didn't know how she had made it through Grandma's service, but she had—and without breaking down in front of everyone. All too often, she got looks of sympathy or curious stares from others because of her handicap, and the last thing she needed today was anyone's pity. All she wanted to do was get through the graveside service, which would soon take place, mingle with their guests awhile during the afternoon meal, and retreat to the solitude of her room.

As Dad's horse and buggy pulled away from the barn, Rebekah glanced out the back window. In perfect procession, Grandma's close family members followed the simple horse-drawn hearse, with the other buggies coming up behind them. Single file, the Amish carriages wound their way down the Stoltzfus driveway and continued onto the narrow road. The mourners passed fields of growing corn, soon-to-be-cut alfalfa, and Amish farmsteads dotting the countryside. The long column turned down an even narrower road and finally came to a halt at a fenced-in graveyard.

The drivers got out first and tied their horses to the fence. Soon everyone was assembled at the graveside, and the pallbearers slid Grandma's coffin from the wagon and carried it to the grave that had been dug the day before. Right beside the new grave was the small, simple headstone of Grandma's husband, Henry Stoltzfus, who had preceded her in death some thirteen years ago.

Wooden poles with long straps extending the width of the grave had been placed across the hole for the coffin to rest upon. Rebekah's family mourned openly when the box was lowered into the ground and the hole was covered with dirt. Their beloved grandma was laid to rest. After the men had all removed their hats, Bishop Benner conducted the graveside service, which included the reading of a few verses from one of their Amish hymns. He closed the service by inviting those present to pray the Lord's Prayer silently with him.

Rebekah's stomach felt like it was tied in one big knot, and she fought to keep her emotions under control. She knew in the days ahead she would pine for the long talks she and Grandma used to have; for the board games they often played; the times spent together caring for Grandma's houseplants; and the meaningful hours she had listened to Grandma read the scriptures to her. There were so many precious memories of the dear woman.

Rebekah glanced at the somber faces surrounding her and knew she wasn't the only one in pain. Aunt Mim wept openly as she leaned against Uncle Amos's shoulder, and

Mary Ellen and her twelve-year-old brother, Henry, stood near their parents with tears streaming down their faces.

To the left stood Uncle Jonas and Aunt Crystal with their fifteen-year-old twin sons, Jacob and John, and eleven-year-old daughter, Maddie. Next to them were Uncle Lewis, Aunt Grace, and their children, Peggy, age twelve, and Matthew, who was seven. To the right stood Rebekah's own family—Mom, Dad, Simon, and Nadine. They were all shedding plenty of tears—everyone but Rebekah, who was determined to remain in control.

This was the first time Rebekah had lost someone so close to her. She'd only been six when Grandpa Stoltzfus died of a heart attack. She barely remembered him, and at the time of his death, she hadn't been so greatly affected.

Despite Rebekah's resolve, a few tears slipped out from under her lashes and splashed onto her cheeks. *Oh, God, why did you have to take my mammi? Why must life be so unfair?*

No answer. Just the whisper of the wind wafting through the trees overhead.

Rebekah wondered if God had even heard her prayer. She wondered if He cared about her at all.

The funeral dinner was held at Rebekah's folks' place, and an array of food and beverages had been prepared and brought in by many of their friends and neighbors. Most of the adults had been served inside the house, but some of the younger ones decided to eat their meal at one of the picnic tables set up on the lawn since it had turned out to be such a warm day.

As Mary Ellen walked across the grass carrying two plates of food, she noticed Rebekah sitting in her wheelchair under the branches of a large willow tree. Her eyes were closed, and her mouth was pursed tightly as if an invisible drawstring had pulled her lips together.

"Are you sleeping?" Mary Ellen asked as she approached her cousin.

Rebekah's eyes snapped open. "No. Just resting my eyes."

"Sure is a hot, muggy day, isn't it?"

"Jah, but then that's typical summertime weather."

Mary Ellen held one of the plates out to Rebekah. "I brought you something to eat."

"Danki, but I'm not so hungry."

"Maybe not, but you need to keep up your strength."

"My strength? My strength for what—crying?" Tears seeped under Rebekah's long lashes and dribbled onto her flushed cheeks. "I—I was determined not to do that, yet here I am, giving in to my tears anyway."

Mary Ellen bent down to place both plates on the ground; then she leaned over Rebekah's wheelchair and gave her a hug. "We'll all miss Grandma, but you probably will feel the greatest loss. She lived with you and took care of your needs for a long time."

Rebekah nodded.

"God knows what's best for each one of us, so I'm sure He will give you the strength to get through this time of loss."

"It was best to take Grandma away?"

"Not better for us, maybe, but for Grandma, it surely was."

"She's dead, Mary Ellen."

"I know that, and I'll miss her, too. But remember that

the Bible says for a believer to be absent from the body is to be present with the Lord." Mary Ellen smiled as she looked up at the cloudless sky. "If we could only know what heaven is really like, I think we would all long to go there."

"Maybe so."

"Grandma's no longer confined in her aging body. She doesn't have to toil here on earth or feel any more physical pain. She's probably having the time of her life, walking all over heaven with Grandpa and Jesus right about now."

Rebekah nodded slowly. "I—I know you're right, but it's ever so hard to let go of my precious mammi because I miss her so much. Every time I go into her room or see something that reminds me of her, I feel as if my heart is breaking in two."

"Grieve if you must, Rebekah, but don't let your grief consume you. Grandma wouldn't want that."

"Last night I had a distressing nightmare about her leaving me. Mom and Dad were in the dream, as well, and they disappeared into the same foggy mist that Grandma walked into after she told me good-bye." Rebekah groaned and held her stomach as though she was in terrible pain. "Do you think that means they'll be leaving me soon, too?"

Mary Ellen shook her head. "Of course not. It was only a dream—a dream that most likely came about because you are grieving over the loss of our mammi."

"You're probably right, but it was so terrifying, and I—I'm afraid of what it might have meant."

"What do you mean?"

"Maybe it was a warning of things to come. . .a time when I'll be all alone with no one to care for me."

"That won't happen because you have plenty of family who will be around to help take care of your needs." Mary Ellen patted Rebekah's arm in a motherly fashion. "I'm sorry about the nightmare, but I'm sure it won't happen again, and you can't let anything steal your joy."

"How can I feel joy when I've just lost Grandma?"

"We all lost her, Rebekah. But life goes on, and we need to keep a positive attitude and look for things to be joyous about."

"It's not so easy for me to feel joy the way you do. You've always been able to smile, even in the face of difficulty. I remember when we were kinner and some of our classmates used to pick on you. Your loving, forgiving spirit was evident even back then." Rebekah slowly shook her head. "I don't know how you managed to stay so sweet and kind."

"My life hasn't always been easy. As you know, I lost my real mamm when I was young, and I had to make many adjustments. It was hard on Pappy, too, but he set a good example and taught me how to love and laugh. Then God brought Mama Mim into our lives, and she's been there for me ever since." Mary Ellen released a sigh. "There's always something for which to be thankful. Maybe you just need to count your blessings, consider all the beautiful things God has made, and focus on how much He loves us."

Rebekah nodded. "I know that's true, and I'll try to do as you suggested."

Mary Ellen lowered herself to the ground beside the wheelchair. She reached for Rebekah's plate and handed it to her. "We'd better eat before the ants find our food and decide to have themselves a little picnic of their own."

Rebekah's lips curved into a tiny smile. "I might be willing to share my food with one of my special aunts, but never with a bunch of picnic ants."

Rebekah's first bite of food tasted like cardboard, and she had trouble swallowing, but after a while, she found herself actually enjoying the meal. A short time later, Rebekah looked down at her plate and was surprised to see that it was empty. She'd been so busy visiting with Mary Ellen that she hadn't even realized she had eaten everything.

"Guess I'm done," she said, handing her plate to Mary Ellen.

"Good for you. I'm glad you ate something."

Rebekah caught sight of Daniel Beachy walking across the yard, and she was surprised when he joined them under the weeping willow tree. Maybe he'd decided this was a good chance to speak with Mary Ellen since Johnny wasn't around to hog the conversation.

"I'm sorry about your mammi," Daniel said, dropping to the ground on the other side of Rebekah's wheelchair. "I didn't know her as well as some in our community, but she seemed like a right nice woman."

"She was the best grandma anyone could ever want," Rebekah said with a nod.

"She wasn't my mammi by blood," Mary Ellen put in, "but she always treated me as such."

Daniel removed his straw hat, and with the back of his hand, he wiped away the rivulets of sweat running down his forehead. "Whew! Sure has turned out to be a mighty warm day. With so many folks here, it's nice that some of us could eat outside."

Mary Ellen nodded. "If June's this hot and sticky, I wonder what we can expect from the rest of our summer."

"Probably more hot, muggy days," he replied with a chuckle.

Mary Ellen joined him in laughter, but Rebekah just sat there, feeling as out of place as a June bug in December. *My cousin looks so cute whenever she laughs. I'm sure that's why all the fellows hang around her so much of the time. That and the fact that she's got two good legs and can join in their fun and games.* Rebekah glanced down at her lifeless legs. Two dead sticks, that's all they were. Sure weren't good for much. *I'd probably never look as cute as Mary Ellen, no matter how much I laughed or smiled.*

"Is this a private party, or can anyone join in?" Johnny Yoder asked in his usual, smooth-talking way. Rebekah looked on in surprise as he plunked on the grass beside Mary Ellen. He held a man-sized plate of peanut butter cookies in one hand, and the smile he wore could have melted a block of ice. "I've brought you some dessert," he said, extending the plate to Mary Ellen.

She reached out and snatched one off the plate. "Danki, Johnny. Peanut butter's my favorite, so I'm beholden to you now."

Johnny's smug expression reminded Rebekah of the way some of their barn cats looked whenever they brought a poor defenseless mouse up to the house to show off their catch.

Johnny nudged Mary Ellen's arm. "Since you're beholden to me, does that mean I'm welcome to join this group?"

"Of course you're welcome to join us. We're glad to have your company, aren't we?" Mary Ellen glanced over at Rebekah and then at Daniel.

Rebekah nodded. "It's fine by me."

Daniel only shrugged, and Rebekah was sure that his wrinkled forehead gave proof of his obvious disappointment. The poor fellow was probably irritated with Johnny for interrupting the conversation he'd been having with Mary Ellen. Rebekah couldn't fault him for that. It did seem as if Johnny always showed up just when Daniel had begun to make a bit of headway with Mary Ellen.

In no time at all, the cookies were gone, though the two young men had eaten most of them. Conversation didn't lag much, either—at least not between Johnny and Mary Ellen. Rebekah thought it most unfair that Johnny seemed to be hogging her cousin that way and hadn't given either her or Daniel a chance to say much.

"The funeral service was long, wasn't it?" Johnny asked, looking over at Daniel for the first time.

"Jah, they usually are." Daniel leaned back on his elbows and turned his face toward the cloudless sky. Apparently he wasn't any more interested in talking to Johnny than Johnny was in talking to him. Daniel was obviously put out because he hadn't been able to say anything to Mary Ellen since Johnny had showed up.

"The funeral was almost as long as a regular preaching service, and sometimes it's hard for people to stay awake that long." Johnny cast a sidelong glance at Mary Ellen. "Say, how about that time you fell asleep in church?"

Mary Ellen jumped up, planting her hands on her slender

hips. "What do you mean, Johnny? I never did such a thing, and you know it!"

"Sure you did," he teased. "You nearly fell right off your wooden bench that day."

"That's not so." Mary Ellen wrinkled her nose at him. "I always pay close attention during preaching."

"I think he's only kidding with you," Rebekah said. "I sure don't remember you ever falling asleep in church."

"Me neither," Daniel put in.

"Jah, well, maybe she wasn't sleepin'," Johnny admitted. "She might've been prayin' for a really long time." He leaned his head back and hooted until his face turned red and tears trickled down his cheeks. Then he jumped up and grabbed Mary Ellen's hand. "Say, why don't you take a little walk with me? We'll head on down to the creek, and maybe that'll help you cool off. A girl with a fiery temper needs a bit of coolin' down, don't ya think?"

Mary Ellen pulled away from him and folded her arms, although there was a tiny smile tugging at the corners of her mouth. "What makes you think I would be willing to go anywhere with you, Johnny Yoder?"

He blinked a couple of times and gave her a jab in the ribs with his elbow. "Because I'm irresistible, and if you don't agree to go with me, then I'll have to get down on my knees and beg like a *hund*. You wouldn't want me to do something that embarrassing, now would you?"

"Oh, all right," Mary Ellen conceded with a shrug. "I couldn't stand to see you beg like a dog." Her gaze fell on Rebekah; then it swung over to Daniel. "You're both welcome to come along."

"No, thanks," Rebekah declined. "I'd rather stay right here under this shady old tree." She glanced at Daniel, who now lay on his back, using his straw hat as a pillow. "You go ahead, if you want to, Daniel."

He crinkled his nose and waved a hand. "Naw, they don't need me taggin' along."

There's that look again, Rebekah noted. *Poor Daniel. He's so smitten with Mary Ellen that he doesn't know what to do. What with Johnny being around all the time, he has about as much of a chance at winning her over as a snowball does of staying frozen until the Fourth of July.*

Mary Ellen and Johnny said their good-byes, then walked away, giggling like a couple of kinner.

"Why didn't you go with them?" Rebekah asked, as she looked down at Daniel. "I'm sure Mary Ellen would—"

"I'd rather not be a fifth wheel on the buggy." He pulled himself to a sitting position. "I'd have gone if you'd been willing, but no, not alone."

Rebekah shook her head. "If I had agreed to go along on the walk, I would have only slowed the rest of you down."

"I could have pushed you in your wheelchair. I've had lots of practice with the plow and my daed's mules, so we'd move along pretty fast, and we wouldn't have slowed anyone down."

Rebekah grunted. "I've never been compared to a team of mules before."

His face heated up, and he gave his earlobe a quick tug. "Sorry. Didn't mean it the way it sounded." *Why do I always seem to say the wrong thing?*

50

"That's all right. It's not important," she murmured.

"Have you written anything interesting for *The Budget* lately?" Daniel asked, taking their conversation in another direction and hoping to draw Rebekah out of her melancholy mood.

"Not really." She stared down at her hands, clenched tightly in her lap. "I–I'm not so sure I want to continue doing it now that Grandma is gone."

"How come?"

She shrugged.

"Do you think your mammi would want you to give up doing things just because she died?"

"I—I guess not. Knowing Grandma, she'd probably want me to keep writing for *The Budget*, the way she used to do before she turned her column over to me."

He nodded and smiled. "I think you're right about that."

"Well, I suppose I'd better go see if Mom needs me for anything." Rebekah motioned to the plates on the ground. "Would you please hand me those so I can take them inside?"

"Want me to take 'em there for you?"

She shook her head with a determined expression. "I can manage something that simple."

"Okay." Daniel placed the plates in Rebekah's lap, wishing there was something he could do or say that might help take away her pain.

"Danki."

"You're welcome."

Rebekah wheeled away, leaving Daniel alone and wondering why he could never seem to say the right thing when she was around.

CHAPTER 4

Grandma had been gone for nearly a month, yet the pain still lingered in Rebekah's heart. She missed the dear woman so much—especially the long talks they used to have. Grandma had always been full of good advice, and Rebekah often wondered where all that wisdom had come from.

Nearly every night since Grandma's death, Rebekah had dreamed about her, often having the same nightmare that involved others in her family being taken from her, too.

"Oh, Lord, what would I do if something happened to Mom and Dad? How would I manage on my own?" she mumbled one morning, as she entered Grandma's old room.

No answer. Like all the other times she had asked God before, He seemed to be ignoring her. Didn't God care how much she was hurting? Didn't He want to give her a miracle?

Rebekah drew in a deep breath and reached for the watering can sitting beside some pots of African violets on the dressing table. Grandma had died so unexpectedly, and Rebekah hadn't been able to do anything about it. Now she was determined to keep Grandma's plants alive and flourishing so she would have something to remember her by.

When Rebekah finished watering and pruning all the plants, she spotted Grandma's Bible lying on the small table next to the bed. The last time she'd seen it, it had been lying across Grandma's chest. Now it was closed just like Grandma Stoltzfus's life.

Rebekah rolled her chair up to the table and reached for the Bible, holding it close to her heart. Unbidden tears seeped under her eyelashes, and she sniffed deeply, trying to keep them from falling onto her cheeks. She had heard about the process of grieving for a loved one, but nothing had prepared her for this terrible, empty ache in her soul. She hadn't realized how much her grandmother had meant to her until she was gone. Now it was too late to tell Grandma all the things that were on her heart.

Why do folks always wait until it's too late to express their real feelings for one another? she wondered. *Why not tell them how much you care while they're still alive?*

She placed the Bible in her lap and opened it to a spot where a crocheted bookmark had been positioned. It was in the exact place where the Bible had been open when Rebekah found Grandma in the deep sleep of death.

"Mom must have put this in here," Rebekah whispered. "Maybe she wanted to save the place where Grandma had last read God's Word." Her gaze traveled down the page until it came to rest on the verses Grandma had underlined. "Proverbs 3:5 and 6," she read aloud. " 'Trust in the Lord with all thine heart; and lean not unto thine own understanding. In all thy ways acknowledge him, and he shall direct thy paths.' "

"Those are some good words to live by, don't you think?"

Rebekah turned her head and saw Mom standing inside

the doorway. She nodded but made no reply. If she spoke, she feared her voice would break and she would dissolve into a puddle of unstoppable tears.

Mom came the rest of the way into the room. She took a seat on the edge of the bed near the wheelchair and placed her hand on Rebekah's trembling shoulder. "It's all right to grieve for Grandma, but she would want you to go on with life and find happiness."

"Go on with life?" Rebekah sobbed. "What life, Mom? What kind of a life can a person with a handicap like mine ever have? What happiness awaits someone like me?"

"Oh, Rebekah, it is possible for you to have a meaningful life. Why, many people in the world have disabilities, and most of them live fairly productive lives." Mom squeezed Rebekah's shoulder. "You were always such a pleasant, easygoing child, and I thought you had come to accept your limitations. However, since you've become a young woman, I've noticed a definite change in your attitude, and I'm not sure I like what I see."

Rebekah sniffed deeply, swiping at the tears running down her cheeks. "When I was a little girl, you all spoiled me. Someone was always around to care for me or just sit and talk, the way Grandma often did. I thought there would always be someone available to provide for my needs. Now I know I'm really a burden, and someday I might not have anyone to care for me."

Mom moved from her place on the bed and knelt in front of Rebekah. She grasped her hands and held them tightly. "Losing Grandma has made us all aware of how fragile life is. None of us will live on this earth forever. Someday, every believer will join Grandma in heaven." She closed her eyes, as though searching for just the right words. When she opened them again, she was smiling. "We're a close family, and I'm sure that, even after your daed and I are both gone, someone will take over the responsibility of your care."

Rebekah nearly choked on the sob rising in her throat. "I–I don't want anyone to *have* to be responsible for me. I want to provide for myself—at least financially." She wiped her eyes with the backs of her hands. "I just don't know what someone like me can do to make enough money in order to accomplish that goal."

"You could sell eggs or do some handcrafts and take them to the farmers' market," Mom suggested.

"Doing small things like selling eggs or crafts wouldn't give me enough money." Rebekah felt as if Mom was treating her like a child, and it irked her just a bit.

"If it means so much to you, maybe you should pray about the matter and search God's Word for wisdom." Mom stood. "Why don't you keep Grandma's *Biewel?* I think she would have wanted you to have it. I know the scriptures gave her a lot of comfort, not to mention answers whenever she needed the Lord's guidance."

Rebekah thought about the underlined verses in Grandma's Bible. Maybe she would continue to search for other scriptures Grandma might have underlined or highlighted. Perhaps the miracle she was looking for could be found in one of those passages.

Sarah returned to the kitchen with a heavy heart, and she flopped into a chair at the table with a moan. If there was only something she could say or do to help her daughter accept her limitations and gain back the joy she had known when she was a child. As a toddler, Rebekah had been so adventuresome, always attempting new things, and full of laughter and smiles, even when she fell down or didn't get her way on something. The first few years after Rebekah's accident, she had been easygoing and seemed positive about her situation.

But things began to change when Rebekah started into puberty, and by the time she'd become a teenager, she had developed a completely different attitude. Things she used to shrug off or even laugh about now became issues. She seemed worried about being a burden to others, lacked the confidence of other young women her age, and sometimes succumbed to depression.

Since Grandma's passing, Rebekah's dismal attitude seemed to have gotten worse, and it concerned Sarah that she couldn't reach her daughter or help ease her despair.

Sarah glanced at the calendar hanging on the wall near the door and shook her head. The handicap convention had already taken place, and there wouldn't be another one until next year, so the idea of taking Rebekah there was certainly out. If only she had been willing to go. If only. . .

Feeling the need to pray, Sarah closed her eyes and lowered her head to the table. *Heavenly Father, please comfort Rebekah, and give me the strength to keep trying to be an encouragement to her.* She paused and swiped at the tears trickling down her cheeks. *If it's Your will for my daughter to become self-sufficient, then please show us the way.*

For the next several days, Rebekah spent every free moment looking through Grandma's well-worn Bible. On almost every page, she found a verse of scripture that had been underlined. In some places she discovered that Grandma had scrawled notes in the margin or at the bottom of certain pages, mentioning how some particular verse had spoken to her heart. There was no doubt in Rebekah's mind— Grandma Stoltzfus had lived and died by the truth of God's Word. Perhaps that's what Rebekah needed to do, too.

One morning after breakfast, Rebekah found herself alone in the house. Mom and Nadine were outside weeding the garden, and Dad and Simon were hard at work in the fields. She decided this would be a good time to read a few more scriptures from Grandma's Bible. Rebekah positioned her wheelchair at the kitchen table and set the Biewel and a glass of cold lemonade in front of her. A deep sense of longing encompassed her soul as she silently prayed, *What words do You have for me today, Lord? I need to know whether You have a special plan for my life.*

She opened the Bible to a place that Grandma had marked with a small piece of ribbon. As she studied the page, she spotted another underlined passage, Jeremiah 31:3-4. "The LORD hath appeared of old unto me, saying, Yea, I have loved thee with an everlasting love: therefore with lovingkindness have I drawn thee. Again I will build thee, and thou shalt be built."

Rebekah sat for several minutes, pondering the scripture. Deep in her heart she knew God loved her, but was

His Word saying He wanted to rebuild her? If so, did it mean rebuild her body? Now, that would take a huge miracle. No, she was fairly sure the scripture referred to being spiritually renewed and rebuilt, and she knew she was in need of that, especially where her lack of faith and tendency to fear the unknown were concerned.

For the next little while, Rebekah continued to seek out verses. She was pleased to discover several that dealt with the subject of fear. Psalm 34:4 in particular spoke to her heart: "I sought the LORD, and he heard me, and delivered me from all my fears." After Rebekah read the verse a couple more times, she had a deep sense that she must not be afraid of her dreams anymore or of being left alone. God would provide for her needs and calm her fears; she just needed to be faithful and learn to trust Him more.

With a feeling of peace she hadn't felt in many months, Rebekah closed the Bible, bowed her head, and offered a silent prayer. *Dear Father, thank You for reminding me that You love me with an everlasting love and want to build up my faith. Please draw me closer to You, and help me remember not to fear but to trust in You. And if it's Your will for me to support myself financially, then please show me how. Guide me, direct me, and prepare my heart for a true miracle from You. Amen.*

When Sarah finished her weeding and returned to the house, she was surprised to see that Rebekah was not in the kitchen where she had been earlier. Figuring her daughter might have gone to her room, she rapped on the door.

No answer.

"Rebekah, are you there?"

Still no response.

"Maybe she went to Grandma's old room." Sarah moved to the next room and knocked on that door.

"Come in."

She opened the door and spotted Rebekah sitting in her wheelchair, watering some of Grandma's African violets that had been placed on the window ledge. "I thought I might find you in here," she said, crossing the room to join her daughter in front of the window.

Rebekah turned her head and gave Sarah a questioning look. "Did you need me for something?"

"Not really, but I did want to talk to you about an idea I have."

"What idea is that, Mom?"

"Your daed's hired a driver to take us to the farmers' market tomorrow, where we plan to sell some of our fresh produce and a few other things. Since you seem so set on wanting to make some money of your own, I thought you might like to take some flowers from the garden or maybe a few of these houseplants to sell," she said, motioning to the violets.

"Sell off Grandma's plants?" Rebekah's eyebrows furrowed as she shook her head. "No, Mom, I could never do that. It wouldn't be right. No, not right at all."

"Why not?"

"Because the African violets were so special to her." Rebekah's smile never quite reached her eyes. "They help keep her memory alive, too."

"Grandma's memory will always be alive in our hearts," Sarah said. "We have many other things to remind us of her besides the plants, and I don't think Grandma would mind if you sold a few violets so you could have some money of your own."

"I do want to start making money, but selling off Grandma's plants? Sorry, but I just couldn't do that and feel good about it."

"Why not take cut flowers from the garden then? I'm sure those would sell, too."

"That would be all right, I suppose." Rebekah stared out the window with a wistful expression. Suddenly, she snapped her fingers and smiled. "I know! I could take some starts from Grandma's plants. All I need to do is put them in some pots full of good soil, and they'll soon become new plants of their own. It might even be good for the bigger plants to be thinned a bit. At least that's what Grandma used to say whenever I asked her why she was pinching some of the leaves off the violets and repotting them in smaller pots."

"I think that's a fine idea. If you want, I'll help you get the cuttings done today."

"Danki for offering, but if I'm to make the money from the plants, then I want to do all the work myself." She blinked a couple of times. "Besides, this is something I can do without any help at all."

"Okay." Sarah clasped Rebekah's shoulder and gave it a gentle squeeze. She turned to leave, but before she got to the door, Rebekah called out to her.

"Mom, there's one more thing."

"What's that, Rebekah?"

"I think I'm ready to start writing some things in my *Budget* column again."

"I'm glad to hear that. Maybe you can write up some-thing about our trip to the farmers' market."

"Jah, maybe so."

"All right then. Tomorrow you can share our sales table at the market, and we'll see how everything goes." Sarah went out the door, feeling a little more hopeful about Rebekah. She knew full well how important it was for her daughter to feel independent, and she would do nothing to stand in the way of Rebekah doing something on her own.

CHAPTER
5

The farmers' market seemed unusually busy, and the proof was in the parking lot, nearly full of cars. "It must be all the summer tourists," Dad said to Mom as they began unloading their things from the back of Vera Miller's van.

She smiled. "Jah, business should be good today."

Rebekah sat in her wheelchair beside the van, holding a box of African violet cuttings in her lap. "I hope so," she put in. "All the pruning and potting I did yesterday had better pay off."

Nadine, who stood behind Rebekah, leaned over her shoulder. "Want me to push you inside the building?"

Rebekah nodded. She hated to ask for assistance, but if she let go of the box in order to manipulate her wheelchair, she would probably end up losing the whole thing.

A few minutes later, they headed for the market building, each carrying a box of their own.

Once Rebekah's father and brother got tables set up, they started making sales. Mom had some vine-ripened, juicy red tomatoes and baskets of plump, sweet raspberries from her garden; Dad had brought some of his delicious, quick-to-make root beer; Simon sold cartons of bulky brown eggs; Nadine had several batches of chocolate cupcakes and ginger cookies for sale; and Rebekah had her freshly cut flowers and starts from several of Grandma's plants.

By noon, nearly all of Rebekah's African violet starts had been sold and many of the cut flowers, as well. It was the first time she'd ever made so much money in such a short time, and she was pleased that she had finally done something that might prove to be financially productive if she had more plants to sell and could come to the market more often.

"How's business?" Mary Ellen asked as she stepped up to the table Rebekah shared with her two siblings.

Rebekah grinned. "Much better than I'd ever imagined it would be. I only wish I had more plants and flowers to sell. If the market was open six days a week, I believe I could actually make enough money to be self-sufficient."

Mary Ellen nodded. "That would be *wunderbaar*, all right."

"Even if it was open all week, I couldn't afford to hire a driver that often." Rebekah shrugged. "Oh, well. It was a nice thought, anyway."

"You really do like flowers and plants, don't you?"

Rebekah's head bobbed up and down. "Jah. Ever so much."

"And as you've said, you've discovered today that they sell quite well."

"Indeed! I've done real well."

Mary Ellen leaned close to Rebekah's ear. "Can you take a little break? I'd like to talk with you—in private."

"About what?"

"I think I might have a great plan for you."

"What is it? Can't you tell me now?"

"We'd probably be interrupted by a customer if we tried to talk about it here."

Rebekah nodded. "Okay. It's time for lunch anyway, so I'll ask Nadine to watch my end of the table, and then I'll get the box lunch my mamm prepared this morning. We were planning to eat in shifts, so I'm sure Mom won't mind if I take my lunch break with you."

Mary Ellen grinned. "Sounds good to me. We can eat under the shade of that old maple tree out behind the building."

Soon after Rebekah wheeled away from their table, Nadine spotted her friend Carolyn Weaver heading her way. A freckle-faced Amish boy who looked to be about Nadine's age walked beside Carolyn. Nadine didn't think she had ever seen him before, but she thought he was awfully cute.

When Carolyn and the boy reached the end of the table where Nadine sat babysitting Rebekah's plants, they came to a halt.

"Didn't expect to see you here today," Carolyn said, offering Nadine a wide smile.

"Didn't expect to be here, neither." Nadine's gaze went to the dark-haired boy who stood beside her friend. Wasn't Carolyn going to introduce him?

As if she could read Nadine's mind, Carolyn nodded at the boy and said, "Nadine, this is my cousin Melvin. He and his family live in Missouri, and they've come to Lancaster County to visit for a couple of weeks."

Nadine put on what she hoped was her best smile. "It's nice to meet you, Melvin." She glanced over to see what her folks were doing and was pleased to see that they were both busy with customers at the moment.

"Nice to meet you, too," he said with a friendly grin.

Nadine leaned her elbows on the table and stared up at him. "I've never been to Missouri before. What's it like?"

Melvin shrugged his broad shoulders. "The weather's not much different than it is here, but the community we live in is a whole lot smaller." He scrunched up his nose. "Not much to do around there—that's for certain sure."

"No big towns nearby?"

"Nope. Just Seymour, and that's a pretty small place. The closest big town is Springfield, but of course, I don't get to go there so often."

"Is there a farmers' market in Seymour?"

"Just during the summer, and it's nothing at all like this place." He made a sweeping gesture to the tables nearby. "Ours is held outside in a vacant lot across the street from the hamburger place, not in a big building such as this."

"Oh, I see."

"Have you had your lunch yet?" Carolyn asked, breaking into their conversation.

Nadine shook her head.

"Want to get a hot dog with me and Melvin?"

Of course Nadine wanted to go. Selling Rebekah's plants was boring, and it would give her a chance to get to know Carolyn's cousin a little better. "Let me ask my folks."

Nadine pushed her chair aside and moved to the other table, where Dad sat with his jugs of root beer, and Mom her mounds of produce. "Can I go have lunch with my friend Carolyn and her cousin?" Nadine asked, leaning close to her mother's ear.

Mom shook her head. "Not until Rebekah gets back. You're needed here right now."

"How come?"

"Someone needs to keep an eye on her flowers."

"But that's not fair. You let Simon go to lunch at the same time as Rebekah."

"And you shall go as soon as they get back."

"But why can't you and Dad watch Rebekah's table?"

"Because the market is really busy, and a lot of customers are heading our way," Dad interjected. "So put on your best smile, sell lots of your sister's plants while she's gone, and no sulking. You hear?"

Nadine grunted and moved back to her end of the table. "Sorry, but I can't go to lunch until my sister and brother get back." She kept her gaze fixed on one of the African violets, afraid if she looked at Melvin as she spoke he might see the tears that were stinging the back of her eyes and threatening to spill over.

"How long will they be gone?" Carolyn asked.

"Probably another half hour or so."

"I guess we could walk around awhile and come back for you then."

Hope welled in Nadine's soul, but before she could give a reply, Melvin spoke up. "I'm really hungry, so if it's all the same to you, I think I'll head over to the hot-dog stand right now."

"Jah, okay. Maybe we can visit some other time," Nadine mumbled.

As Carolyn and Melvin walked away, Nadine pushed one of Rebekah's plants closer to the front of the table and gritted her teeth. *Rebekah always gets to do what she wants. Sometimes I wish I were the one in a wheelchair.*

"It's another hot, sticky day," Rebekah remarked as Mary Ellen took a seat on the grassy patch beside her wheelchair. "I'm glad we have a nice shady place to help keep us cool."

Mary Ellen took a drink of her foamy root beer. "Umm. . . your daed sure makes some good soda. This helps put the fire out on a muggy summer day such as this."

Rebekah giggled when the end of Mary Ellen's nose became covered with the frothy white head of the root beer. "And you wear my daed's soda real well, too."

Mary Ellen reached into her lunch basket and retrieved a napkin; then she swiped it across her nose. "There. Do I look any better?"

Rebekah nodded. "But then, you always look good in the face. It's not hard to figure out why so many of the fellows we know act like silly kinner in order to seek your favor."

"There's only one man whose favor I seek."

"And who might that be?"

"I'd rather not say just yet. Not until I'm sure he likes me, too. Besides, you didn't agree to have lunch with me so we could talk about my love life. I want to discuss a possible business venture with you."

"Business venture?" Rebekah's eyebrows lifted high on her forehead. "You and me?"

"No, just you. I've got my teaching job at the school, remember?"

"Of course I do, but what business venture are you thinking about that would involve me?"

"You've been telling me for weeks that you want to be self-sufficient. Isn't that right?"

Rebekah nodded. "Right as rain."

"Then I think I have an idea that might work quite well for you," Mary Ellen said as a feeling of excitement welled in her soul. She did so want to see her cousin make some money of her own.

"What idea do you have?"

"You need to make money in order to be more independent, correct?"

"Right again."

"Today you found out that you have a product people will buy."

"Jah. The flowers and plants."

"And you enjoy working with them?"

"Very much so."

"Then all you have to do is get more plants and sell more plants."

"That sounds wunderbaar, but you've forgotten one important thing."

Mary Ellen pursed her lips. "What's that?"

"The farmers' market isn't open often enough, and even if it were, there's the problem of me being able to afford transportation to and from."

"I'm getting to that." Mary Ellen tapped her finger against the side of her head as the excitement of her plan continued to mount. "I was thinking if you had a greenhouse near the front of your property, you could sell your plants and flowers from there. News travels fast around here, so I'm sure folks—especially the tourists who come to our area—would soon find out about your business. In no time at all, you would probably have a stream of customers coming the whole year long."

Rebekah's forehead wrinkled in obvious confusion. "That sounds like an interesting business venture, but there's one big problem."

"What problem is that?"

"We have no greenhouse on our property."

"So you have one built," Mary Ellen said, reaching into her lunch basket to retrieve a sandwich.

"It–it's not that simple. Building a greenhouse would take time and money."

"Not if your family and friends did all the work. I'm sure my daed would be glad to help out, and so would your other uncles and cousins. Maybe some of the neighboring Amish men would come, too." Mary Ellen grasped Rebekah's hand and gave it a gentle squeeze. "You really must ask your folks about this."

"Well, I don't know—"

"I'm sure your family wants you to be happy and self-reliant. Won't you at least give my idea some thought and talk it over with them?"

Rebekah finally nodded. "I'll think about it and, of course, pray for some answers. If God wants me to do something like this, then He will have to show me how."

Mary Ellen smiled, pleased that her cousin liked the idea and even more pleased to see Rebekah so excited about something.

CHAPTER
6

The entire Stoltzfus family had been invited to a picnic at the Hiltys' place, and Rebekah looked forward to going. Family picnics were always fun, and it was a good time for the busy farmers and craftsmen to get caught up with one another's active lives. Since preaching services in their Amish community were biweekly and this was an off Sunday, it was a nice way to spend the afternoon.

Mom had insisted that Rebekah wear her leg braces for at least part of the day, reminding her that she needed to get out of that wheelchair once in a while and exercise the lower half of her body. As much as Rebekah disliked the cumbersome braces and the effort it took to walk, she didn't want to make a fuss about it, so with the aid of her crutches, she gritted her teeth and hobbled up the dirt path leading to the Hiltys' front porch.

Mary Ellen had been sitting on the porch swing, but when Rebekah approached, she jumped up and rushed toward her. "Oh, it's so good to see you walking today."

Rebekah frowned and shook her head. "This isn't really walking. I feel like one of those little metal robots I've seen in the toy section at the Wal-Mart store."

"Here, let me help you up the steps," Mary Ellen offered, ignoring Rebekah's negative comment. "We can sit on the swing and visit awhile."

Rebekah allowed her cousin to help her up the stairs, then over to the swing. "What's new in your life?" she asked, once she was seated.

"Not so much," Mary Ellen said with a shrug, but her hazel-colored eyes sparkled as though she could hardly contain herself.

"Are you sure about that? You look pretty happy about something."

Mary Ellen stood for a few seconds, rocking back and forth on her heels. Then her lips turned into a wide smile. "If you must know, Johnny has finally asked if he can court me."

Rebekah had mixed feelings about that bit of news. She was trying to be happy for Mary Ellen because she was her best friend and all, but she felt sorry for poor Daniel. Now that Johnny would be calling on Mary Ellen, Daniel's chances of winning her would be slim to none.

Rebekah plastered a smile on her face, although she really felt like crying. "It's nice to see you're so happy."

"Jah, I truly am." Mary Ellen's face fairly glowed as she took a seat beside Rebekah on the swing and reached out to clasp her hand. "How are things with you these days? Have you thought any more about my greenhouse idea?"

Rebekah nodded, glad for the change of subject. "I have. I even talked to Mom and Dad, and they think it's a good idea, too. Dad says he can begin building it sometime next week." She drew in a deep breath and let it out in a rush.

"Just think, I might actually be able to support myself if this business takes hold."

"That would be wunderbaar, all right." Mary Ellen squinted. "But what will you sell? Do you have enough plants and flowers?"

"Not yet, but with the money I made at the farmers' market, I'll be able to buy some of what I need to get started. I can use more starts from Grandma's plants, and there's always fresh-cut flowers from our garden to sell."

"Sounds like you've got it all figured out."

"I'm working on it. In the beginning, all my profits will have to go back into the business. I'll need to buy more plants, seeds, fertilizers, pots, and potting soil. After the first year or so, I'm hoping that I'll be able to start supporting myself."

Mary Ellen pumped the swing back and forth with her legs—legs Rebekah would have given nearly anything to have owned. "It's good to see you so cheerful. You've been acting kind of gloomy lately."

Rebekah sighed. "That's partly because of those awful dreams I kept having about Grandma dying and then others in my family leaving me, too."

"Are you still having the nightmares?"

"Not since I started praying more and committing to memory some scriptures on trusting God and not fearing the unknown."

"I'm glad to hear it. Which verses have you memorized?"

Rebekah was about to reply when Aunt Mim stepped onto the porch, interrupting their conversation. "I see you two have found my favorite swinging seat," she said, smiling brightly.

"Would you like to sit here?" Rebekah offered. "We can go someplace else to visit."

"You stay right where you are. I can't take time to sit just now, anyway. I have to see about getting some food set out for this family picnic of ours."

"Is there anything we can do to help?" Mary Ellen questioned.

Aunt Mim shook her head. "Maybe later. Sarah, Crystal, and Grace are here to help, so you two can sit right there for now and keep on visiting." With a wave of her hand, she hurried into the house.

"Aunt Mim's a sweet lady. She always seems so full of joy," Rebekah said, nudging Mary Ellen with her elbow.

"Jah. She may not be my real mamm, but she loves me like she is. I thank God for bringing her into our lives when I was a young girl—though she wasn't always so happy."

"What do you mean?"

"Don't you remember when she was our schoolteacher and some of the kinner used to call her en alt maedel with a heart of stone?"

Rebekah nodded. She wondered how many folks thought of her as an old maid. She knew her sister did because she'd already said so. Despite the fact that Nadine had apologized for her hurtful words, things hadn't been the same between them since their last disagreement.

"God can change hearts if we allow Him to," Mary Ellen said, waving her hand at a bothersome fly that seemed determined to buzz their heads.

"Do you think God still performs miracles?"

"Of course He does. Why would you ask such a thing?"

Rebekah's eyelids fluttered, then closed and opened again. "Sometimes I think I might be able to actually *feel* God's presence if He gave me an enormous miracle the way He did for folks back in the Bible days. In fact, I've been praying for such a miracle and trying to trust that He will answer that prayer."

"We don't need big miracles in order to see God. He performs small miracles in people's lives nearly every day." Mary Ellen took hold of Rebekah's hand and gave her fingers a gentle squeeze. "Often we don't see the small miracles because we don't have our eyes wide open."

"Are you talking about me?"

"Not in particular. I'm talking about believers in general. Even when clouds of pain seem to hide God's face, we're never hidden from His miracle of love and His tender mercies."

Rebekah studied Mary Ellen's pretty face. "Just how did a nineteen-year-old woman get to be so smart, anyway?"

Mary Ellen smiled, bringing to the surface her two matching dimples. "I think my wisdom comes from God, but I wouldn't be teaching school if I wasn't putting it into practice every day."

Rebekah nodded and released another audible sigh. "You're probably right. I'm praying that God will give me lots of wisdom, and I hope it's real soon. For as I'm sure you've heard some of the older folks say, 'we grow too soon old and too late smart.' "

Four large picnic tables had been set up on the front lawn

for eating, and two more were loaded with a variety of food and beverages. Rebekah noticed that everyone seemed to be in good spirits and had come with hearty appetites, for not only was a lot of visiting going on, but in no time at all, most of the food was gone, too.

When it appeared that everyone had finished eating, Rebekah's father stood and called for their attention. The hum of talking subsided as he clapped his hands together. "Those who work hard eat hearty, and you've all done right well. Now it's time to share some good news with you." He paused and glanced over at Rebekah. "I want you to know that my oldest daughter is about to become a businesswoman."

All eyes turned to Rebekah, and she felt the heat of a blush creep up the back of her neck and spread quickly to her face.

Dad laid his hand on her shoulder. "Rebekah wants to open a greenhouse that will be built near the front of our property."

Cheers went up around the tables, and everyone smiled at Rebekah—everyone except Nadine. She just sat stony-faced, staring at her empty plate, which only confirmed in Rebekah's mind that things still weren't right between her and her sister.

"If the greenhouse is to be built before summer ends, I'll need some help with the project," Dad continued. "Are there any volunteers?"

"You can count on me," said Uncle Lewis.

Uncle Jonas nodded. "Jah, me, too."

"I'd be more than happy to help," Uncle Amos put in.

"Same here." This came from Cousin Henry, whose eager

expression made Rebekah think he might like to begin build-ing on her greenhouse right away.

"Don't forget about us," John and Jacob said in unison.

"I would help if I was bigger," seven-year-old Matthew piped up.

Dad laughed. "I'll not turn away any help. Danki, to all of you."

"I'm ever so grateful," Rebekah said, feeling tears of joy flood her eyes.

"What will you call this new business of yours?" Aunt Mim questioned.

Rebekah sniffed and wiped her eyes with the backs of her hands as a vision of Grandma Stoltzfus came to mind. "I'm thinking about calling it Grandma's Place. I'll be using lots of starts from her plants, and she loved flowers so much. It seems only fitting to name the greenhouse after her."

"I think it's a wunderbaar name," Aunt Mim said with a nod.

"I do believe we'd better move this conversation in-doors," Mom interjected, "because I just felt something wet splat right on my nose!"

Everyone scrambled to get the dishes cleared off the tables and into the house, but Nadine, arms folded, and chin tucked against her neck, remained seated. Why was it that everything always had to be about Rebekah? *Rebekah needs more understanding. Rebekah should sell plants at the farmers' market. Rebekah will soon be getting her own greenhouse.* Nadine was sick of her sister being the center of attention and getting to do all the fun things she was never allowed to do.

She thought back to the day at the farmers' market when she'd been denied the privilege of having lunch with Carolyn and her cousin Melvin. Rebekah had gotten back late from her lunch with Mary Ellen, and by the time Nadine was free to go, Carolyn and Melvin had already left the market.

It's not fair, she grumbled in silence as the rain continued to fall. *I'm always kept busy with chores, and I hardly ever get to do anything just for fun.*

"How come you're still out here in the rain? I thought you'd gone inside with the other women."

Nadine whirled around. Dad stood behind her with a disgruntled look on his face. At least he hadn't referred to her as a little girl. She supposed that was something to be thankful for.

"I was just sitting here thinking," she mumbled.

He lifted his hand and caught several raindrops in his palm. "You like thinkin' in the rain?"

She gave an exaggerated shrug.

"You'd better get into the house now. This storm is getting worse, and we'll be leaving as soon as we've had our dessert."

With a weary sigh, Nadine climbed off the picnic bench and trudged toward the house, feeling even more frustrated because she wouldn't be allowed the privilege of sitting in the rain by herself.

"Dad, I wish we weren't heading for home already," Nadine complained from the back of their closed-in buggy. "That homemade ice cream Uncle Amos made was sure good, and I wanted a second helping."

"We left because of this storm," Dad called back to her. "It's getting worse all the time, and we need to be home to see that the livestock gets fed and put to bed."

It was obvious by the way their father gripped the reins that he was fighting to keep the horse under control. Jagged streaks of lightning zigzagged across the horizon, thunderous roars shook the sky, and the rain pelted to the ground in torrents.

"I'm scared," Nadine whined. "I hate *wedderleech* and *dunner*. I wish we could have stayed at Aunt Mim's house until the storm was over."

"Aw, a little lightning and thunder is nothin' to be scared of," Simon asserted. "This is just a typical summer storm."

Mom looked back at them over her shoulder. "There's nothing typical about this weather, and I think it would be wise if we all kept quiet so your daed can concentrate on his driving."

Rebekah leaned her head a little closer to Nadine, hoping to calm the girl's nerves. "We'll be home soon enough."

Another shuddering clap of thunder sounded, and the horse whinnied loudly. "Whoa there. Steady, boy," Dad said in a soothing voice.

They were nearing their farm, and as they turned up the gravel driveway, Mom let out a shrill scream. "Fire! Oh, Andrew, our barn's all ablaze!"

"It must have been struck by lightning." Dad urged the horse into a fast trot. When they reached their front yard, he halted the gelding and jumped down from the buggy.

"Go get help!" he called to Mom. "Simon, you and Nadine should start filling some buckets with water right away."

"What about me?" Rebekah asked, feeling helpless and frightened. Wasn't there something she could do to lend a hand?

"You can either go on up to the house or ride with me," Mom said over her shoulder.

Rebekah looked out the window and saw Dad running toward the water trough, with Simon and Nadine on his heels. It was obvious that none of them had the time to help her out of the buggy right now. "I'll ride with you, Mom," she replied, knowing full well that they couldn't afford to waste a single moment.

Mom nodded and quickly turned the buggy around. As they tore out of the yard, Rebekah grabbed the edge of her seat, fearing she might be thrown out. When she turned to look out the back window again, she saw Dad, Simon, and Nadine running frantically toward the barn, each carrying two buckets of water in their hands.

The rain soon turned to a trickle, but the wind continued to blow furiously. Rebekah was painfully aware that, unless the fire department could get to their place quickly, Dad would surely lose the whole barn.

The first stop Mom made was at their English neighbors' house, which was about two miles down the road. She asked them to call the county fire department; then she headed over to Jonas and Crystal's place to let them know what had happened.

Uncle Jonas and his boys left right away to help fight the fire, while Mom and Rebekah moved on to enlist the help of Uncle Lewis, Uncle Amos, and Henry.

Rebekah prayed and kept a close watch out the window to be sure there was nothing in Mom's way. By the time they got home, the wind had subsided, and two Lancaster County fire trucks were parked in the driveway, their red lights flashing this way and that. One look at the barn told Rebekah all she needed to know. The firefighters' efforts had been in vain—the barn had burned clean to the ground.

She glanced toward the corral and realized that Dad must have managed to save the livestock, because the cows and horses he kept inside the barn were now crowded into the corral. At least that was something for which to be grateful.

As the reality of the situation took hold, Rebekah's eyes stung with tears, and she nearly choked on a sob. "Ach my, what will Dad do now?"

Mom reached over the seat and took hold of Rebekah's hand. "He'll do just as all other Amish men do whenever they lose a barn. He shall have a barn raising."

CHAPTER 7

Rebekah figured the news had spread quickly about Dad's barn burning to the ground, for offers of help to rebuild came from far and wide, from both their English and Amish neighbors. It was a comfort to know that so many people cared about them.

"When is the barn raising going to be?" she asked Dad as the family sat around the kitchen table the following morning.

"Simon and I, and probably Amos, Jonas, and Lewis, will spend time today and tomorrow cleaning up the mess left from the fire. Many bales of hay were ruined, and those have to be disposed of, too. Then the foundation will need to be laid, and if all goes well, we should have the barn fairly well finished by next Saturday." He pulled his fingers through the end of his beard and grunted. "I'm sorry, Rebekah, but the building of your greenhouse will have to wait awhile longer. I hope you understand."

Rebekah felt a keen sense of disappointment, but she couldn't let Dad know that. He had enough on his mind. She wouldn't say anything that might cause him to feel guilty about something he couldn't prevent. "It's all right," she said, forcing a smile. "Getting the new barn up is more important than anything else right now."

"We'll all be busy during the next several days," Mom put in as she left the table and headed across the room to get the pot of coffee from the stove. "There will be a lot of food to prepare for the hungry crews and several errands to run as we get everything ready for the barn raising."

Nadine, who sat across the table from Rebekah, seemed to perk right up. "Will some of the boys my age come to help raise the barn?"

"I'm sure many of the young fellows will show up with their daeds," Dad replied. "There will be plenty of work to do, even for the younger ones."

"Maybe I can help by bringing nails and other supplies out to the workers," Nadine volunteered.

"She doesn't really want to work. She just wants to flirt with the boys." Simon reached across Rebekah and jabbed Nadine's arm with the end of his spoon.

"There'll be no time for flirting," Mom said with a shake of her head. "Nadine will be kept busy helping the women that day, not the boys."

"I always have to help the women," Nadine mumbled.

Simon wrinkled his nose. "Oh, quit with all the *gebrutz*."

"I'm not pouting."

"Sure you are," he said with a slow nod. "It seems like you're always pouting or complaining about something these days."

Before Nadine could respond, Dad shot them both a warning look, and they clamped their mouths shut real quick.

When Mom joined them at the table again, she touched Rebekah lightly on the shoulder. "I was thinking of hiring a driver to take me to Lancaster to do some shopping later today. If you'd like to go along, maybe we could stop by the garden center and pick out some plants for that new greenhouse of yours."

Rebekah's spirits lifted a bit. "Do you have time for that? I know you had planned to do some baking today."

"Oh, that can wait until tomorrow, I expect."

"Can I go, too?" Nadine asked with a hopeful expression.

"I'd rather you stayed home today," Mom said. "I have some wash that should be hung, and Dad and Simon will be cleaning up the mess from the old barn so they'll need someone here to make their lunches."

"Does that mean you're not gonna be home from Lancaster by lunchtime?" Nadine questioned.

Mom poured herself a cup of coffee and then one for Dad. "By the time Rebekah and I finish our shopping, it will no doubt be noon, so we'll probably eat someplace along the way."

Nadine crinkled her nose and leered at Rebekah. "That's not fair. She always gets to have all the fun. I wish that I were—"

"What? You wish you were like me? Is that what you were going to say, Nadine?"

Her sister shrugged. "Maybe."

"Come now. Would you really want to be trapped in my crippled body, limited to a wheelchair or those confining leg braces I sometimes must wear? Do you think that's anything to be jealous of?" Rebekah's voice had raised at least

84

two octaves, and her hand shook as she pointed a finger at Nadine. "You don't even know what you're saying. Why, I'd gladly trade places with you or anyone else who could walk and run!"

Rebekah knew she was letting her emotions get the best of her, but she had already begun to say what was on her mind, and she wasn't about to stop until she'd gotten it all said. "Someday you'll grow up and fall in love. Then you'll get married and have kinner. Your life will be full and complete." She gulped on a sob. "I, on the other hand, will never marry or fall in love. So please don't envy me or anything I might be allowed to do, because I would give almost anything if I could do all the things you're able to do."

Nadine's face flushed, and without a word, she jumped up from the table and dashed out of the room.

Dad turned to Rebekah and said, "Don't let your sister upset you. She's young and doesn't understand what it's like to be in your situation. To her, it probably seems as though you get more attention and special favors, so it might help if you could be more tolerant of her, too."

Rebekah nodded, feeling foolish for allowing her temper to get the better of her. "Jah, Dad, I know, and I'll try to be more understanding of Nadine."

As Rebekah and Mom rode to Lancaster in Vera's van later that morning, Rebekah put her nose up to the open window on her side to enjoy the clean, fresh smell. Sometimes after a summer storm had left its mark, the air would turn hot and muggy. Not today, though. Today was much cooler with hardly any humidity at all. For the benefit of the men who would be working on Dad's barn, she hoped it would stay like this until the job was done.

Rebekah's thoughts went to her sister, and she began to fret over the way Nadine always reacted whenever she wasn't allowed to do something Rebekah got to do. If there was only some way to make her sister understand the way things were. Rebekah wished she could be as close to Nadine as she was to Mary Ellen, but unless Nadine's attitude changed, they were unlikely to become good friends.

As they pulled into the town of Lancaster, Rebekah pushed her thoughts aside and allowed her emotions to soar. Opening a greenhouse of her own would be the most exciting thing she had ever done. She could hardly contain herself as Vera steered the van off the main road and into the parking lot at the garden center.

Mom and Vera went around to the back of the van to get Rebekah's wheelchair, and a short time later, Rebekah and Mom entered the store.

With a feeling of anticipation, Rebekah wheeled up and down the aisles, inspecting a variety of houseplants and outdoor foliage as she went along. "Oh, Mom," she said excitedly, "just look at how many plants and flowers there are to choose from."

Mom smiled. "Maybe someday you'll have nearly as many in your own place of business."

Rebekah sucked in a deep breath and released it quickly. "I could only wish for such a miracle."

"I believe miracles are to be prayed for, daughter, not wished for," Mom corrected.

Rebekah shrugged. "Well, you know what I mean."

"Are you looking for anything in particular?" one of the clerks asked, as he stepped up to them.

Rebekah smiled at the tall, gray-haired man. "I need several of your hardiest, most reasonably priced indoor and outdoor plants."

He chuckled. "I see we have a shrewd businesswoman here."

Rebekah felt the heat of a blush creep up her neck. She wondered if she looked old enough or smart enough to be a businesswoman. Or did the clerk only see her as a pathetic crippled girl in a wheelchair, who needed someone to say something nice to her so she would feel better?

"I think I do know a good bargain when I see one," she said. "So if you'll lead the way, as we go along, I'll decide what will best suit my needs."

Rebekah was thankful when Mom walked slowly behind and gave her opinion only when it was asked for. If this was going to be Rebekah's business venture, then she figured she should do as much of the decision making as possible.

It took about an hour for her to select all the plants she needed, and when Vera showed up, the clerk helped load all the boxes into the back of Vera's van. He even offered to help Mom with Rebekah's wheelchair.

"You did real good today," Mom said, as she assisted Rebekah into the back seat of the van. "You got quite a few plants for the amount of money you had. I would think if you took some starts from them, you could probably double—or even triple—your investment in no time."

Rebekah smiled and reached over to touch her mother's

arm. "You knew I was disappointed about Dad not being able to start building the greenhouse this week, didn't you?"

"Jah, I knew."

"And you thought this trip to town might make me feel better?"

"I hoped it would."

"Well, it worked, because I do feel better." Rebekah patted her stomach and grinned. "But I'd feel even better if we had something to eat."

Mom laughed. "Vera and I talked about that earlier. We'll have lunch somewhere on the way home, and right after that, I have one more errand I need to run."

"Oh? What errand is that?"

"It's going to be a surprise for someone."

"A surprise? You can tell me, Mom. I won't spill the beans, I promise."

Mom placed her fingers against her mouth. "My lips are sealed."

Rebekah was allowed to choose where they would eat lunch, and she picked a Pennsylvania Dutch restaurant near the town of Bird-in-Hand, telling Mom she never got tired of traditional Amish cooking. The three women were escorted to a long table where several other people sat. This was part of family-style dining, but Rebekah felt funny about sitting next to folks she'd never met before. She knew most of them were just curious tourists wanting to check out the Plain folks, but that didn't make her feel any less self-conscious.

"Could we have a small table by ourselves?" she asked her mother.

Mom turned to Vera. "Is that all right with you?"

"Whatever Rebekah's comfortable with is fine by me," Vera said with a nod.

Mom smiled at their Mennonite hostess and said, "Would you possibly have a separate table for the three of us?"

The young woman, who was dressed in plain clothes similar to what Rebekah and Mom wore, nodded and led them to a small table near the window, then handed them each a menu.

Rebekah maneuvered her wheelchair as close to the table as possible. It wasn't as easy as eating at home, where the big wooden table had plenty of leg room, but at least they would have some measure of privacy. "I'm just not up to people's curious stares today," she said to Mom and Vera when they'd taken their seats across from her.

"I don't think folks would be staring at us," Mom replied. "This is a Pennsylvania Dutch restaurant, remember? There are several Amish and Mennonite people eating here, too."

Vera smiled. "Most of the help are Plain People, as well."

"I know, but I was thinking more about them staring at me—my disability," Rebekah said with a grimace.

Mom reached across the table and patted Rebekah's hand. "Try not to worry so much about what other people think. Not everyone in the world stares at people with disabilities, you know." She shrugged. "Even if they should stare, how can it really hurt?"

Rebekah fingered her silverware, pushing her knife and

spoon together and then apart again. "It makes me feel uncomfortable when they look at me, that's all."

Another young Mennonite woman came to take their order. "We have two choices for the Dutch family-style lunch," she explained. "One is roast beef, which also comes with baked country sausage, mashed potatoes, green beans, chowchow, pork and sauerkraut, pepper cabbage, and homemade bread." She paused a moment, then added, "The other menu includes baked ham, fried chicken, bread filling, applesauce, pickled beets, noodles in brown gravy, sweet potatoes, creamed corn, bread-and-butter pickles, and homemade rolls." She stopped again and drew in a deep breath. "The beverages we have to offer are coffee, hot tea, iced tea, lemonade, and milk. The choice of desserts for both meals is the same: carrot cake, shoofly pie, cherry crumb pie, tapioca pudding, apple crumb pie, vanilla ice cream, German chocolate cake, and pumpkin roll."

"Ach! With either meal there's so much food to eat," Mom exclaimed. "It's a hard choice to make—that's for sure." She nodded at Rebekah. "What would you like?"

"I think I'd prefer the one that includes baked ham and bread filling. I could eat tasty filling until the cows come home."

Mom glanced at Vera. "Which meal appeals to you?"

"The second one is fine for me," Vera told the waitress.

As soon as the woman walked away, Mom leaned across the table and whispered to Rebekah, "You know, I may have to borrow that wheelchair of yours when we leave this place."

Rebekah squinted. "Huh?"

"They might have to wheel me out of here because I'll be too full to walk."

Rebekah giggled. It felt good to spend the day with Mom like this. She could understand why her sister might be a bit jealous, but Nadine got to do so many other things—things Rebekah couldn't do. She hoped by now that Nadine had forgotten about the little argument they'd had this morning and had found something to feel positive about. Knowing her little sister, she was probably daydreaming about some boy already.

In no time at all, the food started coming, and whenever one bowl emptied, the waitress was there to fill it up again. Rebekah ate until she couldn't take another bite, and as they left the restaurant, she figured none of them would need any supper that night.

"Where would you like to go while I'm on my secret errand?" Mom asked, helping Rebekah into the van.

Rebekah shrugged. "Oh, I don't know. Maybe the bookstore. I might find something there on caring for plants or possibly on business management."

"That sounds fine," Mom agreed. "We'll drop you off first; then Vera can take me to my errand. We'll be back in half an hour or so."

"Okay, Mom."

The bookstore was only a few blocks away, and soon they had pulled up to the brick storefront. Mom went around and got out the wheelchair; then she helped Rebekah into it, walked to the front of the bookstore, and held the door open. "See you soon, sweet daughter."

Rebekah waved and wheeled herself inside. There seemed

to be a lot of tourists milling around today, looking at all the books that had been written about the Amish and Mennonite people and their Plain lifestyle. She moved quickly away from the group of curious onlookers and found the shelf where the books about plants and flowers were kept. She spotted one on the second shelf entitled *Caring for Your African Violets.* Rebekah strained to reach it, but her arm wasn't long enough. She could attempt standing, she supposed, but she had tried that a time or two without the aid of her crutches, and usually ended up flat on the floor. Falling on her face at home was one thing, but making a fool of herself in front of an audience was not on Rebekah's list of things to do for the day.

She glanced around, hoping to catch the attention of one of the store clerks. They all seemed to be busy helping the English tourists.

"You are buying a *buch?*" The question came from a deep male voice.

Rebekah gave her chair a sharp turn to the left. Daniel Beachy stood looking down on her with his straw hat in one hand and a crooked grin on his face. "I'm surprised to see you here, Rebekah. Are you alone?"

"Mom's in town, but she's on an errand so I'm here buying a book." Rebekah's forehead wrinkled. "At least I would be if I could reach it."

"Which one is it? I'll get it down for you," he offered.

Rebekah pointed to the shelf above her. *"Caring for Your African Violets."*

Daniel's long arm easily reached the book, and he handed it to her with another friendly looking smile. "Are you a plant lover?"

She nodded. "Oh, jah. Especially African violets. They were Grandma Stoltzfus's favorite plant, too." She placed the book in her lap. "I hope to open a greenhouse soon, so I want to learn all I can about how to run the business."

Daniel's eyebrows shot up. "A greenhouse, you say? Now that sounds like an interesting business venture. Where will it be located?"

"Near the front of our property. Of course, that won't be until Dad has time to build it. We lost our barn last night, so the greenhouse project will have to wait another week or two."

Daniel's dark eyes looked more serious than usual as he nodded. "I heard about that fire; such a shame it is, too. When is the barn raising going to be?"

"There's a lot of cleanup work that needs to be done, and then the foundation will have to be laid, so the building probably won't begin until at least next Friday or Saturday."

"Tell your daed he can count on my help." Daniel drummed his fingers against his chin. "Maybe I could help build your greenhouse, too. I'm pretty handy with a hammer and saw."

"Danki. I'll appreciate any help I can get."

Daniel shuffled his feet a few times and stared down at his boots. "Well, guess I'd best get going. I picked up some supplies for my daed, and he's probably wondering what's takin' me so long."

"I'm sorry for keeping you."

He patted his stomach. "Naw, it wasn't you. I spent way too much time eating my noon meal. They were serving roast beef at the Plain and Fancy today. I think I ate my share and enough for about five others, as well."

"Mom and I were at the Plain and Fancy, too, with our driver, Vera," Rebekah said. "I didn't see you there, though."

"I was at one of the long tables with a bunch of other folks over on the right side of the room."

"That's probably why we didn't see you, then. We three ate at a small table near the window."

Daniel turned toward the door; then as though he might have forgotten something, he turned back around. "Say, I hear there's going to be another singing in two weeks. It's supposed to be over at Clarence Yoder's place. Do you plan on being there, Rebekah?"

Rebekah thought about the last singing she had attended and remembered how out of place she'd felt. She shook her head. "I've got too much work to do if I'm going to get all my plants ready to open for business in August." A small sigh escaped her lips. "That is, if I have a greenhouse by then."

"The barn raising will only take a good full day if there's plenty of help," Daniel said. "We should have your building up in short order once the work on the barn is done."

"That would be nice."

"Well, I'd best go now. See you soon, Rebekah."

"Have fun at the singing," she called to his retreating form.

"Guess I won't go to this one, either," he mumbled before he disappeared out the door.

"Poor Daniel," Rebekah whispered. "He likes Mary Ellen so much he's probably not going to the singing because he can't stand to see Johnny flirting with her again." She clicked her tongue. "What a shame my cousin doesn't see how nice Daniel is."

As Daniel exited the bookstore, he couldn't get the image of Rebekah out of his mind. She'd looked kind of bewildered and had even acted a bit nervous when he'd first spotted her trying to reach that book. After he'd taken it off the shelf for her and they'd talked about the plans for her new greenhouse, she had seemed to relax some. But then when he'd mentioned the singing, Rebekah had acted kind of distant again.

Maybe some ice cream would cheer her up, he thought as his gaze came to rest on the ice-cream store across the street. *Think I'll get a couple of cones and take one over to her.*

A short time later, Daniel left the ice-cream store holding two double-dip strawberry ice-cream cones in his hands. He had just started up the sidewalk and was almost ready to cross the street, when a young Amish boy riding a scooter whizzed past.

Daniel jumped out of the way just in time to keep from being knocked off his feet, but in the process, the ice-cream cones toppled over, landing on the sidewalk with a *splat.*

"Sorry," the boy mumbled, but he kept on going.

"Jah, me, too." Daniel bent to pick up the smashed cones, tossed them into the nearest trash can, and headed back to the ice-cream store.

A short time later, holding two more double-dip cones securely in his hands, he made his way across the street and into the bookstore. At first glance he saw no sign of Rebekah, so he walked up and down every aisle, looking for her.

"May I help you?" the middle-aged Englishman who ran the bookstore asked as he stepped up to Daniel.

"I–I'm looking for a young woman in a wheelchair. She was here a few minutes ago, looking at a book about African violets."

The man nodded. "She bought the book and then left the store right after that."

"Well, wouldn't ya just know it?" Daniel started for the door but turned back around, lifting one of the cones in the air. "Say, would you like an ice-cream cone?"

The man smiled but shook his head. "Thanks anyway, but I'm a diabetic so I have to watch my sugar intake."

"Jah, okay." Daniel shuffled his way to the front of the store and headed out the door. "Should have never bought any ice cream at all," he grumbled. "Guess I'm gonna have to eat both of these cones now so they don't go to waste."

Friday morning, Rebekah awoke to the piercing sound of pulsating hammers pounding nails into heavy pieces of lumber, and the grating of saws cutting thick pieces of wood. She had slept well the night before and had even had a very pleasant dream about her future greenhouse, where she'd become quite successful.

She grabbed hold of the bed rails, pulled herself upright, scooted to the edge of the bed, and dropped into her wheelchair. Her arms were strong, and she had become quite adept at this morning ritual. It wasn't an easy task, but it was better than bothering someone else to come help.

Rebekah wheeled herself over to the window so she could look out at the side yard and see what was going on. From her downstairs bedroom, she had the perfect view of the spot where the new barn was going to be.

She lifted one edge of the dark shade a bit and took a peek. She was surprised to see so many men and boys scurrying about the place. Why, nearly two hundred of them had come to help out. Some were already laying the floor beams and planks, while others had paired off in groups to prepare the panels, beams, and rafters.

Rebekah caught sight of one of the younger men looking her way, and she quickly turned her chair away from the window. From this distance, she couldn't be sure who had been watching her, but she didn't need anyone's curious stares or pitying looks this morning. Besides, she knew she should hurry and get dressed so she could see about helping with breakfast and whatever else needed to be done.

Aunt Mim, Aunt Crystal, Aunt Grace, and Mom were already in the kitchen when Rebekah made her entrance a short time later. Nadine and their cousins Peggy, Maddie, and Mary Ellen were also helping out. The room was warm and smelled of sweet cinnamon buns, reminding Rebekah of Grandma, who had always liked to bake. A pang of regret shot through her, but it was quickly replaced with a sense of peace. She still missed Grandma and probably always would, but Rebekah had finally come to grips with her loss, taking comfort in the fact that Grandma was in a much better place.

"Why'd you let me sleep so late?" Rebekah asked, as she wheeled up to her mother. "I didn't know anyone was here until I woke up to the racket of all those noisy hammers and saws."

"You must sleep pretty sound. They've been at it for nearly an hour already," Aunt Crystal said with a wink.

"Don't worry about it," Mom said. "As you can see, I have plenty of help. I thought it would do you good to sleep a little longer this morning. Ever since our trip to the garden center in Lancaster, you've been busy cutting and repotting all those plants you bought and studying that book on African violets."

"Your mamm was telling us more about your new business venture," Aunt Mim said as she made a place at the table for Rebekah to park her wheelchair. "It sounds exciting—hopefully prosperous, too."

Rebekah reached for a sticky cinnamon bun and smiled. "I sure hope so."

"Rebekah's going to use some starts from Grandma Stoltzfus's plants in her greenhouse," Mary Ellen put in.

Aunt Mim smiled. "That sounds like a good idea."

"Grandma was real special, and she taught me to appreciate flowers and plants," Rebekah said, reaching for a glass and the pitcher of cold milk, also on the table.

The back door flew open just then, and Rebekah's fifteen-year-old twin cousins, Jacob and John, rushed into the kitchen. "We need somethin' cold to drink!" Jacob wiped his sweaty forehead with the back of his arm. "It's already hot as an oven out there."

John nodded in agreement, his brown eyes looking ever so serious. "That's right, and when a body works hard, a body deserves a cool drink!"

Aunt Crystal nodded. "I think these boys are real workers. We should give them some iced tea. Better send some of it out for the other men, too."

"There are several jugs in there," Mom said, pointing to the refrigerator. "Just help yourself and take the rest outside. I think there are some paper cups on the picnic table."

John stared at the plate of sticky buns sitting on the table. "You wouldn't happen to have enough of those so we could have some, would you, Aunt Sarah?"

She laughed. "There's more on the counter behind you. Help yourself and take some out to the other workers, as well."

The boys piled some of the cinnamon rolls onto a plate, grabbed some jugs of iced tea, and headed back outside.

As soon as Rebekah finished eating her breakfast, she rolled her wheelchair over to the sink, where her mother stood washing dishes. "What can I do to help?"

"Why don't you and Mary Ellen shell some peas for the salads we'll be having with our noon meal? You can go outside on the porch to do it, if you like."

"Okay," Rebekah said with a nod.

Mary Ellen gathered up two hefty pans and a paper sack full of plump peas, and Rebekah followed her out the back door.

Mary Ellen found a metal folding chair that had been propped against the side of the house near the door and pulled it up next to Rebekah's wheelchair. She placed one of the pans in Rebekah's lap and put the other in her own. Then she distributed the peas equally between them.

"How's the courtship with Johnny going?" Rebekah asked as she picked up a handful of pea pods and began to shell them lickety-split.

Mary Ellen's face broke into a wide smile. "It's going real good. He's been over to our place to see me nearly every night for the past week."

"Do you like him a lot?"

"Jah, I do. He's so much fun and pretty good-looking,

too, don't you think?"

Rebekah wrinkled her nose and emitted a noise that sounded something like a cat whose tail had been stepped on. "That's not for me to be saying. Johnny might not take kindly to me making eyes at him."

"I'm not asking you to make eyes at him, silly. I only wondered if you think he's good-looking or not."

Rebekah shrugged her slim shoulders and grabbed another handful of pea pods. "I suppose he's all right. He's just not my type, that's all."

"Who is your type, might I ask? Is there something you're not telling me? Do you have your heart set on anyone special?"

Rebekah shook her head.

"I'll bet it's Daniel Beachy. I've seen the way you steal looks in his direction whenever you think no one's paying any attention."

Rebekah's face turned crimson. "I have no interest in any man, and none have interest in me."

"Maybe they do have an interest, and you're just too blind to see it."

"Don't you think I would know if someone cared for me?"

"Maybe so. Maybe not."

"What's that supposed to mean?"

"It means that you might not be paying close enough attention."

Rebekah made no further comment on the subject, and Mary Ellen decided it was probably best to drop the subject. No point in embarrassing her cousin any further; she had enough to deal with.

"Sure is a hot one today," Rebekah complained. "I don't envy those poor men working out there in the sweltering sun all day."

"Jah, but I'm sure they—" Mary Ellen's sentence was interrupted when a man's heavy boots thudded up the porch steps.

"*Wie geht's*, you two?" Daniel asked with a nod in their direction.

Rebekah waited to see if Mary Ellen would respond, but when her cousin made no comment, she smiled up at him and said, "I'm doing okay. How's the work on my daed's barn coming along?"

Daniel yanked off his straw hat and wiped the perspiration from his forehead with the back of his hand. "It's going well enough. Whew! Today's sure hot and humid, don't you think?" His question was directed at Rebekah, and she swallowed hard as his serious dark eyes seemed to bore straight into her soul.

"Jah, I was just saying that to Mary Ellen before you showed up," she murmured, feeling another flush of warmth, but excusing it as coming from the heat of the day.

"I've talked to your daed about helping with the green-house," Daniel said, shifting his weight from one foot to the other. "He said he hopes to begin working on it sometime next week."

Rebekah swallowed again. Why was Daniel being so nice, and why did he keep looking at her in such a strange way? It wasn't a look of pity, she was sure of that much, but she couldn't decide what his tipped head and lips curved slightly upwards meant. "I—I really appreciate the offer of help," she said. "I'll be grateful to anyone who helps build my new greenhouse."

Daniel stared down at his boots, rocking back and forth on his heels as if he might be feeling kind of nervous all of a sudden. Then he cleared his throat a couple of times and looked up at her again. "Well, guess I. . .uh. . .had better get back to work before my daed comes lookin' for me and accuses me of sloughin' off."

He turned and was about to step off the porch when Rebekah called out to him. "Did you get some cold tea yet?"

Daniel lifted his hat over his head and waved it at her. "I had some, danki." He took the steps two at a time and actually ran back to the job site, leaving Rebekah to wonder about his strange behavior. Had he been nervous because Mary Ellen was sitting there beside her and hadn't said one single word to him? Had he wanted to say something to her but not been able to work up the nerve? Jah, that was probably the case, all right.

"You could have at least said hello to Daniel," Rebekah said, squinting at her cousin, who had seemed intent on shelling peas the whole time Daniel had been on the porch, rather than joining in on their conversation.

Mary Ellen's eyebrows drew together. "I figured if he had something he wanted to say to me, he wouldn't have been talking to you."

"Maybe the reason he was talking to me was because you just sat there, shelling peas like there was no tomorrow and never taking part in the conversation at all."

Mary Ellen merely shrugged in response, but a few seconds later, she poked Rebekah with her elbow and whispered, "Daniel seems like a nice person, don't you think?"

Rebekah nodded but kept her focus on the pan of peas in her lap. *If you think he's so nice, then why aren't you giving the poor fellow a chance?* she silently fumed. *If I had someone like Daniel Beachy interested in me, I sure wouldn't be wasting my time on the likes of that juvenile Johnny Yoder.*

Daniel kicked at a hefty stone with the toe of his boot as he ambled across the yard toward the new building that was rapidly going up. Had he made a fool of himself during his conversation with Rebekah? She'd been friendly enough, he supposed, but she had acted kind of nervous, too. And her cousin Mary Ellen hadn't said a single word the whole time he'd been on the porch—just sat there shelling peas as though he didn't exist.

Does Mary Ellen disapprove of me? Maybe she thinks I'm not good enough for Rebekah. She might have even said some things against me to her.

Daniel didn't have a fancy way with words like Johnny did, and he sure wasn't nearly as funny or persuasive. But he was a hard worker, and he cared about Rebekah—so much so that it actually hurt. He figured that ought to count for something.

He kicked another stone and grimaced. *Maybe I'm just too unsure of myself. Maybe I ought to come right out and tell Rebekah what's on my mind and be done with it. At least then I'd know where I stand with her. If she doesn't care for me at all,*

I should at least give her the chance to say so.

"Hey, Daniel, are you comin' back to work anytime soon, or did you plan to stand there all day kickin' at stones?" Daniel's father shouted from where he knelt on one of the rafters of the new barn.

Feeling a rush of heat cover his face, Daniel cupped his hands around his mouth and hollered back, "I'm on my way, Pop!"

CHAPTER

9

As Nadine stood in front of the kitchen sink, drying the dishes Rebekah had washed earlier, she stared out the window at Dad's new barn. It was now fully erected and had been filled with hay and animals soon after its completion. The men who had helped out had been hardworking and faithful, in spite of the fact that they all had their own chores waiting to be done at home.

Dad said he didn't feel he could ask any of them to return the following week to begin building Rebekah's greenhouse, and even though the uncles said they were still willing to help with the greenhouse, he had turned them all down.

"It wouldn't be fair," Nadine had heard him tell Rebekah last night after supper.

However, with the help of Simon and Daniel, who had insisted on lending a hand no matter what Dad had said, the building would go up, even if it would take a little longer than expected.

Nadine suspected the main reason Daniel had insisted on helping with the greenhouse was because he had an interest in Rebekah. Too bad her older sister seemed too blind to see it.

A knock at the back door drove Nadine's thoughts aside, and she went to answer it. She was surprised to see Daniel standing on the porch holding a large clay pot with an equally large Boston fern inside. She stood in the doorway staring at him and wondering what the plant was for, and he stood staring back at her with a red, sweaty face.

"I'm. . .uh. . .here to help build Rebekah's greenhouse," he mumbled. "Is she at home?"

Nadine nodded and stepped away from the door, motioning him into the kitchen. She pointed to where Rebekah sat at the table, drinking a cup of tea and writing on a tablet. "You've got company, sister."

Rebekah swiveled her wheelchair around. "Guder mariye, Daniel. What brings you by so early this morning?" She eyed the plant he held but made no mention of it.

"This is for you," Daniel said, hurrying across the room and placing the fern in the center of the table. "It's for your new greenhouse—to keep, not sell."

She smiled. "It's beautiful, and I wouldn't think of selling it. Danki, Daniel."

Nadine went over to the sink to finish up the dishes but glanced over her shoulder to see what Daniel would do next. He shifted from one foot to the other, looking kind of embarrassed.

"Is. . .uh. . .your daed still planning to begin work on the greenhouse this morning? I've come prepared to work all day if he is."

"I think so," Rebekah replied, looking rather embarrassed

herself. "Dad's out in the new barn right now, so if you want to talk to him about it, you'll have to go out there."

"Naw, that's okay. I'll stick around here for a while yet." Daniel removed his straw hat and went to hang it on a wall peg. Then he shuffled back toward Rebekah, wearing a silly grin.

Nadine lifted her gaze toward the ceiling, thinking how goofy Daniel was acting and wondering why he wasn't more assertive.

"Say, what's that you're workin' on there?" Daniel asked as he peered over Rebekah's shoulder.

Rebekah smiled, and her cheeks turned pink. "Well, I was writing my latest column for *The Budget*, but that's about done so now I'm ready to begin working on the inventory for my new greenhouse."

"Mind if I take a look-see?"

"No, no, not at all."

Those two are just sickening, Nadine thought as she grabbed another dish to dry. *It's obvious to me that Daniel has his eye on my sister, so why doesn't he quit thumpin' around the shrubs and just come right out and say so?* She pivoted away from the sink and turned toward the table. "Would you like some coffee or a glass of milk, Daniel?"

"Jah, that'd be fine."

Nadine planted both hands on her hips and glared at him. "Well, which one do you want? Milk or coffee?"

"I'll have whatever Rebekah's havin'," Daniel said, barely looking at Nadine.

She shook her head and muttered, "She's drinkin' tea; can't you see that?"

"Okay. Tea's fine for me then." Daniel pulled out a chair beside Rebekah's wheelchair and took a seat. "Do you mind if I see what you have written there?"

"Sure, go ahead." She pushed the tablet toward him.

He studied it intently, commenting with an occasional, "Hmm. . .ah. . .I see now. . . ."

When Nadine thought she could stand it no longer, Rebekah asked, "Well, what do you think? Does it seem like I have enough plants to open for business?"

Daniel scratched the back of his head. "I suppose it'll all depend on how many customers you have at first—and on what they might decide to buy. Sometimes one certain flower or plant seems to be everyone's favorite, so that might sell rather quick."

"How is it that you seem to know so much about flowers and plants?" Rebekah asked.

Before Daniel had a chance to respond, Nadine moved over to the table and set a cup of hot lemon-mint tea and a hunk of shoofly pie in front of him.

"Danki," Daniel said, never taking his eyes off Rebekah. "My uncle Jake lives in Ohio, and he owns a greenhouse. I spent some time there one summer, and I helped him in the greenhouse for a bit."

Rebekah's eyebrows lifted. "Really? Then you could probably give me all kinds of good advice."

He bobbed his head up and down and grinned. "I would be happy to help out. That is, if you really want my suggestions."

Nadine gritted her teeth. "Of course she does, silly. Why else would she have said what she did?" Listening to the way those two carried on was enough to make her wonder why she was so anxious to start courting.

"Nadine's right. I do want your suggestions," Rebekah said. "Of course, that's only if you have the time. I know you keep busy helping your daed with those dairy cows of his."

"I do get some free time, and my brothers, Harold and Abner, help Pop out, too, so I'm sure I can manage to find the time." Daniel stared at his cup of tea as though he might be puzzling over something.

Unable to stand the suspense, Nadine was on the verge of asking him what he was thinking about, but he spoke first. "I wonder sometimes if workin' with dairy cows is what I want to do for the rest of my life. I believe God's given us all special abilities, and I'd sure like the chance to use mine."

Rebekah tipped her head and stared at Daniel. "I know exactly what you mean."

"I would think running a dairy farm would be kind of interesting," Nadine spoke up. "What's it like, Daniel? Can you tell us a little about the operation?"

He nodded. "Well, I guess I'm lucky in that my daed uses diesel-generated milking machines rather than doing the milking by hand the way some dairymen in other Amish communities still do."

Nadine pursed her lips, as she shook her head. "Dad makes either me or Simon milk our two goats twice a day, and I don't enjoy it one little bit."

"Even with the use of mechanical milkers, refrigerated coolers, and battery-operated agitators, dairy farming is still a lot of work." Daniel wrinkled his nose. "I especially don't like the job of cleaning the barn and disposing of all the cow manure."

"Do you do that by hand?" This question came from Rebekah.

"Nope. We use our horses to pull metal devices through the manure trenches. The manure then goes into a tank, which is later pumped into a spreader."

Unable to listen to any more talk about smelly manure, Nadine went back to the sink to finish drying the dishes. A short time later when she had put the last dish away in the cupboard, she moved back to the table. "I'm done with the dishes now, so I think I'll go outside and see if Mom needs help hanging up the wash."

"What?" Rebekah pulled her gaze away from Daniel and angled her wheelchair toward Nadine.

"I said I'm done here. I'm going out to help Mom."

"Okay then."

Nadine headed out the door, but she was sure that neither Rebekah nor Daniel had even noticed. "When I'm old enough to start going to singings," she mumbled under her breath, "I'll be looking for a fellow who at least knows how to speak his mind."

Rebekah and Daniel went back to talking about her greenhouse, and they stayed deeply engaged in conversation about her future plans for nearly an hour. Finally, Daniel looked up at the clock on the opposite wall and whistled. "Wow, it's later than I thought. Guess I'd better get outside and see if your daed's ready to go to work on the greenhouse." He smiled kind of sheepishly. "If he hasn't already gotten half of it built while I've been in here yappin' away and boring you with all my silly notions."

Rebekah shook her head. "You haven't been boring me at all. I appreciate all of your good ideas."

Daniel's chair made a scraping sound as he pushed it away from the table and stood. "Feel free to ask me for help of any kind once you open for business. I enjoy being around plants and would be more than happy to come by and help out whenever I'm able." His gaze dropped to the floor. "Well, I–I'd better get going."

"Don't work too hard," Rebekah called as he went out the door.

For the next several minutes, she sat staring at the list she and Daniel had made for the things she might need in her greenhouse and thinking about how nice it was of him to offer his assistance and how interesting she found him to be. While Daniel couldn't be considered handsome the way Johnny was, his dark chocolate eyes always looked so sincere. His slim, angular nose and full lips made him seem rather appealing, too. At least Rebekah thought so.

Mom and Nadine came into the kitchen just then, each carrying an empty wicker basket in their hands.

Rebekah smiled. "Guess what, Mom?"

"What's that?"

She tapped the notebook with her pencil and grinned. "Turns out that Daniel knows a lot about greenhouses, and he helped me add some more items to my list."

"That's good to hear." Mom set her basket on the floor and moved over to the table where Rebekah sat. "I saw Daniel outside. He and your daed, as well as your brother, were getting ready to work on your greenhouse."

Nadine placed her basket on the end of the counter and rushed over to the table. "Say, Mom, did you know that Daniel's sweet on Rebekah?"

Rebekah's face heated up, and she shook her head vigorously. "No, he's not. He's got his eye on Mary Ellen and has for some time."

Nadine snickered. "Jah, well, you should have seen the way he hovered over Rebekah, stumbling over every word and making cow eyes at her the whole time."

"That's not so!" Rebekah whirled her wheelchair around to face her sister. "And you shouldn't have been spying on us."

"I wasn't spying," Nadine said in a defensive tone. "I was just dryin' the dishes, and it's not my fault I could hear every word that was being said." She clicked her tongue. "And it didn't take me long to realize that you're as sweet on Daniel as he is on you."

Rebekah wanted to deny her sister's accusation, but she couldn't. The truth was, she did care for Daniel, but she would never have admitted that to Nadine or Mom. Especially when she knew nothing could come from her feelings for him. She was painfully aware that, even if by some miracle Daniel returned those feelings for her, they could never have a future together.

With Dad, Simon, and Daniel working on the greenhouse, it took a little more than two weeks to complete the project. The day after the greenhouse was completed, Mom and

Dad hosted a picnic in honor of the official opening of Grandma's Place. All the family had been invited, as well as Daniel since he had done so much of the work.

The picnic supper was served on the lawn out back, and soon everyone was heaping their plates with barbecued burgers and hot dogs, potato salad, coleslaw, homemade soft pretzels, baked beans, pickles, olives, and carrot sticks. For dessert, they served homemade ice cream with both chocolate and strawberry toppings.

When it appeared as if everyone had finished eating, Dad stood and called for their attention. "As you all know, the greenhouse is finally done, so I'd like to offer my thanks to two very helpful people. First of all, my son, Simon, who worked as hard as any man could." He reached over and ruffled Simon's hair, and Simon grinned up at him. Then he nodded at Daniel, who sat on the end of a bench beside Rebekah's wheelchair. "A special thanks goes to Daniel, who came over for several hours nearly every day and did more than his share of the work."

Rebekah couldn't help but notice how red Daniel's face had become as he stared at his empty ice-cream bowl. "Aw, it was nothin'," he mumbled. "I was glad to do it."

"Daniel not only helped build the greenhouse, but he also assisted Rebekah in setting out all the plants and flowers she will sell. I appreciate the fact that Clarence Beachy was so willing to loan out his son," Dad went on to say.

Rebekah stifled a giggle behind her hand. Just thinking of Clarence loaning out his son made it seem as if Daniel was some piece of farm equipment instead of someone's grown son.

"Now my wife has a little something she would like to give to the new owner of Grandma's Place." Dad nodded at Mom, and she stood.

"This is for you," she said, bending down and pulling a large paper sack from under the table.

Rebekah sat staring at the sack Mom had just handed her.

"Well, go ahead and open it," her brother prompted. "We'd all like to see what's inside that sack."

With trembling fingers, Rebekah tore open the bag. When she reached inside and withdrew a large wooden plaque, she gasped. Inscribed in bold, block letters were the words GRANDMA'S PLACE–OWNER, REBEKAH STOLTZFUS.

"Oh, Mom, it's wunderbaar! Danki, so much."

Mom fairly beamed, obviously quite pleased with herself for keeping such a special secret. "It's that surprise I was working on when Vera took us shopping a few weeks ago. You see now why I couldn't tell you where I was going?"

Rebekah nodded and wiped away the tears that had dribbled onto her cheeks despite her best efforts to hold them at bay.

"And now," Dad said in a booming voice, "let's all go down to the new greenhouse and hang up the sign, because Rebekah Stoltzfus is officially in business!"

As everyone stepped inside the greenhouse, Rebekah was filled with a sense of awe. Even though she had been inside plenty of times during the building of it, she was still pleased with how nice it looked and excited about the prospect of making her own money. Grandma's Place was everything

Rebekah could have hoped for. The building was a wooden structure with glass panels set in the middle section. Dad had built a wheelchair ramp up to the door so she could easily come and go on her own. The front of the building, which was divided by a partition, had a long counter where people could place their purchases. A battery-operated cash register, a calculator, several stacks of notepaper, and some pens had been placed on the end of the counter where Rebekah would wait on her customers. Several gas lanterns would light this section of the building, and a small woodstove would heat the building during the chilly winter months.

"This is nice," Uncle Amos said with an enthusiastic nod. "Jah, really nice."

"It's much bigger than I thought it would be," Aunt Mim put in.

"We wanted to make it big enough for expansion in case Rebekah should ever need more space," Dad said, looking rather pleased with himself.

"Let's go into the next area of the greenhouse and check that out now. It's where all the glass panels are set." Rebekah rolled her wheelchair in that direction, and the others followed, chattering as they went.

"See, here," she said, motioning to a row of low-hanging shelves. "These are for me to set some of the plants on." She pointed up. "And those large hooks hanging from the rafters are so other plants can be secured from wire or chains that will be operated by a pulley." Rebekah smiled up at Daniel, who stood near her wheelchair. "Daniel figured that out for me. The hanging chains will make all the plants more accessible for me, and at the same time, the customers will be able to see everything I have for sale."

"Makes good sense to me," Uncle Lewis put in. "Daniel's a right smart fellow."

Daniel's face turned even redder than it had earlier when Dad had made such an issue over how helpful Daniel had been. Rebekah knew it wasn't right to feel *hochmut*, but she couldn't help feeling a little pride at how well this special greenhouse had turned out.

"Due to the glass panels, the building will be well-lit during daylight hours, and it should stay quite warm in here," Dad spoke up. "There's also a small propane heater, which will supplement the sun's natural heat on colder days." He thumped Daniel on the back. "And this young man also suggested that we install several small screens that will be set in place of the glass windows during warmer weather. They'll provide the necessary cross draft that will help keep the room at a more even temperature."

Several others commented about how nice the greenhouse was and what a good job the men had done. Then Rebekah asked everyone to follow her to the back room, where she showed them a small area where she could work on repotting plants and arranging bouquets of cut flowers. It had a long, low table, as well as a small cot where she could rest awhile if she felt the need.

"See here," Rebekah said, motioning to a door not far from the cot. "Dad even plumbed in a small bathroom for me, which is powered by a gas generator. There's also a sink; a compact, propane-operated refrigerator; and a small cookstove, which is also operated on propane." She grinned as a sense of pure joy bubbled in her soul. "Why, I could spend the whole day here if I had a mind to."

"Of course she won't," Mom put in. "She'll be too busy selling all her flowers and plants to friends, neighbors, and eager tourists to be lazing around her private little room all day."

Everyone laughed. Everyone except for Nadine, that is. She stood off to one side with her arms folded and a grim expression on her face. It was then that Rebekah realized her sister hadn't said one nice thing about her greenhouse. Nadine hadn't said anything at all, not even during the picnic supper.

Under different conditions, Rebekah might have been put out by her sister's poutiness and lack of interest, but not today. This was Rebekah's moment to share the joy of owning her own business with her family and friends, and she wasn't going to let anyone or anything spoil it for her.

"In the wintertime, my store hours will be shorter," she said. "But the greenhouse should stay plenty warm and cozy, even on the coldest of days."

"That might be a good time for you to start seeds that could be ready to repot and sell in the spring," Daniel said, as they started back toward the other room.

Rebekah smiled up at him. "Jah, that's what I was thinking, too."

Soon after they returned to the main entrance, Aunt Mim leaned over Rebekah's wheelchair and gave her a hug. "It looks like you've thought of everything, dear girl."

"Actually, it was Dad and Daniel who thought of most of the things I would need in the greenhouse." She extended her hand to her father. "And I'm ever so grateful."

He gave her fingers a gentle squeeze. "I'll bet you'll settle into this greenhouse like it's always been your home."

Rebekah nodded, feeling as if her miracle might be just round the corner. Now all she needed was some paying customers.

CHAPTER 10

T he first official customer to visit Grandma's Place was
Johnny Yoder. It was Tuesday morning, and Rebekah
had just hung the OPEN sign on the front door of the
greenhouse.

When Johnny rang the bell, which hung on a rope outside the door, Rebekah called, "Come on in!"

The door swung open, and Johnny sauntered into the
room, holding his straw hat in one hand, while his white
shirttail hung out of his dark trousers as if he hadn't even
bothered to check his appearance. "Guder mariye. Are you
to home?"

Rebekah wheeled her chair toward him, laughing. "Of
course I'm here. I just told you to come in, didn't I?"

"Jah, you sure did." Johnny grinned and tipped his hat
in her direction.

"Can I help you with something?" Rebekah asked, ignoring his immature antics.

He moved slowly about the room as though he might be
checking everything out. "Say, you wouldn't happen to have
any cut flowers, would ya?"

"This is a greenhouse, Johnny, so of course I have flowers." Johnny had always been such a kidder. Rebekah figured all his joking around might be why Mary Ellen enjoyed his company so much. It probably made her feel good to be around someone so lighthearted and spirited.

He chuckled as he jiggled his eyebrows up and down. "Jah, I reckon that's true enough. Don't know what I was thinkin', askin' such a silly question as that."

"Are you needing some flowers for any particular reason?"

Johnny nodded, and his face turned the color of ripe cherries. It was a surprise to see him blush that way since he never seemed to let things bother him much. "Uh, they're for your cousin Mary Ellen. I've been courtin' her here of late."

"So I've heard." Rebekah motioned him to follow as she wheeled into the part of the greenhouse where the flowers and plants were kept. "Did you have anything special in mind?"

He shrugged. "Not really. I thought you might have a suggestion, seeing as to how you're in the business of sellin' flowers and whatnot."

If Rebekah had known exactly how much Johnny planned to spend, it might have helped in her selection of a bouquet. However, she didn't feel it would be proper to come right out and ask such a question. Instead, she discreetly said, "I have several bunches of miniature roses. They sell for ten dollars apiece. I also have some less expensive gladiolas—or maybe some pink carnations would be more to your liking."

"I think roses would be best," Johnny said, his green eyes twinkling like fireflies doing their summer dance. "I want the gift to be really special—somethin' that will let Mary Ellen know how much I care."

"I think a bouquet of pink and white roses will do the trick." Rebekah moved over to select the flowers and then proceeded to wrap the stems tightly together with a rubber band. A bit of tissue paper gathered around the bottom completed the arrangement. "If you're not going to give these to her right away, maybe you should put them in some water," she said, handing Johnny the flowers.

Johnny grinned, looking as excited as a first-grade scholar. "We're goin' on a picnic today, so I'll see her real soon, I expect." He reached into his pants pocket and pulled out a ten-dollar bill, then handed it to Rebekah.

"Danki," she replied. "I hope you enjoy your picnic, and I hope Mary Ellen likes the flowers."

Johnny started toward the door, but before his hand touched the knob, he swiveled back around. "You know, it looks mighty nice around here. I hope your new business is a huge success." He left the building, tossing his hat in the air and whistling like a songbird on the first day of spring.

Rebekah smiled to herself as she placed the money from her first sale into the drawer of the cash register. Had it not been for the fact that she was so excited about her new business venture, she might have felt a twinge of jealousy hearing that her best friend had a picnic date. While running the greenhouse gave her a feeling of satisfaction, it didn't take the place of love or romance. Maybe if the business made a go and she could fully support herself, she wouldn't miss courting so much.

By the end of August, news of Rebekah's greenhouse had spread throughout much of Lancaster County. She averaged at least twenty customers a day, sometimes even more. Her inventory was quickly receding, and she knew she would either have to restock soon or put a CLOSED sign on the door.

Dad and Simon had been busy harvesting the cornfields, so Rebekah asked Mom if she would schedule a ride with Vera to take her to town in order to buy some more plants.

The following morning, they set out right after breakfast. This time, Nadine was allowed to accompany them. She seemed excited about the trip, and as she sat behind Rebekah's seat in Vera's van, she giggled and talked nonstop about all sorts of silly stuff. Rebekah tried to be patient with her sister's prattling, but her mind was on other things—things more important than how cute Eddy Shemly was or who had recently gotten a new pair of rollerblades.

Rebekah was mentally trying to add up the estimated cost of what she might be able to purchase during this trip. Cut flowers weren't a problem since they still had several varieties in their garden at home. What she needed most were more plants and some seeds.

When Nadine finally took a breath between sentences, Rebekah seized the opportunity and leaned over to her mother, who sat beside her. "Say, Mom, you know I've made a fairly good profit during the last few weeks."

"That's wunderbaar."

"Well, I'm wondering how much of that profit to put back into the business and how much I should save."

"Never borrow, for borrowing leads to sorrowing. Spend less than you earn, and you'll never be in debt. That's the true motto of every good businessman—or woman, in your case," Mom said with a wide smile.

Rebekah bobbed her head up and down. "That's good advice, and I'll try to remember it." She paused but not for long, because she knew if she didn't speak quickly, she would probably be interrupted by Nadine's small talk again. "I've been wondering about something else, too."

"What might that be?"

"Do you think I really can make enough money to support myself? I mean, will things work out all right if I work extra hard in the greenhouse?"

" 'And we know that all things work together for good to them that love God, to them who are the called according to his purpose,' " Mom quoted from Romans 8:28. "I know you love God, Rebekah, so you must learn to trust Him more."

Rebekah fell silent. Trust. That was the hard part. When things were going along fine and dandy, it was easy to put one's trust in God. But when things became difficult, it was hard not to waver in one's faith. She would need to keep Grandma's Bible handy in the days to come for she needed to bathe herself in God's Word every day in order not to give in to self-pity or start fretting about the future.

A short time later, they pulled into Lancaster and had soon parked in front of the garden center. Once inside, it didn't take Rebekah long to select a good supply of plants as well as numerous packets of seeds. She concentrated on indoor plant varieties since winter would be coming soon and people would most likely want something to bring a bit of color and cheer into those dreary days.

The back of Vera's van was nearly full when they left the nursery, but Rebekah still had some money left over. She felt good about the purchases she had made and smiled, thinking that she had Daniel to thank for all the good suggestions he'd given her before the greenhouse had been built.

When they left Lancaster, Vera drove them to the farmers' market in Bird-in-Hand, where Mom planned to buy some whole grains and dried beans that one of her friends was selling there. As soon as they were inside the building, Nadine asked if she could wander around by herself for a while. Much to Rebekah's surprise, and probably Nadine's, Mom agreed. So Rebekah wheeled off by herself, as well, leaving Mom and Vera to visit with Ellie Mast and purchase some of her dried goods.

Rebekah hadn't eaten anything since their early morning breakfast, and she felt kind of hungry. She knew they would be going to lunch soon after they left the market, but she decided that a little snack right now might not be such a bad idea.

She wheeled over to a table where they were selling everything from homemade candy to fresh salads. She wasn't in the mood for anything as sweet as candy, but a small fruit salad sure looked refreshing. She bought one and had begun to maneuver her wheelchair to the corner of the room where she could be out of the way when a teenage English boy bumped into the front of her chair.

"Why don't you watch where you're going?" he grumbled, giving the chair a quick shove.

Another English boy, about the same age, grabbed the handle and swung the wheelchair completely around.

Rebekah's head spun dizzily, and she gripped the armrests, hanging on for all she was worth. "Please, stop it," she pleaded. "You're making me dizzy."

"Hey, Joe, we've got ourselves one of those Plain little gals, and she's in a wheelchair!" the first boy hollered. "She bumps right into my leg and then has the nerve to tell me to stop it. Can you believe the gall some folks have these days?"

The one named Joe let out a hoot and gave Rebekah's chair another hefty shove. She was close to tears for in all the time she'd been crippled, nothing like this had ever happened before, and she didn't have a clue what to do about it.

"How about a ride in your wheelchair?" the first boy asked, wiggling his dark eyebrows up and down. "You wouldn't mind scooting over and letting me sit next to you, now would you, honey?"

Rebekah shook her head, and he pushed the wheelchair in the direction of his friend again. It rolled with such force that the bowl of fruit salad flew out of Rebekah's lap and landed upside down on the floor with a *splat.*

"Now look what you've gone and done, Ray," Joe hollered, shaking his finger in his friend's face. "The poor little gal has lost her lunch." He leaned close to Rebekah, and when he squinted his eyes, it reminded her of a newborn pig. "Say, tell me somethin', honey—why do you Amish women wear such plain-looking clothes?"

Before Rebekah could find her voice, Ray wrinkled his

freckled nose and said, "Yeah, and how come you eat all that healthy food?" He poked his friend on the arm. "You know, Joe, I hear tell that many Amish folk still grow a lot of their own food, just like the pioneers used to do." He stared right at Rebekah. "Is that true, little missy? Is it, huh?"

Rebekah swallowed around the bitter taste of bile rising in her throat, fearing she might be about to get sick. She looked around helplessly, knowing she was completely out of her element and hoping someone would see what was happening and come to her aid. However, the closest table was several feet away, and the people who ran it were busy with customers and never even looked her way.

"I-I've got to find my mom," she squeaked. Her shaky voice was laced with fear—the gripping kind that finds its way to the surface, then bubbles over like boiling water left unattended on the stove.

"Now isn't that sweet," Joe taunted. "The little lady wants her mama." He gave the wheelchair a good yank toward his friend. It wasn't Ray who caught it by the handles this time. It was someone much bigger than either one of the boys. Someone who wore a stern look on his face.

Rebekah felt as though all the air had been squeezed clean out of her lungs. Daniel Beachy's serious brown eyes stared down at her. Since the Amish were pacifists, she knew he wouldn't be apt to fight the young men who had been taunting her, but he sure looked like he might. Daniel's eyes narrowed into tiny slits, and he pursed his lips. Rebekah drew in a deep breath and waited expectantly to see what would happen next.

"I think you fellows owe this woman an apology, and

also some money to buy another salad." Daniel motioned to the mess on the floor. As his gaze went back to the boys, Rebekah noticed that his face had turned bright red and a muscle on the side of his neck twitched like a cow's tail when a fly had buzzed it.

"Aw, we were just having a little fun. We didn't hurt her none," Ray mumbled.

Joe shuffled his feet a few times. "Come on, Ray. She's probably his girlfriend, so we'd better leave 'em alone to do their lovebird crooning."

Daniel moved his body to block the boys. "What about that apology and some money for the salad?"

"It's all right, Daniel," Rebekah said in a pleading voice. "Just let them go, okay?"

Daniel planted his hands firmly on his hips and stared hard at the boys. "Jah, well, I don't want to see you two around here again. Is that clear?"

Rebekah had never seen this side of Daniel before, and his response surprised her almost as much as seeing Joe and Ray tear out of there as fast as their long legs could take them.

Daniel dropped to his knees beside Rebekah's wheelchair, obvious concern etched on his face. "Are you okay? They didn't hurt you, did they?"

Rebekah trembled, closer to tears now than ever. "I—I appreciate you stepping in like that, Daniel. I don't know what would have happened if you hadn't come along when you did." Her eyes stung, and she blinked rapidly to hold back the tide of threatening tears.

Daniel's fingers brushed hers, and their gazes locked. "I

couldn't let 'em hurt you, Rebekah. You're a special girl, and you sure as anything don't deserve to be taunted that way."

Rebekah looked away, hoping to hide the blush she knew must have come to her cheeks. "Danki, Daniel. Danki, so much."

"You're welcome." Daniel remained on his knees for several more seconds. Then he finally stood.

"Oh, there you are, Rebekah. Do you know where Nadine is?"

Rebekah lifted her gaze and saw Mom heading in their direction, waving her hand.

"Please don't say anything about my encounter with those English boys," she whispered to Daniel. "Sometimes my mamm can be a bit overprotective. If she thought letting me go off by myself had put me in any kind of danger, she might have second thoughts about letting me be alone in my greenhouse so much of the time."

Daniel nodded. "I won't say a word."

"Hello, Daniel," Mom said, as she approached. "How's your family these days?"

He smiled. "Oh, fair to middlin'. I'm in town picking up a new harness for one of my daed's plow mules. I thought I'd stop by the market to see what's doin', and I was just figuring on going somewhere to get a bite of lunch pretty soon."

Mom's face seemed to brighten. "Would you like to join me and the girls at the Plain and Fancy Restaurant? If we can ever find Nadine, that is."

"I haven't seen her, Mom," Rebekah said. "Not since we separated earlier."

Daniel motioned across the room. "I saw her over at Kauffmeirs' root-beer stand. She was talkin' to a couple of fellows about her age." He gave Rebekah a crooked grin. "I'd be happy to join you for lunch. The Plain and Fancy is one of my favorite eating spots."

"Well then, let's see if we can round up that stray daughter of mine, and we'll go eat ourselves full," Mom said with a nod.

As Nadine followed the others to a table at the Plain and Fancy, she wondered why she had been scolded by Mom for talking to Luke and Sam Troyer over at the root-beer stand and yet Rebekah had been allowed to bring Daniel Beachy to the restaurant with them. As usual, everything went her sister's way, and it didn't seem fair that Rebekah was so spoiled. *Luke and Sam must think I'm still a little girl who has to check in with her mamm every few seconds,* she fumed.

She looked over at Daniel, who had taken a seat beside Rebekah's wheelchair. *He likes her. I don't care what Rebekah says. And I'm sure she likes him, too, even though she's too stubborn to admit it.* Nadine glanced at Rebekah, who wore a smile on her face, and she was sure the satisfied look wasn't just because they were about to eat lunch at her favorite restaurant.

"Is everyone as hungry as I am?" Vera asked, as she took a seat between Mom and Nadine. "I didn't take time to eat much breakfast this morning, and I think it's finally caught up with me."

"I know I'm hungry," Daniel said, giving his stomach a couple of thumps. " 'Course my mamm says I've been hungry since the day I was born."

"What's wrong, sister?" Rebekah asked, glancing across the table at Nadine. "You look like you might not be feeling so well."

"It's nothing. I'm fine."

"Probably drank too much root beer at the farmers' market," Mom put in. "That is where I found her, after all."

"I didn't drink any root beer at all," Nadine said with a frown. "I never got the chance because you dragged me away from there, saying it was time for lunch."

"I didn't *drag* you anywhere, Nadine." Mom clicked her tongue. "How you do exaggerate sometimes."

Vera cleared her throat. "If I might change the subject. . ."

"Certainly," Mom said, giving their driver a pleasant smile. "What did you want to talk about?"

"Well, I subscribe to *The Budget*, and when I was reading it the other day, I noticed that there's going to be a barbecue next week for the volunteer firemen in our area and their families. I know that two of Andrew's brothers are volunteers, so I was wondering if you would all be going to that."

"I'd like to go," Nadine spoke up before Mom could open her mouth to reply. "My friend Carolyn went to the one last year, and she said—"

"We'll have to wait and see how it goes," Mom interrupted. "We might be busy with other things that day."

"I'll bet if Rebekah wanted to go, you'd say it was okay."

"Not if we had other plans, I wouldn't."

Nadine was about to say something more on the subject,

but Mom put her finger to her lips and shook her head. "We'll talk about this later."

Rebekah glanced over at Daniel and noticed that he seemed to be staring at the place mat underneath his silverware. Was he thinking about that incident at the market with the English fellows? He might be wondering if he should tell her mother about it, after all.

Rebekah hoped he wouldn't go back on his promise because it had been stressful enough to go through that ordeal without having Mom in some kind of a stew over what could have happened to Rebekah had Daniel not come along when he did.

"How's your new business going?" Daniel asked suddenly, breaking into Rebekah's thoughts.

"It's doing real well," she said, feeling a sense of relief that he wanted to talk about something on a more positive note. "We went to the garden center in Lancaster this morning, so I could buy more plants and some packets of seeds that I can start during the winter."

Daniel's eyes seemed to brighten. "I think spending all day around plants and flowers would be wunderbaar. I wish I could do something more enjoyable like that. I've got a love for flowers that just won't quit, but my daed says being a dairyman is important work." He crinkled his nose. "My uncle Jake—the one I told you about who lives in Ohio—has invited me to move out there and help in his greenhouse."

"Why don't you go then?" The question came from Nadine, who leaned her elbows on the table and looked intently at Daniel. "Or is something keeping you here?"

Daniel shrugged. "I've thought about his offer, but Ohio's kind of far from my family and friends, and I'm afraid I'd be lonely out there." He glanced over at Rebekah, but she averted her gaze.

"Living near one's family can be important in times of need," Mom put in. "None of my immediate family lives close, but I appreciate having Andrew's family to call my own. They've always been there for us—through the good times and the bad."

Rebekah's thoughts drifted back in time—back to when she'd had her accident. She still remembered how everyone in the family had rallied with food and money for the hospital bills. That's when Grandma had decided to move in with them. She had a heart full of love and wanted to help out.

"When I marry someday, I hope to teach my kinner the value of a loving family," Daniel said with a note of conviction.

If you married Mary Ellen, you'd be getting a wonderful family, Rebekah thought ruefully. *What a shame she's passing up someone as good as you, Daniel. Maybe when I see Mary Ellen at church on Sunday, I'll tell her that, too.*

Daniel enjoyed the Pennsylvania Dutch meal they had been served, which consisted of fried chicken, meatloaf, buttered noodles, potato filling, homemade rolls, chowchow, and green beans, but he didn't enjoy watching the disagreeable looks Nadine kept shooting at Rebekah. Had their mother noticed it—or even Vera, the English driver Sarah had hired today? If so, what must they be thinking?

Had something happened between Rebekah and her sister earlier in the day, or was Nadine taking out her frustrations on Rebekah because her mother had caught her flirting with the Troyer boys? Whatever the reason, Daniel could tell that Nadine wasn't happy, and her sulky attitude seemed to put a damper on everyone's meal. For the last ten minutes, Rebekah hadn't said more than two words to Daniel, and he figured it might be because she was upset with Nadine. Either that or she was still fretting over the incident with the rowdy English fellows at the farmers' market.

Daniel clenched his teeth. It had been hard for him to control his temper and not give in to the temptation to punch those two in their snooty noses. But that wasn't the Amish way, and he was pleased that he'd been able to run them off by his words. He could understand why Rebekah didn't want her mother to know about the unpleasant episode. If Sarah was upset because one of her daughters had run off to flirt with some Amish boys, he could only imagine how she would have reacted to Rebekah being tormented by those rude Englishers.

He glanced over at Rebekah again and watched as she ate the piece of apple-crumb pie their waitress had just brought. "This is pretty tasty, jah?" he commented, after he'd taken a bite of his own piece of pie.

She smiled and nodded but gave no other reply.

"If you need some help setting out those plants you bought this morning, I'd be glad to come over later today and assist."

"That's nice of you, Daniel, but I'm sure there are things at your place that need to be done, and I wouldn't want to impose."

"It's no imposition. I'd be glad to help in whatever way I can."

"Well, if you really want to, I won't turn down the help."

He nodded enthusiastically. "I'll go straight home after I've finished my dessert, drop off the harness I picked up for my daed, and then head on over to the greenhouse."

"Danki," Rebekah said with a heart-melting smile. "I really appreciate that."

"Danki for runnin' to town for me this morning," Daniel's daed said, when Daniel entered the barn and handed him the harness he'd picked up at the harness shop near Bird-in-Hand.

"You're welcome."

"Did you make it by the farmers' market to get some of that fresh-squeezed apple cider your mamm likes so well?"

Daniel nodded. "Picked up a couple of jugs when I first got there and put 'em in my buggy while I looked around for a bit."

"So that's why you're late gettin' home, huh?" Pop placed the harness on a shelf inside one of the horse's stalls and turned back to face Daniel. "I thought maybe you might have gone out to lunch at your favorite restaurant."

Daniel's face heated up. "Actually, I did—after I left the market."

Pop nodded and gave Daniel a thump on the back. "That's no reason for ya to be lookin' so embarrassed. I know you've got a hole in your leg that has to be kept filled up."

Daniel chuckled. Pop always had liked to tease about his ravenous appetite.

"So, where'd you eat? At the Plain and Fancy?"

"Jah. I shared a table with Sarah Stoltzfus and her daughters. Her English driver was with 'em, too."

"Ah, I see. Did you run into them at the restaurant then?"

"Actually, I saw Rebekah along with her mamm and sister at the market, and Sarah—well, she invited me to go with 'em for lunch, and I said I would."

Pop moved toward the barn door. "Sarah's a good woman, and she's had a lot on her hands since Rebekah got hurt and ended up in a wheelchair."

Daniel nodded as he followed his father out the door. "Speaking of Rebekah—I was wondering if it would be all right if I went over to her greenhouse this afternoon. I want to help her set out the plants she bought in Lancaster this morning."

Pop shook his head and kept right on walking. "I'm needin' your help here. Got a fence that needs mending in several places, and your brothers are already out there workin' on one section of it."

"How long is it gonna take? Couldn't I go over to the greenhouse after I'm done?"

"From the looks of things, we'll be workin' on fences at least until suppertime, and then we'll have the milkin' to do after that."

Daniel felt a keen sense of disappointment all the way to his toes. He'd been counting on seeing Rebekah again today, and he'd as much as promised that he would go there and help out. What would she think if he didn't show up?

"Can I at least drive over there and tell her I'm not comin', so she won't think I went back on my word?"

Pop halted and turned to face Daniel. "You should never have given your word in the first place. You knew when you left here this morning that there would likely be some kind of chores waiting when you got home."

"But Pop—"

"Enough said. Now grab a hammer, and let's get busy."

"Would you like me to stay and help with those?" Mom asked Rebekah after she and Vera had finished hauling the plants into the greenhouse for her.

Rebekah smiled but shook her head. "I appreciate the offer, but Daniel said he'd be coming by soon to help."

"That's awfully nice of him. He seems to have taken an interest in you, daughter."

Rebekah was glad Nadine had gone up to the house. If she'd heard what Mom had just said, she would have probably put in her two cents' worth and insisted that Daniel was sweet on Rebekah.

"He's interested in flowers, Mom," Rebekah said, maneuvering her wheelchair over to the table where her plants had been put. "There's nothing more to it than that."

Mom gave her a knowing look, shrugged, and then headed for the door. "I'll ring the bell when supper's ready."

"Jah, okay." Rebekah was glad Dad had thought to build a ramp leading up to the front door of her greenhouse. That way she didn't have to bother anyone to help her get to and from her place of business. When it was time for supper, she just wheeled herself right out the door and up to the house.

As soon as the door closed behind Mom, Rebekah grabbed the ledger she kept on the shelf under the front counter and got busy recording the names and prices of all the plants she had bought. By the time she finished that job, she hoped Daniel would have arrived.

Sometime later, Rebekah glanced at the clock on the far wall and frowned. It was almost three and still no Daniel. *I wonder what could be keeping him?*

She rolled her chair across the room and peered out the window. No sign of Daniel's rig. She pressed her nose up to the glass. No sign of any buggies going by on the road, either. Had Daniel forgotten about coming, or had he changed his mind and decided not to come after all?

"Jah, that must be it," she muttered, a keen sense of disappointment threatening to weigh her down. She should have known better than to let herself get so worked up about the idea of spending a few hours this afternoon with Daniel in the greenhouse.

She sighed and rolled her wheelchair away from the window. "Guess I'd better get busy and set these plants out myself, because it surely won't get done otherwise."

CHAPTER 12

The preaching service that week was held at Uncle Amos and Aunt Mim's house. It was the first Sunday of September, and the weather was still unbearably hot, feeling stickier than the flypaper hanging from the rafters in Dad's barn. All the doors and windows were flung wide open, but Rebekah thought it was still much too uncomfortable to be inside with a bunch of warm-bodied folk today.

She maneuvered her wheelchair next to the backless bench where Nadine sat with several girls her age. Her eyes scanned the other benches on the women's side of the room, searching for Mary Ellen. She wasn't in her usual place, and Rebekah worried that she might have gotten sick and wouldn't be in church at all today.

"I wonder where Mary Ellen is," Rebekah whispered to her sister.

Nadine shrugged. "How should I know?"

"I hope she isn't sick," Rebekah said, choosing to ignore Nadine's curt words.

"I don't think so." Nadine pointed to the door. "Here she comes."

Rebekah wished she had been able to talk to her cousin before church started, but she guessed what she had to say could wait until the service was over. She had lain awake for several hours last night, rehearsing what she would tell Mary Ellen about her decision to let Johnny court her. She had planned to suggest that Mary Ellen give Daniel a chance, but after he'd promised to show up at the greenhouse the other day and hadn't followed through, Rebekah wondered if it might be better for Mary Ellen not to get involved with Daniel, either, because apparently he couldn't stick to his word.

"And now, before we close our service for the day," the bishop said, "I'd like to announce some upcoming weddings that will be held in our community. The marriage of Johnny Yoder and Mary Ellen Hilty will take place on the second Thursday of November."

Rebekah's mouth fell open, and she sat in her wheelchair too stunned to move. She was so shocked by Bishop Benner's announcement that she didn't hear the other names he published before the congregation.

What on earth was Mary Ellen thinking? How could she have agreed to marry Johnny without consulting her best friend about it first? Surely she would have wanted to get Rebekah's opinion on something as important as this. In the past, they had always talked things over whenever either one of them had a big decision to make. Rebekah had discussed her plans to open a greenhouse with Mary Ellen, so it made no sense that Mary Ellen would become betrothed to Johnny without mentioning it to Rebekah.

Maybe their friendship wasn't as strong as it used to be.

Maybe Mary Ellen cared more about Johnny than she did Rebekah.

Of course, Rebekah reminded herself, *when a person falls in love, no one else matters so much anymore. Once Mary Ellen and Johnny become husband and wife, they'll put each other first, and I guess that's the way it should be.*

When the service was finally over and the people had been dismissed, Rebekah drew in a deep breath and forced herself to move her wheelchair toward the front door. Mary Ellen would probably expect hearty congratulations from her family and friends—especially her best friend. But how could Rebekah offer such congratulations when she felt so betrayed? She knew it was the right thing to do, but it wouldn't be easy.

Rebekah swallowed against the burning sensation pushing at the back of her throat and wheeled onto the front porch. Was the pain she felt because she hadn't been told about the engagement, or was it the fact that she was intensely jealous? She and Mary Ellen had shared nearly everything up until now. When they were young girls, Mary Ellen had gotten a rabbit, and she'd made sure that Rebekah had one, too. When they were a few years older, Grandma had given Rebekah a faceless doll. Immediately, she had asked Grandma to make one just like it for Mary Ellen.

Things had begun to change of late, however. Mary Ellen was moving on with her life in a direction Rebekah was sure she could never take. She also knew it wouldn't be fair to expect her cousin to give up love, marriage, and a family of her own because Rebekah couldn't have those things, but it hurt, nonetheless. If Mary Ellen thought

Johnny was the best choice for a husband, then who was Rebekah to say otherwise? She would simply have to accept it. Maybe Johnny would settle down once he and Mary Ellen were married. It might turn out that his playfulness would be exactly what his wife would need during times when things didn't go so well.

Rebekah scanned the yard and caught sight of Mary Ellen walking across the grass with Johnny. With a sense of determination to do the right thing, she glided the wheelchair down the ramp Uncle Amos had built for her sometime ago and headed in the direction of the young couple.

As Rebekah drew near, she reminded herself to be happy for her best friend no matter how much her heart was breaking. She had nearly reached the spot where Mary Ellen and Johnny stood when she was greeted by yet another surprise.

"Have ya heard the news about Aunt Grace and Uncle Lewis?" her cousin John asked as he and his twin brother, Jacob, walked beside her.

Rebekah shook her head. "What news is that?"

"She's in a family way. They're gonna have a *boppli*," Jacob put in.

"Really? I hadn't heard."

"Their boy, Matthew, is already seven years old, and I'll bet he's gonna think a little *bruder* or *schweschder* is a real bother." John's forehead wrinkled as his eyebrows drew together. "I can still remember when our little sister was born. It seemed like Maddie cried all the time."

Rebekah chuckled despite her dour mood. "Kumme now, John. You and Jacob were only four when Maddie joined your family. You weren't much more than a baby yourself, so I doubt you can remember much about it at all."

"Jah, I can," Jacob asserted. "All Maddie ever did was eat, sleep, cry, and wet her *windle*. *Bopplin* are such a bother!"

"When you get married and start a family of your own, you'll change your mind about babies," Rebekah said.

John chuckled and thumped Jacob on the back. "That might be true, but I doubt my brother will ever like anything about dirty diapers."

"That will never be a problem because I ain't never gettin' married." Jacob shook his head with such vigor that his hat fell off.

"Jah," John agreed, "Jacob and I have decided that we're gonna stay single for the rest of our lives."

Rebekah smiled and grasped the wheels of her chair. "If you two will excuse me, I've got to congratulate the happy couple." She rolled away quickly before she lost her nerve.

Rebekah found Mary Ellen and Johnny surrounded by several well-wishers, so she stayed off to the side, awaiting her turn. She would be glad to be done with this so she could get off by herself for a while to think things through. When the others finally cleared away, she maneuvered her wheelchair close to the smiling couple.

"Congratulations, you two." She tried to make her voice sound cheerful, even though her heart ached something awful. "You're full of surprises; that's for sure."

Mary Ellen's smile widened, and Johnny nodded enthusiastically. "It was a surprise to most, but surely not to you, Rebekah," he said. "You're Mary Ellen's best friend so she must've told you about our plans."

Mary Ellen's smile faded, and she stared at the ground. "No. I—I didn't tell Rebekah you had asked me to marry you."

"You didn't? Why not?" Johnny's tone was one of surprise, and his eyebrows lifted high on his forehead.

Rebekah looked over at her cousin, wondering the same thing.

"Could we speak privately for a minute?" Mary Ellen asked, bending down to whisper in Rebekah's ear.

Rebekah glanced up at Johnny for his approval.

"Jah, sure, go ahead. It's fine by me," he replied with a shrug.

"Let's go down by the pond," Mary Ellen suggested. "I don't think anyone else is there right now since everyone's waiting to eat."

"Shouldn't we help the other women get lunch on?"

"We won't be gone long, and there are plenty of others here to help so we probably won't even be missed."

"Well, okay then." Rebekah wheeled off in the direction of the pond, and when they reached the taller grass, making it hard for her to maneuver the chair, Mary Ellen took over pushing.

A couple of ducks on the water dipped their heads up and down and flapped strong wings as if they didn't have a care in the world.

"They look so happy," Mary Ellen said, dropping to a seat on the grass.

"Almost as happy as you and Johnny seem to be," Rebekah mumbled.

"Oh, we are," Mary Ellen's voice bubbled like a sparkling stream, but when she looked up at Rebekah, her dreamy expression turned suddenly sorrowful. "I'm sorry for keeping our betrothal from you. It's just that—well, I was afraid you might be upset."

"Upset? Why would you think I'd be upset?"

"We've always done everything together. If I got a bunny, you got one, too."

"If I got a doll, so did you."

Mary Ellen nodded. "But this time, I was afraid you would be hurt that I was getting married and you weren't."

"That's just the way of things," Rebekah said flatly. No use telling Mary Ellen how she really felt. "There comes a time when little girls must grow up. I've come to realize that I can't have everything my friend has."

"Oh, but you can." Mary Ellen touched Rebekah's shoulder. "Well, maybe not at the exact same time as me, but someday you'll fall in love and get married."

Rebekah groaned. "We've had this discussion before. I'm not able to get around like you, and I doubt that any man would want to be stuck with a handicapped wife."

"Other women—some much worse off than you—get married and even have children."

"It doesn't matter because no one is in love with me." Rebekah shrugged. "Besides, I have my new business now, and if I can become self-supporting, then I won't have need of a husband."

"Love can change all that."

"As I said, there's no one to love."

" 'Commit thy way unto the Lord; trust also in him; and he shall bring it to pass,' " Mary Ellen recited the verse from Psalm 37.

Rebekah gave her wheelchair a sharp turn to the left. "We'd better get back. I'm sure they're probably getting ready to serve up the noon meal by now, and we should be there to help."

Mary Ellen looked like she might want to say something more, but instead, she grabbed the handles of Rebekah's wheelchair and directed it toward the house.

Many of the families lingered for most of the day, enjoying the good food and the fun of being together. It was a time for laughter and games, stories to be told and retold. No one seemed in a hurry to return home to the evening chores that waited to be done.

But Rebekah wasn't anxious to stay around the Hilty farm and be reminded of her cousin's happiness. Even the news about Aunt Grace expecting a baby had sent a pang of regret to her tender, aching heart. She knew it was wrong to harbor feelings of jealousy, and she also knew she had been unkind to Mary Ellen earlier. Since her family had no plans to leave early, the noon meal was over, and everyone seemed occupied, she decided it would be a good time for her to find a place of solitude and talk to God about a few things.

Rebekah wheeled off toward Aunt Mim's garden, where an abundance of flowers and herbs grew. Maybe after some time in the beauty of colors and fragrances that only God could have created, she might find forgiveness for her attitude and could return to the yard feeling a bit more sociable.

A firmly packed dirt path ran through the middle of the

garden, and Rebekah had no trouble navigating it with her wheelchair. She rolled right between two rows of pink roses and stopped to drink in their delicious aroma.

Closing her eyes and lifting her face toward the warming sun, Rebekah sent up a silent prayer. *Dear God: Help me to be a gracious friend and accept the fact that Mary Ellen will soon be a married woman even though I'll always be single. Help my business to do well so I can keep busy and make a good living. Amen.*

Even after Rebekah had finished her prayer, she kept her eyes closed, allowing her imagination to run wild. *Wouldn't it be like heaven to stand in a garden like this one and whisper words of affection to a man who had pledged his undying love to me?* She could almost feel his sweet breath on her upturned face as she envisioned the scene in her mind. She could almost hear his steady breathing as he held her in his arms, whispering words of endearment.

"The roses are sure beautiful this time of year, jah?"

Rebekah's eyes flew open, and she whirled her chair in the direction of the deep voice that had pulled her from the romantic reverie.

Daniel stood a few feet away, hands in his pockets and a peculiar expression on his face. "I'm sorry if I scared you. I could see that you were probably meditating, but I figured you would have heard me come into the garden." He grinned, causing the skin around his eyes to crinkle. "My mom always says my big feet don't tread too lightly."

Rebekah had to smile in spite of her melancholy mood. "You're right. I was meditating." She chose not to mention what she had been meditating on or that she was still a little put out with him for not coming over to help set out the greenhouse plants as he'd said he would do.

As if he could read her mind, Daniel knelt on the grass beside her wheelchair. "I'm sorry about not comin' over to the greenhouse the other afternoon. My daed needed me to help fix some broken fences, and I couldn't get away."

"I figured you were either too busy or had changed your mind about coming," she said, staring down at her hands, clasped tightly in her lap. "It took me awhile, but I finally got all the plants set in their proper place."

Daniel shook his head. "I didn't want to be too busy, Rebekah. I really wanted to help you, and I would have come over to let you know I wasn't able to help out, but Pop wouldn't let me leave." He drew in a deep breath and blew it out with a puff of air that lifted the ties on Rebekah's kapp. "I'll be glad when I'm out on my own and don't have to answer to my daed anymore."

Rebekah wasn't sure how to respond to that comment. It wasn't like Daniel to speak out against either of his folks, but she figured he was probably talking out of frustration.

"Have you gotten any starts from your aunt's rose garden?" Daniel asked, taking their conversation in a different direction.

She shook her head. "I've never thought to ask."

"Mim seems to like you a lot. I'm sure she wouldn't mind sharing some of them with you."

"Maybe I'll talk to her about it."

"I was surprised when I showed up here and found you sitting all alone. I figured you'd be up on the lawn, joining in the young people's celebration."

"Mary Ellen and Johnny's betrothal?"

He nodded, and Rebekah was sure that same look she'd seen on his face a few times before had cast a shadow of sadness on it now. The bishop's announcement must have jolted Daniel like it had her. He was probably hurting every bit as much as she, only for a different reason. She was jealous because she would never have the kind of happiness Mary Ellen was experiencing. Daniel probably wished it had been him, not Johnny, who had won Mary Ellen's heart.

Rebekah swallowed hard, struggling for words that wouldn't be a lie. "Celebrations are for those who can run and play games. I'd much rather be enjoying these *lieblich* flowers."

"They are lovely," Daniel said. "But don't tell my daed I said so 'cause he might think I was *ab im kopp* for caring so much about flowers and plants." He grunted. "All Pop ever thinks about is those cantankerous dairy cows of his."

Again, Rebekah didn't know how to respond. She didn't think Daniel was off in the head, but she certainly didn't want to criticize his father so she sat there quietly, drinking in the delicious aroma of Aunt Mim's flowers and enjoying this special time alone with Daniel.

Daniel stood and moved toward her like he might be about to say something. Then he stared down at his boots a few seconds and slowly raised his gaze to meet hers. "Would ya like me to push your wheelchair? We can walk around the rest of your aunt's garden if you like."

Rebekah's first thought was to decline. She didn't need anyone's help pushing her wheelchair, and she certainly didn't need Daniel's pity. She hesitated only a moment as pride took a backseat and a desire to spend more time with

Daniel took the front seat. "Danki, I'd like that," she finally murmured.

Daniel smiled and stepped behind her wheelchair. "You'd better hang on tight, Rebekah Stoltzfus, because I've been known to be a reckless driver!"

The days sped by with a delicate shifting of summer to fall. A few tourists still visited Rebekah's greenhouse, but most of her customers now were Amish or English people who lived in the area.

Rebekah began to fret over the possibility that her business might fail and had to remind herself frequently to pray, trust God, and search the scriptures for more of His promises. Her faith was still weak, and she knew it.

One Friday since she had no customers at the moment, she decided to lie down on the cot in the back of her store to rest awhile and seek God's will. *Heavenly Father,* she prayed, *I'm still looking for a miracle. I really need to be able to support myself because I don't want to be a burden to others. Please bring in more customers, and show me what to do to make the business more successful.*

The sharp ringing of the bell outside the greenhouse pulled Rebekah from her prayer. "Come in!" she called.

As she struggled to a sitting position, she heard the door creak open. "Rebekah? Are ya here?"

Rebekah recognized the familiar male voice, and she had

to take several deep breaths in order to quiet her pounding heart. Why did Daniel make her feel so giddy? She knew he only cared for her as a friend, but she couldn't seem to stop thinking about him and wishing for more. Daniel's kind face flashed before her eyes as she remembered that Sunday afternoon at the Hiltys' when he'd pushed her wheelchair through Aunt Mim's garden. They'd laughed and talked so easily then, and he had actually made her forget the pain over hearing the news about Mary Ellen's plans to be married.

Rebekah forced all thoughts to the back of her mind as she called, "I'm back here, Daniel. Just trying to get my crutches strapped to my arms."

Daniel poked his head around the partition, and his wrinkled forehead let her know he felt concern. "Are you all right? Why aren't you in your wheelchair? Were you lyin' down?"

Rebekah laughed. "So many questions, Daniel. And don't look so poker-faced. I'm wearing my leg braces today and using the metal crutches that help me stay upright." She dropped one stiff leg to the floor. "Mom hollers at me if I spend too much time in the wheelchair, so I'm trying to humor her today." The other leg followed the first, landing on the floor with a thud. "I was only lying down to rest awhile, but sometimes getting up again isn't so easy."

Daniel moved closer to the cot. "Need some help?"

Rebekah swallowed hard. There it was again. That "I feel sorry for you" look on Daniel's face. She winced, wishing he could see her as a woman and not some *elendich*—pitiful—handicapped girl. She didn't need his pity.

"Are you hurting?" he asked, dropping to his knees in front of her.

She drew in a deep breath. "I'm fine, really." Her crutches were propped against the wheelchair, next to the cot. She reached for one and bumped the other, sending it crashing to the floor. "Always trouble somewhere," she muttered.

Without waiting to be asked, Daniel lunged for the crutch. "Trouble usually has an answer, though," he said, handing it to her with one of his heart-melting smiles.

Rebekah's eyes misted. She hated to be dependent on others, but receiving help from someone as thoughtful as Daniel made it almost a pleasure. "You always seem to be around whenever I need something," she murmured.

"Jah, well, that's what friends are for." Daniel looked Rebekah right in the eye. "I only wish we could be more than friends."

More than friends? What was Daniel saying? Did he actually see her in some other light—something that would involve more than friendship? Rebekah wasn't sure what to say or do next. "You. . .you want to be more than friends?"

He nodded.

"What are you really saying, Daniel?"

He adjusted his weight from one foot to the other. "I'm sayin' that if it were possible, I'd like to be your partner."

"Partner?" Rebekah could barely get the word out.

To her surprise, he touched her arm, sending a jolt of electricity all the way up to her neck. "Jah. I'd like to be your business partner."

Business partner. The words echoed in Rebekah's head like a woodpecker thumping on the side of Dad's barn. She drew in a long, steady breath, hoping to calm her nerves. She should have known Daniel wasn't asking her to be his marriage partner. What a dunce she was for even letting such a ridiculous notion pop into her head. She and Daniel weren't courting, and he'd never shown the slightest interest in her in a romantic sort of way. In fact, she was still sure he was in love with Mary Ellen. How could she have been so stupid as to misread his intentions?

With the aid of her crutches, now strapped to her arms, Rebekah pulled herself to a standing position. "Why would you want to be my business partner?" she asked, once she had found her voice.

Daniel frowned, looking as though it almost pained him to say the words. "I've told you before that I have a love for flowers. Running a greenhouse would be the most exciting thing I could imagine. I envy you, Rebekah."

"Envy me? How could anyone envy a woman with a handicap such as mine?" Tears gathered in the corners of her eyes, and she squinted, hoping to keep them there.

"I–I'm very sorry. I didn't mean to upset you," Daniel sputtered.

With both crutches securely in place, Rebekah plodded across the room. When she stepped into the area where the plants and flowers were kept, she came to an abrupt stop, turned, and almost bumped into Daniel. "Oh, I didn't know you were there."

"Followed you out," he mumbled.

Rebekah glanced around the room, feeling suddenly self-conscious. "I love these green-leafed, blossomed creations God made, so I do understand why you'd want to run a greenhouse." She clicked her tongue. "There are two small problems, though."

He scrunched his forehead until it wrinkled. "Two problems? What would they be?"

"First of all, my greenhouse is a new business. I've been open only a few months, and it's not showing enough profit to support two people. I'm not even sure if it's going to support me."

"And the second problem?"

"Probably the most obvious problem is my parents. They'd never allow such a thing."

"Why not?"

"We'd be spending many long hours together—alone—with no chaperones."

"We're both adults, Rebekah." A slight smile tugged at the corner of Daniel's lips, and a twinkle danced in his usually serious brown eyes. "Of course, my daed don't always see me that way."

Why must Daniel look at me like that? Especially when he sees me as nothing more than a possible business partner? "If we were both the same sex, then maybe it wouldn't be a problem."

"I see what you mean." Daniel shrugged. "Besides, I doubt my daed would want me to quit helping with the dairy business."

"If it were possible," she said with feeling, "I'd actually consider becoming partners. You know a lot about flowers, and you've proved to be pretty handy to have around."

Her words brought a smile to Daniel's face, and when he gave her a surprising wink, her heart fluttered so much she had to will it to stop. "So, what brings you here today? I'm sure it was for something more than to retrieve my crutch."

He chuckled. "I'm here to buy a plant for my mamm. Her birthday's tomorrow, and I want to give her a gift that will last awhile."

"How about a purple African violet?" Rebekah suggested, moving over to the area where all the violets were kept. "I have a beautiful one that came from a start off one of Grandma Stoltzfus's plants."

Daniel bent over and scrutinized the plant in question. "I'll take it."

She giggled. "You haven't even asked the price."

He shrugged. "Well, what does it matter? I like the plants, my mamm needs a gift, and you probably can use the money."

Rebekah gave him a mock frown. What should she do with the likes of Daniel Beachy?

A few days later, Daniel decided to pay Rebekah another visit. "Back so soon?" she asked as he stepped inside her greenhouse. "Did your mamm not like the plant you bought her? I can exchange it for something else, if you like."

Daniel shook his head. "She liked it just fine." He glanced around the room, feeling kind of nervous and wondering how Rebekah would take to the idea he hoped to present.

Rebekah turned her wheelchair toward him. "Then what can I help you with?"

Daniel nodded in her direction as he gathered up his courage. "I was hoping I could help us both."

She lifted her chin to stare up at him. "What are you talking about?"

He shuffled his feet a few times while sticking his thumbs under the edge of his suspenders. "I know I can't work with you here every day, but I think I've come up with a way we can make some extra money, and we'll be doin' exactly what we both enjoy." He wiggled his eyebrows, hoping the playful act might give him an edge the way it seemed to do for Johnny whenever he wanted Mary Ellen to agree with him on something.

Rebekah tipped her head as though she was studying him. Did she think he was joking with her?

"I really do have a good idea," he said, moving closer to her. "Can I tell you about it?"

"If you like," she responded with a shrug.

"All right then. I'll be right back." Daniel spun on his heels and rushed out the front door. A few minutes later, he returned with a large cardboard box. He placed it on the floor, dropped to his knees, and lifted the flaps.

Rebekah wheeled her chair closer as he pulled out several wooden bird feeders, a few whirligigs for the lawn, and some homemade flowerpots.

"Daniel, those are so nice," she exclaimed. "Did you make them yourself?"

He grinned up at her. "In my free time, I like to do a bit of woodworking."

"You do a fine job. However, I don't see what it has to do with—"

"You can try to sell these things here in your greenhouse. I could leave 'em on consignment, and we'd each get a percentage of the profit when they sell."

Rebekah clicked her fingernails against the armrest of

her wheelchair. "Do you think folks coming here would buy items like these?"

"I'm sure they would. My uncle in Ohio sells all kinds of things in his greenhouse. It helps bring in more customers—especially the tourists. They all seem to want something that's been made by one of us Plain People, you know." Daniel paused and moistened his lips. "So, what do you say, Rebekah? Shall we give 'em what they want and make a profit for both of us, as well?"

"It might work. Jah, I suppose it's worth a try."

Daniel grinned, as a new sense of hope welled in his chest. "Silent partners then?"

She nodded. "Jah, silent partners."

Daniel made two more trips over to the greenhouse that day bringing several more boxes filled with bird feeders, birdhouses, flowerpots, and lawn ornaments. With Rebekah's permission, he placed them around the greenhouse in various locations. He also put a few outside the building, saying he hoped to entice more customers into the store. After setting the prices for each item, he and Rebekah reached an agreement that she would get 25 percent of all the money collected from Daniel's handiwork.

"I need to get home now," Daniel said later that afternoon, "but I wanted to make a suggestion before I go."

"Oh? What's that?"

"I was thinking maybe you could also stock vegetable and flower seeds, potting soil, and fertilizers to sell. Since winter will be coming soon, I thought maybe you should get some small holly bushes and several poinsettia plants, too."

Rebekah nodded and followed him to the door in her wheelchair. "You sure do have some good ideas, Daniel."

His smile stretched from ear to ear. "Here's another one of my ideas. What would you think about taking out an ad in *The Budget*, as well as in our local Amish paper, *Die Botschaft?*"

She tipped her head in contemplation. "Hmm. . ."

"I think it would help get things going here even more, and I'd be happy to put up several flyers around town to advertise Grandma's Place."

"Jah, okay. I'll put the add in *The Budget* the next time I send in some information for my column, and I'll do the one for *Die Botschaft* tomorrow morning." Rebekah smiled. Things were looking more hopeful for her business, and she was gaining a kind of self-confidence she had never known before. Having to deal with customers helped her feel less self-conscious, and opening the greenhouse seemed like an answer to prayer. It just might be that miracle she had been looking for.

I hope Mary Ellen likes this quilt," Rebekah told her mother as the two of them sat in front of their quilting frame, stitching on the dahlia-patterned quilt they planned to give Mary Ellen as a wedding present.

"I'm sure she will be very pleased," Mom said. "You do real well with a needle and thread, and you're doing a fine job with this lovely quilt."

Rebekah smiled. "I've always liked quilts—even when I was a kinner."

"Jah, I know. I remember when you and Mary Ellen were barely old enough to walk, the two of you used to like to crawl underneath the quilting frame at whoever's house the quilting bee was being held. I think you thought none of us women could see you under there."

"Maybe we thought it was a tent and were playing that we'd gone camping."

Mom chuckled. "I doubt that since you weren't even out of diapers yet and had never been on a camping trip."

Rebekah thought about the camping trip Dad had taken Simon on last summer, when they'd done some fishing.

Simon had come home dirty, tired, and plenty sunburned, but he'd had a good time and said he couldn't wait until the next camping trip. Rebekah had felt a little envious of her brother, wishing that she, too, might have gone camping. But with her being so limited in what she could do, it would have been difficult on her as well as Dad if he'd tried to take her camping.

"I wish Nadine had shown some interest in helping us make this quilt," Mom said, breaking into Rebekah's reflections. "That girl doesn't seem to want to do anything these days unless it has something to do with boys."

Rebekah nodded. "Jah, she has become pretty interested in the opposite sex, but maybe she'll calm down once she finds a boyfriend and starts courting."

"Let's hope so, although I'm in no hurry for my boy-crazy daughter to begin courting." Mom's needle flew in and out of the material, and she never missed a stitch as they continued to visit.

"I think it's just as well that you let Nadine go over to visit her friend Carolyn today," Rebekah said. "She's never been able to sew a straight stitch, and I don't want anything to ruin Mary Ellen's wedding quilt." She released a sigh. "Besides, if my little sister had stayed around, the two of us would have probably ended up in another disagreement. Seems like every time we're in the same room together, something is said or done that causes Nadine to become upset with me."

Mom stopped sewing and reached over to take Rebekah's hand. "She's having a hard time understanding why you get to do some things she can't."

"Me?" Rebekah's voice raised a notch, and she drew in a deep breath to calm herself. "She's the one who gets to do all the things I can't do. Doesn't she realize how much I envy her for being able to walk around normally, run, skip, jump, or take the stairs two at a time? Can't she see how hard it is for me to sit back and watch others without limitations and not feel sorry for myself?"

"She's young and headstrong," Mom said quietly. "Give her some time to mature and come to a place where she has more compassion and understanding."

"If she listened to the sermons being preached during our church services, she would already know about compassion and understanding." Rebekah tied a knot in her piece of thread and cut the end with the scissors. "There are so many places in the Bible that speak of having consideration for others and being accepting and supportive."

Mom nodded. "That's right, and God's words aren't just for your sister. You need to take them to heart, too."

Rebekah blinked a couple of times as her mother's words registered. Was Mom saying she wasn't kind or understanding? Did she think Rebekah was as selfish and self-centered as Nadine?

"I'm not saying you're inconsiderate," Mom said. "I'm just saying you need to be a little more understanding of Nadine and look past her immaturity—maybe try to set the example for her rather than casting judgment or arguing with her all the time."

A lump formed in Rebekah's throat, and she swallowed hard, trying to push it down. She did want to be a good example to her sister and to everyone she knew. It was just that sometimes when Nadine accused her of being spoiled or always getting her way, Rebekah became irritated and a bit defensive. "I'll try harder where Nadine's concerned," she murmured. "I'll ask God to give me more understanding, too."

Mom smiled and resumed her sewing. "I'm pleased to hear that. Jah, very pleased indeed."

The days of fall moved along quickly, and soon it was time for Mary Ellen's wedding. She had asked Rebekah to be one of her *newehockers* along with Lena, another close friend. The day before the wedding, the two bride's attendants and some who would be table waiters showed up at Mary Ellen's house to help out, as did several aunts, uncles, and close neighbors.

The bench wagon was brought from the home church district to the Hiltys' along with another bench wagon from a neighboring district because they would need a lot more seating at the wedding than during a regular Sunday church service. Much of the furniture had been removed from the house and stored in the cleaner outbuildings, while smaller items were placed in the bench wagons after the men had unloaded the benches, unfolded the legs, and arranged them in the house.

Many hands were needed in the kitchen that morning, preparing the chickens that would be served at the wedding meal, as well as fixing mounds of other food items. The four couples assigned as "roast cooks" divided up the dressed chickens and took them home to roast in their ovens. Mama

Mim had asked Aunt Crystal, who was her best friend and a very good baker, to make most of the doughnuts. Some of the other women relatives had made a variety of cookies.

Mama Mim and Mary Ellen were already hard at work in the kitchen when Aunt Sarah, Rebekah, and Nadine showed up. Mary Ellen grabbed hold of Rebekah's wheelchair and pushed her into the kitchen and up to the table, where she had a pot of tea waiting. "Oh, Rebekah, I'm getting such butterflies! I wonder if I'll be able to eat anything at all between now and tomorrow morning." She extended her trembling hands. "Just look at me—I'm shakin' like the branches of a maple tree on a windy day."

Rebekah reached up and took Mary Ellen's hands in her own. "Try not to think about it. That's what Mom always tells me whenever I'm anxious about something."

Mary Ellen grunted. "That's easy enough for you to say. You're not the one getting married tomorrow."

Rebekah recoiled as if she'd been stung by a hornet.

"Oh, Rebekah, I'm so sorry," Mary Ellen quickly apologized. "I didn't mean—"

"It's okay," Rebekah interrupted with the wave of her hand. "You're right. I'm not the one getting married, and I don't even presume to know what you're feeling right now. I was only trying to help quiet your nerves."

"I know, and I appreciate it." Mary Ellen took a seat at the table and blew on her tea before taking a tentative sip. "I never thought I could be this happy. I love Johnny so much, and I know we're going to be content living together as husband and wife."

"I'm truly happy for you," Rebekah said. "And I'm glad

you asked me to be one of your newehockers."

Mary Ellen felt as if she could burst with the excitement she felt coursing through her veins. "Jah, well, who else would I ask to be one of my attendants but my very best friend?"

Rebekah smiled. "What do you need me to do today?"

"Let me check with Mama Mim. She's the one in charge of things around here."

After consulting with her stepmother, Mary Ellen asked Rebekah, Lena, and Nadine to cut, wash, and dry the celery pieces.

"Sounds easy enough," Rebekah said. "At least it's something I can do from a seated position."

For the next little while, Rebekah sat at the kitchen table, blotting the celery stalks dry with a clean towel after Nadine and Lena had cut and washed them. As she methodically worked, her thoughts went to her greenhouse business, which was doing better than she had ever expected it would. Daniel's wooden items were selling almost as fast as he could make them. She had taken his advice and purchased potting soil, fertilizer, and seeds, not only to use in the business, but to sell, as well. She'd also placed an order for several Christmas cacti, holly plants, and poinsettias to offer her customers during the winter months.

Rebekah's musings about the greenhouse turned naturally to a more personal nature. She always seemed to be thinking about Daniel, especially when she thought of her flowers and plants. If she were truly being honest, she thought of him other times, too. Daniel's kind face was never far from her thoughts. She couldn't understand this attraction because she felt sure it was one-sided. Truly, even if it weren't, there was no hope for any kind of a future for them as a couple.

"You look like you're a million miles away," Mary Ellen said, handing Rebekah another batch of celery to dry.

Rebekah looked up and smiled. "I was thinking about my business." She chose not to mention the part that included Daniel. Why give Mary Ellen something to goad her about?

"Is the greenhouse doing well then?"

Rebekah nodded. "It truly is."

"I'm glad to hear it." Mary Ellen pursed her lips. "I haven't been over in quite a while, what with all the wedding preparations and whatnot, but I've heard from some others that you've made some changes there."

"Daniel Beachy brought several of his handmade wooden items over to sell. The bird feeders are going real fast—probably because everyone likes to feed the birds during the fall and winter months. Daniel does good work, and most of his things sell nearly as quickly as he can make them." Rebekah grinned. "He seems to like flowers and plants as much as I do, and he's given me some helpful suggestions about re-potting, taking cuttings, and which plants need more water than others. He's been a real help."

Mary Ellen poked Rebekah's arm. "So has he started calling yet?"

"Daniel comes over to the greenhouse at least once or twice a week. He likes to see if I need any more items to sell or whether I want help with anything," Rebekah answered as she took up another piece of celery to pat dry.

"No, no, not calling at your greenhouse. Is he calling at your home? Are you two courting, or am I not supposed to ask?"

Rebekah dropped the celery with a thud, and it nearly rolled off the table. "Is that what you think—that Daniel and I are a courting couple? Do you suppose others think that as well?"

Mary Ellen shrugged. "I can't say what others are thinking, but I for one have noticed that he seems to hang around you a lot. I've seen the way you look at him, too."

"Of course he comes around. I just told you, he brings things over to sell at the greenhouse." Rebekah grabbed another hunk of celery out of the pile. "Furthermore, I don't look at him in any special way. He's a good friend, nothing more."

Mary Ellen took an apple from the bowl in the center of the table and bit into it. "All right then. Whatever you say."

Thursday morning dawned bright and clear, a cool, crisp, November day. But the birds were singing, and the sun had rolled over the horizon like a giant ball of fire. It was the perfect day for a wedding. Rebekah figured Mary Ellen had probably been awake since sunup, beside herself with anticipation of her special day. And who could blame her? She was, after all, marrying the man of her choice.

Rebekah sat at her bedroom window, watching two turtledoves in the old maple tree. *Mary Ellen's so happy with Johnny, but I'll never love—leastways not like a woman loves a man.* She groaned, knowing full well that self-pity had stolen into her heart again. Yet she seemed powerless to stop it.

A knock on the door caused her to jump, and she lifted a hand to wipe away the tears rolling down her cheeks. "Come in."

"You didn't show up when I called for breakfast," Mom said, poking her head inside the door. "I was hoping you weren't still asleep. We must hurry if we're to get to the wedding on time."

Rebekah turned the wheelchair toward Mom and forced a smile. "I'm up and, as you can see, even dressed. I guess I was too busy with my thoughts to hear you calling."

Mom moved swiftly across the room, falling to her knees in front of Rebekah's chair. "Is something troubling you this morning? You look so sad."

Rebekah shrugged. Something was troubling her all right, but she didn't want to talk about it. What was the point? Nothing could be changed by talking about it. "I'm fine. I just need a little time for thinking and dreaming."

Mom smiled. "I agree. Without dreams and goals, our lives would never move forward. I believe God has a plan for each of us, but we must be open to His will in order to discover what that plan is."

Rebekah wondered if Mom was trying to tell her something specific. It made her feel so *verhuddelt*. "I guess we'd better get to breakfast," she said, forcing a cheerful voice and ignoring her confused emotions. "After all, this is my best friend's wedding day."

While Rebekah and Nadine washed and dried the breakfast

dishes, Sarah hurried outside to speak with Andrew. She found him in the buggy shed, hitching their horse to the carriage they would ride in.

"What is it, Sarah?" he asked in a tone of concern. "You look like you might be worried about something."

She nodded and took hold of his arm. "I'm concerned about Rebekah. She's not acting right this morning."

His eyebrows arched high on his forehead. "Is she feeling *grank*?"

"No, I don't think she's sick. At least not in a physical sense."

"What is it then?"

"I think she's having a hard time dealing with the fact that her best friend is getting married today."

"Is that all?" Andrew snickered and gave his horse's flanks a couple of pats. "Did you remind her that couples have been gettin' married for hundreds of years?"

Sarah grimaced. "I'm sure she knows that. I just think it's hard for her not to have a suitor of her own."

"That will happen in God's time."

"Maybe so, but Rebekah has told me often enough that she doesn't think anyone would want to marry her because of her disability."

"*Puh!*" He waved a hand. "That's just plain *lecherich*."

"You may think it's ridiculous, but our daughter is convinced she will be en alt maedel for the rest of her life."

"She'll only be an old maid if she closes her mind to love." Andrew's eyebrows drew together. "Maybe I should ask my sister to have a little talk with her because Miriam knows firsthand what heartache that kind of thinking can bring."

"But Mim's happily married now."

"That's just the point. She used to be en alt maedel, but she finally woke up and realized she could be happy being married to Amos."

Sarah shook her head. "Need I remind you that it wasn't so in the beginning of their marriage? It took some time before Mim allowed herself to fall in love with Amos."

"You're right, which just goes to show that given a little time, Rebekah might fall in love with some lucky fellow, too."

"Any idea who that could be?"

He shrugged. "I might have a clue or two."

"You think it's Daniel Beachy?"

"Could be. From what I've noticed whenever he's around Rebekah, I'd say he's got more than a passing interest."

"Can you think of any way we can get the two of them together?"

Andrew let go of the harness and drew Sarah into his arms. "I think we need to leave that matter in God's hands, don't you?"

"I guess you're right," she said, nestling against his muscular chest. "But it wouldn't hurt for us to pray about the matter."

"No, of course not."

"And maybe a little talk with Mim about this wouldn't hurt, either."

"If I don't forget, I'll mention it to her."

Sarah stood on tiptoes and kissed the end of her husband's nose. "I love you, Andrew Stoltzfus."

"And I love you," he said, kissing her upturned mouth.

CHAPTER 15

When Rebekah and her family arrived at the Hiltys' for Mary Ellen and Johnny's wedding, she noticed right away that already there were several gray-topped buggies lined up in the yard, along with a few of the black, open courting buggies. Some of their English friends and neighbors were also present because a couple of vans and several cars were parked nearby, too.

As soon as Dad had parked their buggy and unhitched the horse, they were greeted by one of the six teenage boys, known as the "hostlers," whose job it was to lead the horses away and tie them in the barn.

Their hostler, Paul Troyer, greeted them with a smile. "Looks like there's gonna be a lot of people here today. Guess my biggest job will be to help feed all the horses around noontime."

Dad nodded. "That will be quite a job all right, but I'm sure you boys are up to the challenge."

"Jah, and because there ain't enough room to tie all the horses on the lower level of the barn where they'll be fed, the horses from the upper level will have to trade places with the others when it's their turn to eat," Paul said as he grabbed hold of Dad's horse. "That will make it an even bigger job."

Dad nodded; then he smiled down at Rebekah. "Guess we'd better get you inside. Since you're one of Mary Ellen's new-ehockers, you'll need to get yourself in place soon, I expect."

Rebekah returned his smile, even though her stomach was doing little flip-flops. She would be losing her best friend to Johnny Yoder today, which was hard enough to deal with, but knowing she would never have the privilege of becoming a bride herself was almost too painful to bear.

The wedding began promptly at eight thirty with the chant-like singing of a song from the Amish hymnal, the *Ausbund*. As the people began the third line of the hymn, the ministers stood and made their way up the stairs to a room that had been prepared for them on the second floor. Mary Ellen and Johnny followed, but their attendants waited downstairs.

Rebekah sat in her wheelchair, fidgeting with the corner of her apron and wondering what was being said to the bride and groom in the room above. She nearly broke into tears when she glanced over at Daniel and saw his somber expression. Surely his heart must be broken because Mary Ellen had chosen Johnny and not him.

When the wedding couple returned to the main room and had taken their seats again, the congregation sang another song. The ministers reentered the room during the final verse and also sat down. Abe Landis, one of the ministers, gave a message, which was followed by a period of silent prayer and scripture reading. Then, Bishop Benner rose and began the main sermon.

Rebekah glanced at Daniel again, and he must have caught

her looking at him, for he flashed her a grin. Rebekah's heart did a silly little dance, and she averted his gaze. She figured he was only being friendly, but oh, how she wished it could be more.

The truth hit Rebekah with such force she felt like one of Dad's bulls running at full speed had slammed into her. She was in love with Daniel Beachy. The problem was she couldn't do anything about it. Daniel didn't share her feelings of love, and even if he did, her disability would stand in the way of them being together.

The bishop asked the bride and groom to stand before him then, and Rebekah's attention snapped to the front of the room.

Mary Ellen, looking happy and more beautiful than ever, wore a blue cotton dress draped with a white cape and apron. Johnny looked quite dashing, too, in his white shirt, black trousers, black vest, and matching jacket.

Rebekah listened attentively as the young couple answered each one of Bishop Benner's questions, asking if they would be loyal to one another in sickness or adversity and stay together until death separated them. When the bishop placed Mary Ellen's right hand in Johnny's left hand and pronounced the blessing, Rebekah's eyes stung with tears. She squeezed them shut, hoping to keep the dam from bursting wide open. *Why do I have to be handicapped? Why can't I be like the other young women I know?* She swallowed hard, struggling against the sob rising in her throat. *Dear God, please fill my life in such a way that I won't miss having love or marriage. Give me peace in my heart, like only You can give.*

Rebekah opened her eyes in time to hear the bishop say,

"Go forth in the name of the Lord. You are now man and wife." Johnny and Mary Ellen seemed to radiate a blissful glow as they returned to their seats. In a short time, the wedding feast would begin, and so would Mary Ellen's new life as Mrs. Johnny Yoder.

After the tables had been set up to replace the benches that had been used during the wedding service, and then each of them covered with tablecloths, the eating utensils were put in place. From the temporary kitchen located in the basement, to the eating areas in the living room and upstairs kitchen, foot traffic was heavy and continuous. Food for all courses was soon placed on the tables, beginning with the main course, which included roasted chicken, bread filling, and mashed potatoes. Creamed celery—a traditional wedding dish—coleslaw, applesauce, pies, doughnuts, fruit salad, pudding, bread, butter, jelly, and coffee finished out the meal.

As soon as everything was ready, the bridal party made its entrance, with the bride, groom, and their attendants entering single file.

When Rebekah wheeled her chair in behind Mary Ellen and Johnny, she noticed the jars of select celery she'd dried the day before, which had been spaced at regular intervals on each of the tables so that the leaves formed a flowerlike arrangement. She was pleased to see that the two bouquets of flowers Mary Ellen had selected from her greenhouse were also on the tables.

A special tablecloth from the bride's hope chest adorned the *eck*, the corner table where the bride and groom would sit. On this table sat three cakes that had been made by some of Mary Ellen's friends. A more elaborate cake that had been bought from a bakery in town bore the words, "Congratulations, Johnny and Mary Ellen," across the top in yellow icing.

Also on the eck were pretty dishes filled with candy, nuts, and fancy fruits, as well as some platters full of lunch meats, crackers, and dips.

After each of the tables had filled with the first group of guests, everyone paused for silent prayer. Then, as the people ate, the waiters and waitresses scurried about supplying more food and tending to everyone's needs. When they had all eaten their fill, another silent prayer was said, and the tables were quickly vacated so the next group could be fed.

After the meal, the young folks had some free time to mill around and visit. Mary Ellen invited several of the young women to go upstairs with her and look at some of the wedding presents she'd received, while Johnny went out to the barn to visit with some of his friends.

Rebekah, feeling the need for some fresh air and not wanting to put anyone through the trouble of carrying her upstairs, declined Mary Ellen's offer to view the gifts and said she wanted to go outside for a while.

"You do look flushed," Mary Ellen said with a note of concern. "Are you feeling all right?"

"I'm fine. It's just a bit too warm and stuffy in here for me."

Mary Ellen leaned over and gave Rebekah a hug. "All right, then. See you a little later."

Rebekah wheeled out the door and down the ramp. As soon as she was on the lawn, she caught sight of Daniel standing under a leafy maple tree with one of his brothers. He smiled and nodded as he clasped Harold's shoulder.

Rachel turned her wheelchair toward Aunt Mim's garden, wondering how Daniel could appear so happy when he had just lost the girl he loved to Johnny. As she reached the edge of the garden, she noticed a few late-blooming chrysanthemums and geraniums, as well as several kinds of flourishing herbs. Their pungent aroma drifted on the wind, and Rebekah sniffed deeply, drinking in the serenity of it all. "A garden is my favorite place to be," she murmured.

"Jah, mine, too."

Rebekah jerked at the sound of Daniel's deep voice. "I—I didn't realize anyone else was here."

"I saw you come out and thought I'd join you. That is, if you don't mind my company."

"Of course not."

Daniel grabbed the handles of her chair and pushed it down the wider path. They moved in silence for a time, until he stopped and stepped in front of the wheelchair. "What did you think of the wedding, Rebekah?"

"It was very nice, and I ate more than my share of the good food we were served."

He grinned and nodded in agreement. "Do you think God brought Johnny and Mary Ellen together?"

"I believe Mary Ellen and Johnny would say so."

"They do seem to be very much in love, don't they?"

"Jah." Rebekah was tempted to ask if Daniel was terribly disappointed that he hadn't been Mary Ellen's choice for a husband, but she didn't think that would be a fitting thing to say. Besides, if Daniel was grieving, the reminder might make him feel worse than he already did.

Daniel went back to pushing her chair until he came to a wooden bench. He stopped next to it and took a seat. "I was wondering," he said, looking straight ahead.

"What were you wondering?"

"There's going to be another singing this Sunday night over at the Yutzys' place. Do you plan to go?"

Rebekah shook her head. "I don't think so."

He stole a quick glance at her. "I thought I might go to this one. They'll be having a bonfire with a hot-dog roast and marshmallows. It might be kind of fun, and it may be the last time we can have an outside gathering such as this before the snow flies."

Rebekah pursed her lips as she stared down at her hands, folded in her lap.

"What's wrong?"

"It's just that—well, it's hard for me to go to singings and such when I can't do much of anything but sit and watch from the sidelines."

"I understand, but—"

"No, you don't understand! You're not stuck in a wheelchair like me. No one with a pair of good legs understands what it's like to be confined in this chair or to be forced to walk with stiff leg braces and cumbersome crutches."

Tears welled in Rebekah's eyes, and she was powerless to stop them from dribbling onto her cheeks. She sniffed and reached up to wipe them away.

Daniel sat for several seconds, staring at the garden foliage. Finally, he turned to Rebekah and said, "Okay, so I don't understand what it's like to be in your place, but I don't think you should let your handicap keep you from living."

"I–I'm not. I own a greenhouse now, and that keeps me plenty busy. If that's not living, then I don't know what is."

"You do keep busy working, but what about having fun?"

She nearly choked on the lump in her throat and had to swallow a couple of times before she could respond. "I–I enjoy playing games and putting puzzles together with my family. That's fun. And of course, I still have the column I write for *The Budget*. It's fun whenever someone tells me something humorous that has happened to them."

"That's all well and good, but don't you think you should spend more time with other young people your age?"

"I do. Sometimes. I mean, I spend time with my sister and brother, and of course, Mary Ellen."

"Jah, well, I think you should go to the singing next Sunday, because I'll be there—and it wouldn't be the same without you."

Hope welled in Rebekah's soul. Was Daniel asking her to meet him at the singing, kind of like a date? If she went, was there a chance that he might ask if he could take her home in his courting buggy afterward? She wanted that more than anything, even if they couldn't have a future together. It would be so wonderful to experience what other young women did when they got to ride home with some special fellow—if only just once.

Throwing her doubts and fears aside, Rebekah looked over at Daniel and smiled. "Jah, okay. I'll try to be at the singing."

Now that the time had come to go to the singing, Rebekah had second thoughts about attending. However, the idea of seeing Daniel again won out, and she and Simon were on their way to the Yutzys' in his open courting buggy. The wind whipped against Rebekah's face and stung her nose like a swarm of buzzing bumblebees, but she didn't mind. The sky was clear and full of twinkling stars, and the air was as cool and crisp as a tasty winter apple. To her way of thinking, this was perfect weather for a bonfire—and the perfect night for what she hoped would be her first ride in Daniel's courting buggy.

It will seem odd not to see Mary Ellen there tonight, Rebekah thought regrettably. Now that Mary Ellen and Johnny were married, they would no longer be attending any of the young people's activities. Mary Ellen's days of flirting with the boys and running around looking so cute had come to an end because she was now a *hausfraa*.

Rebekah moaned softly. *I wonder what it would be like to be a housewife with a home of my own to manage? Even a house right next door to Mom and Dad or one that was built on the same property as theirs would make me feel so thankful and independent. Maybe if I become financially self-reliant, Dad will build me a small house. It would have to be near family, of course—in case of an emergency.*

Rebekah supposed she would always need someone in the family to look out for her unless she could make enough money to hire a maid to do the things she couldn't do for herself. But since she couldn't be sure how well the greenhouse would do in the days ahead, there were no guarantees of that, either.

"Now what's that old frown about?" Simon asked, nudging Rebekah's arm with his elbow. "We're on our way to a singing, and there's bound to be lots of good food, fun, and games, so you should be smiling, not frowning like some old sourpuss. Are you feeling sad about something, sister?"

Rebekah managed a weak smile, knowing if she didn't, he would probably needle her all the way to the singing. "I'm not really sad. I was just thinking about something, that's all."

"Like what?" he asked, flicking the reins a couple of times to get the horse moving faster.

"It was nothing important, and I'd rather not talk about it, if you don't mind." She wasn't about to tell her brother that she was nervous about seeing Daniel tonight or that she'd been fretting over whether she might be able to support herself. He would just accuse her of being a worrywart, and he'd probably tease her about Daniel, too.

"Well, if you want to be an old stick-in-the-mud, then suit yourself. I'm really looking forward to tonight, and I plan on havin' fun whether you do or not."

"I wouldn't think of standing in the way of your good time." Rebekah glanced down at her stiff legs. "Make that, sitting in the way of your good time."

Daniel had just hitched a horse to his courting buggy and was preparing to head out to the singing, when his father called out to him. "Where do you think you're goin', son?"

"To the singing over at Yutzys' place."

"Not before we get the milking done. You know that don't wait."

Daniel released a groan. He had been in such a hurry to see Rebekah that he'd plumb forgotten about milking the cows. "Okay, Pop. I'll be right there," he called.

A few minutes later, Daniel entered the milking barn, where his two brothers were already hard at work on one end of the room. His father owned a diesel-operated milking machine so they didn't have to milk all the cows by hand, but even so, the job would take more of his time than he wanted it to.

Sure hope I don't have to do this for the rest of my life, he thought as he squatted down by one of the cows in order to get her hooked up to the milking apparatus. *I'd much rather be raising plants and flowers than milking a bunch of moody old cows.*

A large, annoying horsefly buzzed Daniel's head, and he reached up to swat it away. The fly kept on circling and buzzing, flitting from Daniel's head to the cow's hind end and then back again. The nervous cow mooed, twitched her tail, and then sidestepped, making Daniel feel more exasperated by the minute.

Finally, when he thought he had everything ready to go, the cow let out a raucous *moo-oo*, kicked out her back leg, and slammed her foot into Daniel's leg with such force that he was thrown against the wall behind him. Searing pain shot through his leg, and when he tried to stand, he knew without question that his leg had been broken.

"Pop!" he shouted. "You'd better come on over here 'cause my leg is busted."

It seemed to Rebekah as if all the young people in her community were at the singing. Everyone had crowded into the Yutzys' barn to play games and sing, and as usual, she sat on the sidelines in her wheelchair, listening to the lively banter and watching the door for some sign of Daniel.

I wouldn't think he would want to miss out on all the game playing. Could he have changed his mind about coming? Of course, something might have come up to detain him.

Knowing it would do no good to worry or fret, Rebekah forced her attention onto the game of kickball several of the boys were playing on the other side of the barn. Simon was among those involved, and he was running around, trying to get control of the ball as if his life depended on it. Several young women sat on the sidelines, cheering the fellows on, but Rebekah couldn't muster up the enthusiasm for cheering. If Daniel didn't show up tonight, then she had come to the singing for no purpose whatsoever.

She sighed, and her eyes drifted shut as an image of Daniel's kind face came to mind. If she thought hard enough, she could almost feel his warm breath on her upturned face—could almost sense him looking at her.

"Rebekah, are you awake?"

Her eyes snapped open, and she sat up with a start. Someone *had* been breathing on her, but it wasn't Daniel. Harold Beachy, Daniel's sixteen-year-old brother, stood in front of her with his head bent down so his face was a few inches from hers.

Rebekah drew in a deep breath, trying to calm her nerves. "Don't scare me like that, Harold."

"Sorry, but I need to speak with you about my brother."

"Daniel?"

"Jah. He had a little accident in the milking barn awhile ago."

"Wh-what happened?"

"A nervous cow kicked him real good."

Rebekah's heart slammed into her chest. "Oh, no! Was he hurt bad?"

Harold nodded. "From the looks of things, I'd say his leg was broke."

"I-I'm so sorry to hear that."

"Our daed called 9-1-1 from the phone he keeps in the shed because of his business, and now Daniel and our folks are on their way to the hospital in our neighbor's van."

"How come you're not with them?"

"Daniel asked me to come here and let you know what happened. He was worried that you might think he'd changed his mind about comin' to the singing." Harold gave her a crooked grin. "Don't tell him I said anything, but I think he was planning to give you a ride home tonight in his courtin' buggy."

Under different circumstances, hearing that Daniel had planned to take her home after the singing would have made Rebekah's heart sing, but learning that his leg was probably broken made her feel sick all over.

"Well, I'd better get going," Harold said. "My driver's waiting out front to take me and Abner to the hospital so we can see how Daniel's doing."

She nodded soberly. "Tell Daniel I'm real sorry about his leg and that I'll be praying for him."

Harold gave a quick nod, turned, and sprinted out of the barn.

Rebekah closed her eyes as she fought to keep the tears behind her burning lids from spilling over. She didn't want to be here any longer. All she wanted to do was go home, where she could be alone to read her Bible and pray for Daniel.

"I hope Daniel will like the plant I picked out for him," Rebekah said to her mother as the two of them headed down the road in their buggy toward the Beachys' place. The morning after the singing, they had received word that Daniel's leg was badly broken and he would have to spend a few days at the hospital, since he might require surgery. Word now had it that he was doing as well as could be expected and had been home from the hospital for two days. Rebekah was most anxious to see how he was doing and hoped that her visit might help cheer him up because he was no doubt in a lot of pain.

Mom smiled and reached across the seat to touch Rebekah's arm. "I'm sure Daniel will like the plant you chose."

Rebekah glanced at the cactus sitting in a cardboard box at her feet. "Sure is too bad about him getting kicked by that cow. He probably won't be able to help his daed in the dairy barn for some time now that his leg is broken."

"Maybe there are some things he can do from a seated position, same as you're able to do."

"Jah, but the kinds of things I do in my greenhouse aren't the same as what Daniel's expected to do with those ornery old dairy cows."

"I'm sure he and his daed will work something out. And Clarence does have the help of his other two sons, so they'll probably manage okay even without Daniel's help."

Rebekah nodded and leaned her head against the seat, trying to relax. As she closed her eyes, a vision of Daniel popped into her head. If it weren't for her handicap, maybe someone as nice as him might want to court her. But under the circumstances, she couldn't allow herself the privilege of even hoping for love or romance. She would have to be satisfied with Daniel's friendship. After all, it was better than nothing.

Daniel was lying on the sofa with his leg propped on two pillows when Rebekah came rolling into the living room in her wheelchair holding a cactus with red blossoms in her lap. "It's good to see you," he said, as he started to sit up.

She shook her head. "Stay where you are. No need to sit up on my account."

He dropped his head back to the pillow and grimaced. "I sure hate bein' laid up like this."

"I can understand that." Rebekah wheeled up to the table near the sofa and set the plant on one end. "This is for you, Daniel."

"Danki, that was nice of you." Just seeing Rebekah was a gift in itself, but her thoughtfulness made Daniel realize why he'd come to care for her so much. "Is it from your greenhouse?"

"Jah. It's a Christmas cactus."

"I thought so. I've never tried raising one before, but I hear they can be kind of tricky."

"Not really. Just be sure you water it once in a while—but not too often," she added with a smile.

"I'll do my best not to kill it." He grunted. "Until I can be up and around more on my crutches, there isn't much for me to do, so havin' a plant to care for will be something at least." Daniel knew his limitations were temporary, but it frustrated him not to be able to do the things he was used to doing. Even milking the cows would seem like fun compared to lying around on the sofa all day with his leg propped up on pillows.

Rebekah just sat staring at the cactus with a tiny smile on her face.

"Sorry I missed the singing the other night. Sure was lookin' forward to seeing you."

"Same here."

"So how'd it go? Did you have a good time?"

"Not really. Since I can't play any of the games that require two good legs, it's not so much fun to sit and watch." She lifted her gaze to meet his, and her cheeks turned rosy red. "After your brother came by to let me know about your accident, I asked Simon to take me home."

Hope welled in Daniel's soul. Had Rebekah left because of him not being there? Or had she simply gotten tired of sitting on the sidelines watching the festivities? He was about to ask when his mother stepped into the room with a tray of cookies and two glasses of milk.

"Sarah and I are having tea in the kitchen, and I thought maybe you two would like some refreshments," she said, placing the tray on the table beside the cactus.

"Danki, that'd be real nice." Daniel grabbed the sides of the sofa cushion and pulled himself to a sitting position. "I'm always in the mood for some of your good cookies."

Mom chuckled and ruffled his hair. "I've got a hunch you're only telling me that so I'll keep making more." She smiled at Rebekah. "How about you? Are you hungry enough to eat a little snack?"

Rebekah nodded and patted her stomach. "Jah, I've got the room."

As soon as his mother returned to the kitchen, Rebekah handed Daniel a glass of milk and a napkin with four cookies on it.

"So when's the next singing, do you know?" he asked, placing the napkin in his lap.

"In a few weeks. I think it's supposed to be over at the Hiltys' place."

He bit into a cookie and washed it down with a gulp of milk. "Maybe by then I'll be able to go. In fact, I'm countin' on it."

Rebekah nibbled on the end of a cookie.

"How about you?" he persisted. "Will you go if I do?"

"I—I suppose I could."

He grinned and chomped down the rest of his cookie. "That's good news, Rebekah. It'll give me somethin' to look forward to until then."

She smiled, and the light from the gas lamp nearby reflected in her eyes. "Jah, me, too."

CHAPTER

17

I'm sorry to be so late," Daniel apologized as he hobbled into the Hiltys' barn on his crutches. "I hope you didn't think I wasn't comin'."

Rebekah, who sat in her wheelchair near the door, stared up at him. "I wasn't sure. I thought maybe your leg might be hurting, so you had decided not to come to the singing."

"I told you I'd be here, and I wasn't about to stay home because of my leg." Daniel glanced around the room. "Have I missed much?"

She shook her head. "Not really. Just some songs and a few games. We haven't had anything to eat yet, but some of the men started the bonfire awhile ago, so we should be having the hot-dog roast soon, I expect."

"Now that is good news because I'm a hungry man." Daniel propped his crutches against the wall and lowered himself to a bale of straw near Rebekah's wheelchair.

Rebekah smiled. Daniel made her feel so lighthearted. The sense of peace she felt while sitting with him made her wish the feeling could last forever. But she knew she needed to prepare herself for the day when Daniel would meet someone, fall in love, and get married. Then Rebekah and Daniel's special friendship would be over.

"How's the Christmas cactus doing?" she asked. "Is it still thriving?"

He nodded. "Haven't killed it yet, and it sure is pretty. Makes me think of you every time I look at it."

Rebekah's face heated up. Surely Daniel hadn't meant that he thought she was pretty. He probably had meant that seeing the cactus made him think of her because they both liked flowers and plants.

"Would you like to go out by the fire?" Daniel asked. "Maybe if some of us wander out that way, the Hiltys will get the hint and set out the food."

Rebekah nodded. "You could be right."

Daniel stood and grabbed his crutches. Then, following Rebekah in her wheelchair, they left the barn and headed across the yard to the bonfire.

The cool night air was chilly, and Rebekah suppressed a shiver.

"Are ya cold?" he asked in a tone of concern. "We can move closer to the fire, or I could get a quilt from my buggy."

She shook her head. "I'm fine. I think my shawl will be enough." She pulled the heavy woolen cloak a bit tighter around her shoulders.

"Rebekah, there's something I'd like to ask you," Daniel said in a most serious tone.

She looked up at him expectantly. "Oh? What's that?"

"Well, I was wondering—"

Daniel's words were chopped off when a group of young people rushed out of the barn, laughing and hollering like a bunch of schoolchildren. Karen Sharp along with several other young women began setting food on a nearby table. Then someone yelled, "God is good, and it's time to eat!"

Rebekah glanced over at Daniel and smiled. "I guess this is what we've been waiting for."

He nodded. "Would you like me to get you a hot dog and a stick for roasting?"

"Don't bother. I can get it."

"It's no bother." Daniel hobbled off and returned a few minutes later with two long sticks and a couple of hot dogs. "Would you like me to roast yours for you?"

"Roasting a hot dog is one of the few things I can manage to do for myself." Rebekah knew her words had sounded harsh, and she quickly apologized. "Sorry. I—I didn't mean to sound so ungrateful."

He handed her one stick and a hot dog. "It's all right. Since my accident, I've come to understand a little better how you must feel about not being able to do many things."

"It is hard to rely on others so much of the time." Rebekah rolled her wheelchair closer to the fire so she could reach the stick into the sizzling coals. Her stomach rumbled as she thought about eating some of the delicious food that awaited them. Besides the hot dogs and buns, there was potato salad, coleslaw, potato chips, sweet pickles, baked beans, chocolate cake, and, of course, plenty of marshmallows for roasting.

Since Rebekah had two free hands, and a lap to hold

a plate, she dished up some food for Daniel and handed it
to him after he'd found a seat on a bale of straw. Then she
went back to the food table and filled her own plate. She
had just returned to the spot where Daniel sat when Simon
sauntered up to her.

"Rebekah, I need to talk to you," he whispered.

"What? I can hardly hear you, Simon."

"I need to talk to you!"

"What do you want?"

"I've asked Karen Sharp if I can give her a ride home
in my buggy."

"That was nice of you. I'm sure we can make room
for her."

Simon shook his head. "I don't think you understand.
I want to take her home—alone. So I was wondering if you
might be able to find another ride."

His words and the implication of their meaning finally
registered, and Rebekah grimaced. The last thing she wanted
to do was beg someone for a ride home.

"I can give Rebekah a ride," Daniel said before Rebekah
had time to think of a reply.

"I'd sure appreciate that." Simon grinned and thumped
Daniel on the back. Then he walked away quickly before
Rebekah could say a word.

Her heart sank. Little brother was growing up—about to
begin his own courting days. It wouldn't be fair to hold him
back. It wasn't right to hold Daniel back, either. She studied
him as he sat perched on the bale of straw, with his broken
leg extended in front of him. She wondered how he must
be feeling right now, having been put on the spot by her

brother like that. She had hoped Daniel might ask to take her home tonight but not because he felt forced to do it.

"You're not obligated to see that I get home, Daniel. If you'd planned to ask someone else, then it's—"

Daniel held up a hand as he swiveled around to face her. "I didn't agree to take you home as a favor to your brother, Rebekah. I was plannin' to ask you anyways."

Rebekah blinked a couple of times. "You. . .you were?"

"I was." He smiled at her so sweetly she thought her heart might burst wide open. "So how about it? Will you accept a ride home in my courting buggy?"

Rebekah's common sense said she should probably say no, but the desire deep in her heart won out. "Jah, Daniel," she said with a nod. "I would like a ride home in your buggy tonight."

"Your horse is so *gross*," Rebekah commented once she and Daniel were settled inside his open buggy.

Daniel chuckled. "Toby's a big one, all right. He handles well, though, and we get along just fine."

"Your buggy's real nice, too."

"Danki. I was pretty excited about getting it when I turned sixteen. I've had this buggy over four years now, and I still think it looks pretty good."

"I can see that you take great care with it," she said, letting her hand travel over the black leather seat, so smooth and shiny.

Daniel answered with a smile and a nod as he took up the reins and moved the horse forward.

They rode in silence for a while, with the only sounds being the steady *clip-clop, clip-clop* of the horse's hooves and the rhythmic rumble of the carriage wheels bumping against the pavement.

Rebekah felt such joy being in Daniel's courting buggy on this beautiful, star-studded night. *It's almost like a real date*, she thought wistfully. But then she reminded herself that it was merely one friend giving another friend a ride home from the singing. There was no meaning attached, and she didn't dare to hope that there was, either.

"Do you ever drive any of your daed's buggies?"

Daniel's sudden question pushed her thoughts aside. "Dad's taught me how, but he never allows me to take the horse and buggy out alone," she answered. "He says it would be taking too much of a chance because something unexpected might occur."

"Some unpleasant things have been known to happen, all right. Why, just the other day a buggy was run off the road by a bunch of rowdy teenagers speeding down Highway 6 in their fancy sports car." Daniel shook his head and grunted. "I guess some of those English fellows don't care about our slow-moving buggies. They probably think we're just a nuisance who like to get in their way."

"It does seem so," Rebekah agreed.

"We need to be especially careful when we're out at night. Even with our battery-operated lights and reflective tape, cars don't always see us so clearly."

"I remember once my aunt Mim got caught in a snowstorm and lost control of the buggy, causing it to flip over. She was trapped inside for some time until Uncle Amos came along and rescued her."

"Those two stories are reason enough for your daed not to let you drive alone," Daniel said with a note of conviction. "None of us would want anything to happen to you; that's for certain sure."

Rebekah's heart did a flip-flop at Daniel's thoughtful words. Did "none of us" include him? Was he trying to tell her that he would care if something bad happened because he had romantic feelings for her? She shoved the thought aside, sternly reminding herself that Daniel was only a friend, nothing more.

The ride to Rebekah's house was over much too soon. She'd been having such a good time that she wished it could go on forever.

When they pulled up near the house, Daniel climbed down from the buggy, using the aide of his crutches. "I'll be right back."

"Where are you going?"

"To ask for some help in getting you down."

Rebekah watched as Daniel hobbled up to the steps. Just as he was about to knock on the door, her father stepped onto the porch.

"I spotted your buggy pulling in," she heard Dad say. "Do you need some help gettin' my daughter out of your buggy?"

Daniel nodded. "If it weren't for my bum leg, I'm sure I could manage fine on my own, but under the circumstances, I will need your help."

"No problem." Dad stepped off the porch and hurried out to the buggy. He removed Rebekah's wheelchair first, then lifted her down with ease and placed her in the chair as though she weighed no more than a child.

"I appreciate the ride home," Rebekah said to Daniel as Dad pushed her wheelchair up the ramp and onto the porch.

Daniel smiled and leaned against the porch railing as if he was in no hurry to leave. "I'm glad I could do it."

Rebekah felt relief when Dad grabbed hold of the doorknob and said, "I'm sure you two would probably like to visit awhile, so I'll just go inside now and see what your mamm's up to." He gave Rebekah a sly grin, opened the door, and stepped into the house.

As soon as the door shut behind Rebekah's father, Daniel moved to the front of her wheelchair and leaned over so his face was close to hers. The full moon sent a shaft of light shimmering down from the starry sky, and Daniel's mahogany-colored eyes seemed to dance in the glow of it. "Rebekah, I was wondering something."

"What's that?"

"Well—could I maybe come calling on you one night soon?"

Daniel's whispered words made Rebekah's head feel kind of woozy. Was he asking if he could court her? Oh, surely not. He must mean—

"Rebekah, did you hear what I said?"

Her chin quivered slightly. "What was it, Daniel?"

"We have so much in common, what with our love for flowers and all, and I want to court you."

The rhythm of Rebekah's heartbeat picked up. She hadn't misunderstood him after all. He really did want to court her. It was almost too much to comprehend. "Daniel, I'm honored that you would ask such a thing, but I don't—"

He looked away, and his shoulders slumped. "You don't care for me? Is that it?"

Rebekah felt the sting of hot tears at the back of her eyes, and she blinked a couple of times. "That's not the problem. I...well, aren't you in love with Mary Ellen?"

"Mary Ellen?" he sputtered.

She only nodded in reply.

"But Mary Ellen's a married woman, for goodness' sake!"

Rebekah gritted her teeth. What was wrong with Daniel? Did he think she was verhuddelt? "I know my cousin's married, but before she and Johnny started courting, it seemed as though you were quite smitten with her."

"Now why would you think that? What have I ever done to make you believe such a thing?"

"You were always hanging around her."

He chuckled. "And you didn't know why?"

Rebekah didn't see what was so funny. It irked her that he would laugh about such a serious matter as this. "I—I thought you, like so many other fellows, had your eye on my cute, outgoing cousin."

"The only thing my eyes have ever wanted to look at is you, Rebekah Stoltzfus. I only hung around Mary Ellen because you were usually with her. I wanted to be near you, but I never had the courage to say so before."

Rebekah swallowed against the lump in her throat, and despite her best effort, several tears dribbled onto her cheeks. "Oh, Daniel, I'm flattered by your words, but I—I can't agree to let you court me."

"Why not?" His poker face couldn't hide his obvious surprise at her response. "I think I've made it clear that I'm not in love with Mary Ellen, so there shouldn't be a thing wrong with us courting—unless you don't care for me."

Rebekah's eyelids fluttered. "That isn't the problem, Daniel."

"What is the problem?"

"Courting for us would be pointless."

"Pointless? What could be pointless about two people who enjoy each other's company and have so much in common agreeing to court?"

Rebekah drew in a deep breath and reached up to swipe at another set of tears. "For most couples, courting often leads to a more permanent commitment."

"What's wrong with that? Love and marriage go well together, you know," he said with an impish smile.

Rebekah smiled, too, in spite of her tears. Daniel was everything a woman could want. He was all she wanted; that was for sure. She felt certain that any normal girl would never have considered turning down his offer.

However, that was the problem. Rebekah was not any normal girl. She was crippled and always would be. To her way of thinking, her handicap didn't make her a good candidate as a wife. There were many things she couldn't do without the use of two good legs. And children—she wanted to be a mother so badly. Daniel probably wanted to be a father, too. But it was unlikely that she would ever conceive, and even if by some miracle she could get pregnant, how would a mother in a wheelchair or walking stiff-legged with cumbersome crutches ever care for a baby?

The very thing Rebekah wanted most—to be courted by a man—particularly this man, was being offered to her right now. As much as it hurt, she knew she had to turn it down. She gazed into Daniel's serious brown eyes and blinked rapidly. "I'm a cripple, and I'll always be one."

"I know that already."

"But you don't understand what it's like for me."

"I do understand, Rebekah." He lifted one crutch and nodded at his broken leg.

"But your handicap is only temporary. Once your leg heals, you'll throw those crutches away and walk like a normal man again." She pushed her wheelchair toward the door. "Our relationship could never go any further than just the fun of courting, and as much as it pains me to say this, my answer has to be no."

Daniel stepped between Rebekah and the door and stood for several seconds, staring at her like he didn't quite believe what she'd said.

"Gut nacht, Daniel." Rebekah opened the door and wheeled into the house without another word.

It had been four weeks since Daniel asked if he could court Rebekah, but the pain she felt over her decision made it seem like only yesterday. She dreaded facing Daniel at the preaching service again today, but there was no way she could get out of going because church was to be held in their home this time.

"Oh, you're up," Mom said as Rebekah rolled her wheelchair into the kitchen. "We must hurry and get breakfast on if we're to be ready in time."

Rebekah glanced out the kitchen window. Huge snowflakes fell like powdered sugar from the sky. "It's starting to snow," she said. "Maybe no one will come."

Mom smiled. "It's not coming down so hard. Besides, a little bit of snow isn't likely to keep any of our people from worshiping God."

"I suppose you're right." Rebekah sighed and wheeled away from the window. "What can I do to help?"

"You can set the table and cut the breakfast pie. I'll have Nadine get out some cereal and milk when she comes in from collecting eggs."

As if on cue, Nadine opened the back door and hustled into the kitchen. Her cheeks were pink from the cold, and she stamped snow off her feet. "Brrr. . .it's sure chilly out there. I think winter's definitely on the way." She set the basket of eggs on the counter, slipped out of her jacket, and hung it on a wall peg. "Soon I can get my sled out of the barn, and I'm sure it won't be long until the ponds in the area will be frozen over. Then we can all go ice skating."

Winter, with its drab, gray days and bitter chilling winds always makes me feel sad, Rebekah thought. *Sledding and ice skating for me are out of the question, and Nadine knows that. Is she trying to rub vinegar on my wounds or start another argument with me this morning? Oh, if only. . .*

"Rebekah, are you going to the singing at the Rabers' tonight? Will your beau be bringin' you home again?" Nadine asked suddenly.

Rebekah nearly dropped the plate she'd been about to place on the table. "My what?"

"Your boyfriend. We all know Daniel Beachy gave you a ride home in his courting buggy last month, and I saw him leaning real close to you after Dad came inside, so I'm guessing he's pretty sweet on you, sister."

Rebekah's face heated with embarrassment. She hadn't said a word to anyone in the family about Daniel's offer to court her, and with good reason. "You don't know what you're talking about, Nadine. Furthermore, you shouldn't go around spying on people."

"I wasn't spying. I just happened to be looking out the living-room window when Daniel's buggy pulled into the yard." Nadine puckered her lips. "I'll bet he even kissed you when he thought no one was looking."

"He did no such thing!" Rebekah's voice shook with emotion. So much for her resolve to get along better with Nadine and have more understanding.

"I'll bet you're just too embarrassed to admit it."

Rebekah was about to offer a comeback, when Mom spoke up.

"Nadine, this little discussion has gone on long enough. Stop bothering your sister now. Rebekah will decide when to let us know what's going on with her and Daniel, and she doesn't need your teasing."

Rebekah's eyes filled with tears, clouding her vision. "The simple fact is that there'll never be anything going on between me and Daniel except friendship. Now, can we get on with breakfast?"

Mom gave Rebekah a sympathetic look. "Jah, it's on the way."

All during breakfast, Nadine sulked, barely able to eat anything she had put on her plate. It didn't seem fair that Mom always took Rebekah's side on things, but it had been that way ever since Nadine could remember. She'd only been a baby when Rebekah had lost the use of her legs, so she had no memory of her sister ever walking in a normal way. Nadine had grown up watching her folks, especially Mom, treat Rebekah as if she was someone special—someone who always needed to be stuck up for and sheltered.

"Anything wrong with your eggs?" Dad asked, tapping Nadine on the shoulder.

She shook her head. "I'm not so hungry this morning."

"You're not feeling grank are you?" Mom asked with a look of concern. "If you are, then you'd better get upstairs and into bed."

"I'm not sick."

"Then why the sour face?" Simon asked, giving her arm a nudge.

First Dad and then her little brother. Nadine wished she had sat in another chair.

"I think she's put out with me," Rebekah spoke up before Nadine had a chance to respond.

"Why would that be?" Dad questioned.

"Because I got upset with her for spying on me and Daniel when he brought me home from the singing four weeks ago."

Dad shook his finger in Nadine's face. "You know better than to spy on your sister. What were you thinkin' of, girl?"

"I wasn't spying. I can't help it that I happened to be looking out the window when Daniel and Rebekah were on the porch."

"You were looking out the window so you could see what was going on." Rebekah squinted at Nadine from across the table.

"No, I wasn't trying to see what was going on. I was just—"

Mom held up her hand. "I've heard this once already, and I'm not in the mood for another go-round." She pointed to Nadine's plate. "Now hurry and finish your breakfast so we're all ready when the others show up for church."

Nadine's stomach clenched as she picked up her fork and stabbed a piece of egg. Rebekah had won again.

As Rebekah rolled her wheelchair into the living room, she noticed that everything was in place and ready for the church service. The large hinged doors that separated the living room from the rest of the house had been flung open wide, and the furniture had been replaced with the traditional backless benches used in their worship services.

Soon everyone began to file into the house. The women and girls took their seats on one side of the room, while the men and boys sat on benches across from them.

Rebekah spotted Daniel sitting on a bench between his brothers, Abner and Harold, and she was pleased to note that the cast on his leg had been removed. When he smiled and nodded at her, she felt her face flame so she averted her gaze, hoping no one had noticed. There was no point in giving Daniel any reason to believe she might have changed her mind about them courting, and she certainly didn't want to give anyone the impression that she was interested in him. It was bad enough that Nadine believed it to be so.

The three-hour service seemed to take longer than usual, and the room grew hot and stuffy, despite the cold day. Rebekah fidgeted in her wheelchair, wishing she could be someplace where there was some fresh air to breathe. In spite of the fact that the padded seat of her wheelchair was a lot more comfortable than the hard, wooden benches, she was getting tired of sitting and felt relief when the service was finally over and she could wheel into the kitchen to help with the noon meal.

Several tables were set up throughout the house, and the

guests ate a nourishing lunch of soup and sandwiches, followed by cookies and plenty of hot coffee and apple cider.

The men and boys were fed first, and Rebekah made certain that the group she helped serve were the ones farthest away from the table where Daniel and his brothers sat. Nadine had been assigned to that table, and Rebekah was grateful.

When the men and boys were done eating, they headed outside to the barn. Then the women and girls sat down to their meal. It was during this time that Rebekah was able to visit with Mary Ellen.

"How's it going with being a full-time wife and not teaching school anymore?" she asked.

Mary Ellen shrugged as she offered Rebekah a wide smile. "I'm getting used to it now. Besides, being married to Johnny makes me happy."

Rebekah didn't know quite how to respond. She wanted to express happiness for her friend. She would have liked to say that she, too, was in love and hoped to be married. However, she said neither, for she was sure she would never marry or find that kind of joy.

"I hear you and Daniel Beachy have begun courting," Mary Ellen said suddenly.

"What?" Rebekah's mouth fell open. "Where did you ever hear such a thing?"

"Someone who attended the last singing said Daniel took you home." Mary Ellen grinned at Rebekah. "I always did think he had an interest in you."

"So he says."

"Then you've agreed to begin courting?"

"I told him no."

"You what?" Mary Ellen's wide-open eyes revealed her obvious surprise. "Oh, Rebekah, why? Don't you care for Daniel at all?"

Rebekah nodded. "I care very much for him."

"Then why won't you let him court you?"

"You, of all people, should know the answer to that. You've been my friend a long time, and I've shared many things with you."

"It's about your handicap, right?"

Rebekah nodded, her eyes filling with tears. "I care for Daniel, but if we started courting, he might want marriage—and later, kinner. I can't give him those things, and you know it."

"I know of no such thing, and neither do you. If you'll just trust God and give yourself half a chance—"

"A chance to do what? I'm not a complete woman. I could never make Daniel happy."

"Don't say that."

"Don't say what?" Nadine asked as she joined the women at their end of the table.

Rebekah's head snapped up. "Nothing. It was nothing important."

"I think you two must have been talkin' about boys. Everyone always closes up like a star tulip whenever I come along. Mom especially does that. She thinks I'm too young to be thinkin' about boys." Nadine clicked her tongue. "It's just because I'm the boppli of the family—that's all."

Mary Ellen squeezed Nadine's arm. "Just hold on a bit longer, for your time is coming. Sooner than you think, you'll end up like me—an old married woman."

Nadine shook her head. "You're not old, Mary Ellen, but you sure are pretty. No wonder Johnny wanted to marry you." She glanced over at Rebekah. "My sister has a boyfriend, too, only she won't 'fess up to it."

Rebekah slammed her empty coffee cup down with such force that she thought it might be broken. When she realized it wasn't, she gave it a little shove, then pushed her wheelchair away from the table. "I'm going outside for some fresh air!"

As Rebekah left the room, Mary Ellen looked over at Nadine and shook her head. "I wish I knew what's gotten into your sister today. She sure seems upset."

"Rebekah's always upset about something." Nadine grunted. "Of course, she gets away with it because of her handicap."

"What do you mean by that?"

"Mom's always taking Rebekah's side, and she favors her over me."

"Your mamm has always taken good care of Rebekah, but from what I've seen, she's not treated her any different than you or Simon."

"*Humph!* You don't live at our house, and you don't see how Mom takes Rebekah's side on every little thing. Why, just this morning, Rebekah and me were having a disagreement about her relationship with Daniel, and Mom told me to quit bothering Rebekah." Nadine folded her arms. "Why doesn't she get after Rebekah for her negative attitude instead of always scolding me?"

"I don't know the answer to that, but I do know that it must be hard for your sister to be confined to either her wheelchair or those rigid leg braces and crutches she sometimes uses." Mary Ellen studied Nadine's serious face. "I know it's not easy for you, but maybe you should try a little harder to have more understanding for Rebekah instead of arguing with her about things that don't really matter or feeling resentful because she receives a little more attention than you do at times." She paused a moment to gauge Nadine's reaction, but the young woman just sat staring at the table.

"Your folks love you and Simon as much as they do Rebekah," Mary Ellen continued. "And I'm sure it hurts them when any of their kinner has a disagreement. So won't you try a little harder to get along with your sister and be more understanding?"

Tears welled in Nadine's eyes, and she nodded slowly. "I'll try, but I promise you, it won't be easy."

"I'll be praying for both you and Rebekah," Mary Ellen said.

"Danki." Nadine scooted off the bench. "Guess I'll go visit with some of my friends for a while."

A few minutes after Nadine left, Mary Ellen noticed that Mama Mim was heading her way. Maybe she would have a talk with her about Rebekah's gloomy mood and see what she had to say.

CHAPTER

19

Rebekah sat on the front porch, wrapped in a heavy shawl and breathing in the crisp, cool, afternoon air. The sun peeked out between fluffy white clouds, casting a golden tint on the gently rolling hills. A light dusting of powdery snow rested on most of the trees.

A group of boys played tug-of-war in the driveway, and a few men stood on the lawn, visiting. *The rest of the men must be out in the barn,* Rebekah decided. She was glad Daniel wasn't among those who were still outside, for she didn't want to face him.

She released the brake on her wheelchair and rolled down the wooden ramp. Up the path leading to her greenhouse she went, feeling the need for some solitude. A time to think and enjoy all the plants might help get her mind off Daniel.

When Rebekah entered the greenhouse a few minutes later, she lit a gas lantern so she would have more light. It was chilly in the first section of the building, so she added a few logs to the burning embers inside the woodstove, thankful that Dad had placed them within easy reach.

Once the fire was going well, Rebekah moved into the glassed-in section of her greenhouse. Between the kerosene heater and the solar panels, this area was always plenty warm. She rolled her wheelchair up and down the aisles, drinking in the rich colors and fragrant smells coming from the variety of plants.

"If this is the only miracle You ever give me, Lord, then I'll learn to be content," Rebekah whispered. Even as she said the words, a feeling of emptiness settled over her like a heavy fog. Was the greenhouse really enough? Could she learn to be content?

She reached for a lacy-edged, pink African violet and held the pot as though it were a baby. She thought about Aunt Grace, who would be holding a real baby in just a few months, and about Mary Ellen, recently married. Unlike her aunt or cousin, Rebekah's fingers might often caress a delicate plant but never a husband's bearded face. Like as not, her hands would change potting soil, not dirty diapers. As much as she enjoyed working with plants, they weren't the same as a living, breathing human being, who could offer love in return.

Rebekah startled when she heard the front door of the greenhouse creak open, then snap shut. "Who's there?" she called out, drawing in a quick breath.

"It's me, Rebekah—Aunt Mim."

Rebekah expelled her breath, feeling a sense of relief that it wasn't Daniel.

"I'm back here!"

Aunt Mim poked her head through the doorway and smiled. "I haven't been in here since your opening day. I see you've made quite a few changes."

Rebekah nodded. " I'm selling more items now. Daniel Beachy gave me plenty of good ideas, and all the wooden items you see are his handmade creations."

"So your business is doing well then?"

"Better than I ever expected." Rebekah placed the African violet back on the shelf. "Of course, winter's almost here, and I won't have nearly as many customers now as I did in the summer."

"No, I suppose not," her aunt agreed. "But then, a young woman can certainly find other ways to fill the long winter hours."

Rebekah shrugged. "I suppose I can always quilt or do some other type of handwork. And there's the column I write for *The Budget*. That keeps me busy."

Aunt Mim gave her a wide smile and moved closer to the wheelchair. "It wasn't sewing or writing news about our community I had in mind, Rebekah."

"What did you have in mind for someone like me?" Rebekah asked with a catch in her voice.

Aunt Mim pulled out a wooden stool and sat down beside her. "I was thinking more about courting. I hear you have a suitor these days."

"Mary Ellen Hilty—I mean, Yoder. You are such a blabbermouth!"

"Don't be so hard on Mary Ellen," Aunt Mim said softly. "She only cares about your happiness."

"Jah, well, she can care without meddling. I suppose she saw me come in here and asked you to have a talk with me."

Aunt Mim shook her head. "She shared her concerns,

but it was my idea to speak with you." She placed a gentle hand on Rebekah's arm. "I believe I can help. I think you should hear my story."

"Your story?"

"Jah."

"You used to read me stories when I was a kinner. Why do you think I need to hear one now?"

"Because, sweet niece, I think my story might teach you something."

Rebekah leaned her head against the back of her wheelchair and closed her eyes. "I'm ready to hear your story."

"Once there was a young woman named Miriam Stoltzfus. She fell in love with her childhood sweetheart, and he broke her heart when he moved away and married someone else. Miriam became bitter and angry. She didn't trust men and resolved never to marry. Miriam even blamed God for all her troubles. Her pupils at the one-room schoolhouse often talked behind her back, saying she had a heart of stone."

Rebekah nodded. She remembered hearing such talk.

"And so," Aunt Mim continued, "the bitter old-maid schoolteacher decided she could do everything in her own strength. She even forgot how to pray.

"Then one day after school had been dismissed, she told her young niece that she would give her a ride home. A few minutes later after the child had gone outside to wait for her, Miriam heard a clap of thunder, then an awful, ear-piercing snap, followed by a scream. She rushed outside, only to find her favorite niece lying on the ground with the limb of a tree lying across her back."

Aunt Mim paused a moment as though it pained her to relive the past. After inhaling a deep breath, she finally continued. "The doctor said Rebekah's spinal cord had been injured and that she would probably never walk again. Miriam's heart was broken, and she blamed herself for the tragic accident."

Rebekah's eyelids fluttered. "You—you blamed yourself? I never knew that."

Aunt Mim nodded, her eyes brimming with tears. "I'm the one who said you could wait outside, and I felt responsible for what had happened."

"I never faulted you at all, Aunt Mim." Rebekah's vision blurred with her own tears. It nearly broke her heart to think that her aunt had blamed herself.

Aunt Mim touched Rebekah's shoulder. "I know you didn't. As a young girl, you were always so happy and accepting of your limitations. However, as you grew, I saw a change come on. You began to withdraw and seemed unsure of yourself." She made a sweeping gesture at the room. "When you opened this new business, I thought things might be different. I was hoping you would see that your handicap couldn't keep you from reaching your goals. I prayed that God would send the right man into your life so you would find the joy of being in love, too."

Rebekah slowly shook her head. "I couldn't put the burden of my handicap on Daniel. It wouldn't be fair."

Aunt Mim's forehead wrinkled. "I think we'd better get back to my story."

"All right then. I'm all ears." Rebekah leaned her head back again, but this time she kept her eyes open.

"Well, Miriam Stoltzfus almost made a huge mistake. She met an English man, and after a while, he tried to talk her into leaving the Amish faith."

Rebekah's mouth fell open. "An English man? He asked you to leave the faith?"

"Jah. Do you remember when a reporter came into your hospital room shortly after the accident?"

"The picture man?"

"Right. The one who took your picture and put it in the English newspaper."

Rebekah squinted. "He's the one who asked you to leave the faith?"

Aunt Mim nodded. "We'd become friends, and there was a certain magnetism between us." She sighed. "But despite my attraction to Nick, I knew I could never give up my Amish way of life—although I still wasn't right with God at that time."

"So what did you do?"

"I made the wisest decision of my life. I married Amos Hilty." Aunt Mim crinkled her nose a bit. "When he first asked me to marry him, I turned him down."

"Didn't you care for him?" Rebekah could hardly imagine such a thing. Aunt Mim and Uncle Amos seemed to be so much in love.

Aunt Mim shrugged. "I didn't give myself a chance to find out whether I cared or not. I was so certain that Amos would let me down just as my first beau had done. I didn't think I could trust God to bring happiness into such an empty, bitter life as mine."

"But you did marry Uncle Amos, and you seem to be very happy."

Aunt Mim's eyes filled with another set of tears, and she sniffed deeply as she swiped them off her cheeks. "Jah, I'm happy and have been for a good many years. You see, one day God showed me something very important."

"What was that?"

"He let me know that my bitterness and blaming myself for so many things was of my own doing. He showed me that I could shed all my doubts and hurts from the past. God can do that for you, too, Rebekah. He wants you to be happy, and if you'll only trust Him, He can work a miracle in your life, just as He did mine."

A *miracle*. Wasn't that exactly what Rebekah had been looking for—an honest-to-goodness, true miracle from God? But could she take a leap of faith toward love and possibly marriage? She wanted to—more than anything—but she was afraid of failing.

"Well, I think I'd better stop now. Stories from my past are good, but Rebekah, you'll never know what God can do until you give Him the chance. If Daniel loves you, then he will accept you—imperfections and all."

Rebekah blinked back a fresh set of tears. "I'll try to take the step of faith I need to find love. Will you pray that I'll have the strength to do it?"

Aunt Mim bent down and gave Rebekah a hug. "I'll be praying, and may the Lord be with you, sweet niece."

Rebekah's wheelchair rattled down the path toward the barn. She could only hope that Daniel and his family hadn't left for home yet. If she could just have the chance to speak with him alone for a few minutes, it might be that they could talk things out. If he hadn't changed his mind about them, maybe she would allow him to come calling on her after all.

When Rebekah reached the barn, she pushed open the side door and peered inside. Several clusters of men and boys filled the area—some talking, some playing games. She didn't see any sign of Daniel or his family, though.

Dad spotted her and came over to the door. "What's up, Rebekah? Did you need something?"

She shook her head. "I was looking for Daniel Beachy, that's all."

"I saw him leave with his folks awhile ago, and his brothers and sister left even before that."

"Do you know where Simon is, then?"

"I think he's outside. He and some of the other fellows his age were planning to get a game of corner-ball going."

"Okay, danki." Rebekah wheeled into the chilly air again. She knew what she had to do, but she'd better do it before she lost her nerve.

Dad had been right. She spotted Simon and a group of boys playing ball—in the snow, of all things. Rebekah sat on the sidelines until Simon looked her way; then she motioned for him to come over.

He kept playing a few more minutes but finally ambled her way. "What do you want, and why are you sittin' out here in the cold? Don't you know it might start snowing again?"

"Jah, I know it's cold, but I—I need your help." Rebekah clung desperately to her brother's arm.

"What do you need my help for?"

"Could you please hitch one of our more gentle horses to the buggy and help me get inside?"

His eyebrows lifted high on his forehead. "Inside the buggy?"

"Of course, inside the buggy. What else would I be talking about?"

"Where are you going, and who's going with you?"

"I–I'd rather not say. I just need to go, that's all."

Simon's mouth dropped open. "I hope you're only jokin' about this, sister."

"No, I'm not. I need to go someplace, and I know Dad won't allow me to head out alone so I'm asking for your help."

"You want me to go with you?"

She shook her head. "I need to do this alone. I just want you to get the buggy ready and help me inside. I'll leave my wheelchair in the buggy shed."

"Oh, sure, so I can be the one Dad hollers at? You know I'll be in big trouble if he finds out I helped you do such a stupid thing."

"Then we'll have to be sure that he doesn't find out."

Simon grunted. "All right, then, but you'll owe me big for this one."

CHAPTER 20

Any other time, Rebekah might have been nervous about driving the buggy alone. But at the moment, she was too excited about the prospect of seeing Daniel and telling him she had changed her mind about them courting to think of the possible dangers involved. Dad had taught her how to handle the horse, and just because she had no one with her didn't mean she should be afraid. After all, the Beachys' farm was only a few miles up the road, and it wouldn't take long to get there.

One thing Rebekah hadn't counted on was bad weather. She'd gone about a mile or so when a heavy snow began to fall, making it more difficult to see. The road quickly turned slippery, and it became harder to maintain control.

Rebekah gripped the reins a little tighter and talked soothingly to the horse. She knew it was important for her to remain calm and stay focused on the road ahead, or she could end up in trouble. She snapped on the switches for the battery-operated windshield wipers and the lights. With icy snow pelting her windshield, she had to be sure she could see well enough, not to mention the need to alert any oncoming cars that her buggy was on the road.

Rebekah might not have been scared when she'd started this little trip, but she sure felt nervous now. What if she lost control and her horse and buggy skidded off the road and into a ditch? The buggy could overturn and end up on its side. *Who would help me then?* she worried.

Rebekah drew in a deep breath, hoping to steady her nerves, then did what she should have done at the start of her ride. She prayed. Prayed for all she was worth. *Heavenly Father, I know I was wrong for taking the horse and buggy out alone and without Dad's permission. I probably don't deserve Your help, but I'd be obliged if You would get me to the Beachy farm safely. When I get back home, I promise to tell Mom and Dad what I've done and accept responsibility for my reckless actions. Amen.*

Rebekah was almost to the cross street leading to the road where the Beachy farm was located when she saw another Amish buggy. It was lying on its side along the shoulder of the road. The windows were all steamed up, and she couldn't see inside. With her heart pounding and hands so sweaty she could hardly hold the reins, she pulled up beside the wreck and opened her door. "Is anyone there? Are you hurt?" she called, her voice carrying in the crisp, cold air.

"We're okay, but the door's jammed," a man responded. When she recognized Daniel's voice, her heart slammed against her chest.

"Daniel, it's Rebekah. What happened?"

"We hit a patch of ice. Our horse broke free and bolted. Me and the folks are trapped inside my daed's buggy!"

She lifted a trembling hand to still her racing heart. "Is anyone hurt?"

"We're all okay; just can't get out is all."

"What can I do to help?"

"Is Andrew with you?" Clarence Beachy spoke, and he sounded almost desperate.

"No, I'm alone," Rebekah replied in a shaky voice.

"Rebekah Stoltzfus, what are you doing out by yourself in this horrible weather?" Daniel scolded.

"I was heading for your place. I needed to speak with you."

"Could you possibly go for help?" This question came from Daniel's mother, Frieda, whose high-pitched voice gave clear indication that she was quite agitated. "It's cold in here, and I'm uncomfortable in this awkward position."

"I'll turn around and head back home right away."

"Be careful now," Daniel called.

"I will."

"I'll be praying for you."

"I'll be praying for you, too." Rebekah choked on a sob, and after turning her buggy around, she started back down the road. "Please, God," she fervently prayed, "I need You to guide me safely home. The Beachys are in trouble, and I seem to be their only source of help right now."

Sarah had just set a fresh pot of coffee on the table and was about to serve some apple pie to Miriam, Amos, and Henry Hilty, who had stayed on to visit after the other guests had gone home, when Simon entered the kitchen. His face was bright red, and his jacket was covered with snowflakes.

"Where's Rebekah?" Sarah asked. "Is she in the barn?"

Simon shook his head as he flicked some snow off his jacket.

"I hope she's not sitting out on the porch. It's way too cold for her to be outside this evening."

"She's not on the porch."

Andrew, who was getting ready to pour them all a cup of coffee, looked up at their son and frowned. "Do you know where Rebekah is?"

Simon shuffled his feet a few times and stared at the floor. "Jah, but. . .uh. . .I'd rather not say."

A muscle on the side of Andrew's neck quivered as he set the coffeepot down on the table. "What do you mean, you'd rather not say?"

"I. . .uh. . .kind of led her to believe I wouldn't snitch on her."

"Snitch on her?" Sarah moved over to stand beside her son. Their guests sat quietly, but curiosity covered their faces. "What could Rebekah have done that she wouldn't want us to know about?"

Simon kept his focus on the floor and mumbled, "She's headin' over to the Beachy place to see Daniel."

"How could she be heading to Daniel's when we're all here and the horse and buggies are in the shed?" Andrew asked before Sarah had a chance to respond.

Simon lifted his gaze and turned to face his father. "I got one of our easygoing horses out and hitched it to a buggy so—"

"You did what?" Andrew's fist came down hard on the table, clattering his cup, and nearly spilling the pot of coffee. He jumped up and stormed across the room, shaking his finger in Simon's face. "If anything happens to Rebekah, you'll be to blame for it, is that understood?"

Sarah, fighting to keep her tears at bay, left the table and took hold of her husband's arm, hoping to calm him down. "Yelling at Simon won't solve anything, Andrew. What you need to do is go after Rebekah."

Andrew nodded, then pointed to the door. "Simon, run out to the barn and get a horse hitched to one of our other buggies."

"We'll come, too," Amos said as he and Henry both pushed away from the table.

"Should I get Rebekah's wheelchair?" Simon asked. "We left it in the buggy shed."

"I'll see to it," Andrew said.

Mim and Nadine joined Sarah at the window, and they watched as the men headed out into the snow. "It'll be all right," Mim murmured. "We just need to pray."

Sarah nodded, tears filling her eyes. "Prayer is always the best thing."

"That was a good church service we had today, jah?" Johnny asked as he took a seat on the sofa next to Mary Ellen.

She smiled and nodded. "To me, they're always good."

"Jah." Johnny took a drink from the cup he held in his hands and smacked his lips. "This is real tasty. Hot cider always hits the spot on a cold winter's night."

"I agree." Mary Ellen reached for her own cup, which she had placed on the low table in front of the sofa. "Are you hungry? Should I fix us something to eat?"

"Might have a piece of apple-crumb pie after I get all the animals fed and bedded down for the night." Johnny glanced out the window. "I see it's started to snow real hard. Looks like we might be in for a storm."

"Oh, I hope not," she said with a sigh. "It's not so easy to get around when the roads are icy."

"That's when it's time to bring out the sleigh." He reached over and patted her knee. "Always did enjoy goin' on a sleigh ride with my best girl."

She smiled and took hold of his hand. "Always have liked riding in one, too."

He wiggled his eyebrows and grinned. "Lots of snow means we can have a snowball fight if we want to."

"Oh, Johnny, you're such a tease."

He lifted her hand to his mouth and kissed each one of her fingers. "And that's what you love about me, right?"

"Jah, that's exactly right."

They sat in companionable silence for a while, drinking their cider and holding hands. Then Johnny set his empty cup on the table and stood. "As much as I hate to leave your good company, I'd best get myself out to the barn. The animals won't feed themselves, that's for sure."

"Okay. I'll have a hunk of pie and another cup of cider waiting when you come back inside."

He grinned down at her. "I'm gonna hold you to that, *fraa*."

When Mary Ellen heard the back door open and click shut, letting her know that Johnny had left the house, she leaned her head against the back of the sofa and closed her eyes. An unexpected vision of Rebekah popped into her mind, and she shivered. Was something wrong with her best friend? Was she in some kind of trouble and in need of prayer?

Heavenly Father, Mary Ellen silently prayed, *I don't know why Rebekah's face has come to mind at this time, but I feel it necessary that I pray for her. Wherever Rebekah is, whatever she's doing, please bless her, guide her, and keep her safe from all harm. Amen.*

The snow fell harder, the chilling wind swirled in a frenzy, and the light of day quickly faded into darkness. With sheer determination and lots of prayer, Rebekah managed to keep the horse and buggy on the road. "Steady, boy," she coaxed. "Together we can do this. We have the Lord on our side." A verse from the Old Testament book of Nahum popped into her mind: "The Lord is good, a strong hold in the day of trouble; and he knoweth them that trust in him."

A sense of peace settled over her like a mantle of calm, and she knew instinctively that everything would be all right.

A short time later, Rebekah pulled up in front of her house. "Dad! Dad, come quickly," she hollered when she spotted him standing on the front porch with Uncle Amos and Cousin Henry. She also noticed that her wheelchair was sitting on the porch.

"Rebekah, we were getting ready to come looking for you. What on earth possessed you to take that buggy out alone?" he bellowed.

"I don't have time to explain things right now!" she cried. "The Beachys' buggy overturned not far from their house, and they're trapped inside. Your help is needed right away!"

"Go get some rope," Dad called to Simon, who was heading for the barn; then he raced over to Rebekah's buggy, jumped in, and gently pushed her into the passenger's seat. "You really should get into the house where it's warmer."

She shook her head with a determined expression. "I want to go along. I need to see with my own eyes that Daniel and his family are okay."

"All right then, but we'll be talkin' about this shenanigan of yours when we return home," he admonished.

Rebekah didn't argue. She knew Dad was right. It was a shenanigan she had pulled, and they needed to talk, even if she was in for a strong tongue-lashing.

Simon came running out of the barn just then. Holding a rope in one hand, he jumped into the backseat of their buggy. Uncle Amos and young Henry climbed into their own buggy.

Dad nodded and moved the horse forward. Uncle Amos's horse and buggy followed.

Rebekah's cheeks burned hot, and her hands shook so badly that she had to clench them in her lap in order to keep them still. "They're going to be all right, aren't they, Dad?"

With eyes straight ahead, he answered, "I hope so. Did they say if any of 'em were hurt?"

"Daniel said they weren't, but it's so cold, and what if a car comes along and doesn't see them there? They might be hit, and then—"

"Now don't you go borrowing trouble," Dad said in a calming voice. "If you want to make yourself useful, then you'd better start praying."

"I have been praying, and I won't let up until everyone's safely out of that buggy."

"Sure wish our other three kinner hadn't gone home so much earlier than we did," Daniel's father said as he tried unsuccessfully to open the door on his side of the buggy. "If we'd all left at the same time, they would have seen our rig tip over and been able to help. As it is, they don't even know we're in this situation."

"I'm sure after a time either Abner, Harold, or Sarah Jane will become worried, and then they'll come looking for us," Daniel's mother said.

Daniel shook his head. "Why would they? None of 'em knew what time we planned on leaving the Stoltzfuses' place. For all they knew, we were planning to hang around there until evening."

"Well, whatever the case, Rebekah's gone for help now, and we should be out of this buggy soon," said Daniel's father.

"I hope Rebekah will be all right," Daniel's mother put in. "It's not good for her to be out alone in this kind of weather."

How well Daniel knew that, and if it were up to him, she never would have taken her father's buggy out in the first place. But then, if she hadn't, how long might it have been before someone spotted their overturned buggy?

"I'm sure Rebekah will be fine," Daniel's father said. "We're all praying for her, so we need to trust God to get her home safely and bring us some help."

Daniel squeezed his eyes shut, remembering that Rebekah had said she'd been heading for his place because she needed to speak with him. He hadn't thought much about it until now, but he wondered what she could have wanted to talk to him about that would cause her to take her father's buggy out in the snow alone. Had she changed her mind about them courting? He prayed it was so—and he prayed God would guide her safely home to get them some help.

Rebekah and her father and brother traveled in silence until they came upon the accident a short time later. "There it is. I see their rig!" Simon shouted.

"I see it, too." Dad pulled his buggy as far off the road as possible, and Uncle Amos did the same with his buggy. "Get out and set up some flares, Simon. They're in my toolbox behind your seat."

Simon did as he was told, and Dad climbed down, reaching for the rope Simon had put in the buggy. He handed the reins over to Rebekah. "Hold the horse steady while I get the rope tied around the Beachy buggy."

Rebekah's hands trembled as she held the reins firmly, and her heart pounded so hard she thought it might explode any minute. *Please let them be all right, Lord.*

She strained to see out the front window. Dad, Uncle Amos, and Henry had tied a rope to the back of the overturned buggy. When it was secured, Dad climbed back inside while Simon joined the other men to help stand the Beachy carriage upright. Uncle Amos, Henry, and Simon put their full weight against the buggy as Dad backed up and pulled on the rope until it was taut. It took several tries because the slippery road made things difficult, but the buggy finally righted itself. The men undid the rope and then tied it to the front of the other buggy.

Rebekah's father drove around until he was in front of the Beachy buggy; then the rope was tied to the back of Dad's buggy. In this manner, he towed the Beachy family safely to their farm.

When they arrived, Dad pulled on his reins and said, "Whoa now, boy!" Uncle Amos, who had been following, stopped his buggy, too.

Everyone got out except for Rebekah, who sat with her nose pressed against the window, waiting to see if Daniel and his parents were really all right. She felt so helpless and wished there was something she might do to assist.

"Your door is surely stuck," Dad called to the Beachys after he pulled on the handle and nothing happened. "Are you all okay?"

"We're fine," Clarence Beachy responded. "We'll push on this side of the door, and you can pull. If it still won't open, then you might want to look for a crowbar in my barn, so you can pry it open."

It took two tries, but the door finally opened, nearly spilling all three of the Beachys onto the snow-covered ground.

"Danki," Clarence said, pounding Rebekah's father on the back.

"We're just glad everyone's all right." Dad glanced over at his own buggy then. "Actually, it's Rebekah who deserves the biggest thanks, for she's the one who found you and drove home to give us the news."

As soon as Daniel's feet touched the ground, he hurried around to Rebekah's side of the buggy and flung open the door. "Rebekah Stoltzfus, I should be furious with you for driving the buggy by yourself—and in the middle of a snowstorm, no less."

"It wasn't snowing so badly when I left home," she said.

Lifting Rebekah into his arms, he held her close. "You're an angel of mercy, and even though you did take a chance doing what you did, I thank you for being so reckless."

"I only did what I had to do."

"You might have saved our lives," he said in a voice raw with emotion. "Who knows what could have happened if some car had come along and hit our rig while it was tipped on its side?"

"I know. That's what I was so worried about."

"What were you doin' out there on the road, anyhow?"

"I was driving over to tell you that if you still want to court me, I'm willing."

"Really? You mean it, Rebekah?"

She nodded. "If you still want to, that is."

Daniel's lips curved into a smile. "Of course I still want to. What happened to change your mind?"

Rebekah opened her mouth to reply, but Daniel's sister and brothers came rushing out of the house just then.

"What happened?" Sarah Jane cried when she caught sight of their mangled buggy.

"Has anyone been hurt?" Abner and Harold hollered at the same time.

"We're all fine, thanks to Rebekah and her family." Mom stepped up beside Daniel and nodded at Rebekah, who was still held securely in his arms. "It's getting colder by the minute, so you'd better bring her inside to warm up awhile before she and her family have to start for home."

"There's some coffee and hot chocolate on the stove," Sarah Jane said. "And I'll get one of my brothers to make a batch of popcorn so everyone can have a little snack before they head out."

"I could definitely use a cup of coffee." Uncle Amos clasped Henry's shoulder and grinned. "And I'm sure my growing son wouldn't turn down an offer to eat popcorn, now would ya, boy?"

Henry snickered and started walking toward the house. Everyone else followed.

"How are your arms holding up?" Rebekah asked, looking up at Daniel. "I'm probably getting kind of heavy."

"To me, you're light as a feather, but I do want to get you in out of this cold." He wondered how it looked to the others to see her being held in his arms in such a familiar way, but she had to get inside somehow, and he wanted to be the one to get her there.

Rebekah leaned her head against Daniel's shoulder, and he enjoyed the feeling as he carried her across the yard, up the steps, and into the house.

Soon, everyone had gathered around the kitchen table, and Mom poured cups of coffee for the men and hot chocolate for the young people. Harold got a batch of popcorn going while Sarah Jane sliced huge pieces of spicy gingerbread for the hungry crew.

Daniel placed Rebekah in one of the empty chairs; then he pulled out the one next to it for himself.

"Well, Rebekah, I would have to say that you're the heroine of the day," Daniel's father said, looking over at her with a grateful smile. "We're mighty thankful that God sent you along to find our overturned buggy when you did."

"My daughter took the horse and buggy out without my permission." Andrew gave Rebekah a brief frown, but then his lips curved into a smile. "Still, she did something meaningful today, and it was all on her own. While it may have been rather foolish, it was a brave thing to do, and I'm grateful she was able to bring help to those of you who were trapped in the buggy."

"Jah, and we truly thank you," Daniel's mother said as she handed Rebekah a cup of hot chocolate.

Rebekah blushed, and Daniel figured she wasn't used to being the center of attention—at least not this way. He knew the recognition she usually got was because of her handicap.

"I was pretty scared when the snow started coming down real hard, making it difficult for me to see," Rebekah said. "I know I shouldn't have been driving the buggy alone, but I thank God for watching over me so I could get you some help."

"And I thank God that you changed your mind about us," Daniel whispered in her ear.

"Shouldn't Rebekah and the menfolk have come back by now?" Nadine asked her mother as the two of them stood by the living-room window, looking out at snow that seemed to be coming down harder all the time. "I'm gettin' kind of worried."

Mom draped her arm across Nadine's shoulder and gave it a gentle squeeze. "I'm sure they'll be all right. We just need to pray."

"That's right," Aunt Mim chimed in from across the room, where she sat in the rocker holding a cup of tea.

"I wish Rebekah had thought to ask me to go with her when she went after Daniel in the first place." Nadine swallowed around the lump in her throat. "But then I guess she wouldn't have wanted her little sister taggin' along when she was going to see her boyfriend. Especially since the two of us haven't seen eye to eye on much of anything lately."

Mom offered Nadine a sympathetic look. "Why do you think that is, daughter?"

"I—I suppose it's my fault because I'm always accusing her of being a *verdarewe* child."

"Is that what you really believe, Nadine—that your sister is a spoiled child?"

Tears welled in Nadine's eyes, blurring her vision, as she nodded.

"I've tried to explain things to you many times before," Mom said, taking hold of Nadine's shoulders and turning her around so she could look directly at her. "But you still refuse to understand that Rebekah is not our favorite child, nor do we intentionally spoil her."

Nadine opened her mouth to comment, but Mom rushed over to the front door and pulled it open. She stepped onto the porch, grabbed the handles of Rebekah's wheelchair, and pushed it into the living room. "Have you ever tried to put yourself in your sister's place, imagining what it would be like to be stuck in this chair, unable to walk normally or do all the fun things you're able to do?"

Nadine shook her head.

Mom grabbed a blanket off the sofa and threw it over the wheelchair, which Nadine knew must be cold from setting outside all this time. "Have a seat, Nadine."

"Huh?"

"I said have a seat."

Nadine hesitated a moment but finally did as Mom asked. "Now what?"

"I want you to pretend that you can't use your legs and that you're stuck in that chair. Imagine that a group of young people are having a skating party on one of the frozen ponds in the area, and you want to go with them. Would you be able to go ice-skating from your wheelchair?"

Nadine shook her head.

"And how about if I asked you to go into the kitchen and get the jar of cookies sitting on top of the refrigerator? Could you do it?"

"No, Mom."

"Now do you understand a little of what your sister goes through?"

"I—I think I do."

"Would you like to be in her place, unable to do so many things that you take for granted?"

"No, I wouldn't like it at all." Nadine's voice faltered, and she drew in a shaky breath. "I guess if I had to pick between gettin' more attention and bein' able to do everything I can do,

I'd choose bein' me."

"I'm glad to hear it." Mom smiled. "So do you think you can try a little harder to get along with Rebekah?"

"I guess it's my fault that Rebekah gets so annoyed. If I was a better sister, she might not get so exasperated with me." Nadine released a little sob. "If somethin' bad happens out there in the storm, I'll never forgive myself for not makin' things right with her before it was too late."

Aunt Mim stepped up to the window then, and motioned Nadine to join her.

Nadine looked to her mother for approval, and when Mom nodded, Nadine left the wheelchair and went to stand beside her aunt.

Aunt Mim slipped her arm around Nadine's waist. "Did Rebekah ever tell you that I used to blame myself for her handicap?"

Nadine's mouth dropped open. "How come?"

"Because I allowed her to wait outside for me while I cleaned up the schoolhouse. If I'd made Rebekah stay inside with me, she wouldn't have been standing beneath that tree branch when it broke."

"But you had no way of knowin' the branch would break and fall on Rebekah. It's not right that you should have blamed yourself for something that was nothing more than an accident."

"You're right about that, and I finally came to the same conclusion." Aunt Mim gave Nadine's waist a gentle squeeze. "I'm sure Rebekah and the others will be fine, but it will do you no good to blame yourself for not making things right with her before she left. The important thing now is for us all to pray, and when Rebekah gets back home, you need to talk things out between you."

Nadine nodded. "I know."

"Both of you need to show more patience and understanding with one another, but blaming yourself, or even your sister, will do neither of you any good at all."

"Guess I need to ask God to help me be a better sister," Nadine said tearfully. "Jah, with His help, I'll do my best."

All the way home from the Beachys' place, Rebekah thought about Daniel and how she had agreed to let him court her. She was pleased that he was still willing, but she had a few misgivings yet. Would they find enough things to do together—things that Rebekah was capable of doing? Would Daniel eventually become bored with her and find someone else to court? And what if he wanted something she couldn't give him—marriage and children?

Psalm 34:4, which she had committed to memory, popped into her mind: "I sought the LORD, and he heard me, and delivered me from all my fears." Then she thought of Psalm 37:5: "Commit thy way unto the LORD; trust also in him: and he shall bring it to pass." She'd found that passage in Grandma's Bible and had quoted it often as a reminder that she should trust the Lord in all things, while she committed her way unto Him.

She leaned her head against the seat and closed her eyes, resolving to have more faith and allow God to work things out between her and Daniel.

Winter had definitely come to Lancaster County, as the thick blanket of pristine snow lying on the ground proved. All the trees were dressed in gleaming white gowns, and every pond in the area was frozen solid. Many Amish families exchanged their buggies for sleighs in order to accommodate the dangerously slick roads.

Rebekah loved riding in an open sleigh, especially when it was with Daniel. At least that was something she could do, since she sure couldn't join the other young people in their area who had gone sledding and ice-skating a few times already. Now that she and Daniel were courting and had found some things they could do together, she didn't feel so left out and didn't miss many of the things others her age were able to do that she couldn't.

In spite of the wintry weather, Daniel and Rebekah had managed to go to several more singings, and Daniel called on Rebekah at her home as often as he could. They played board games, worked on puzzles, or just sat by the fire eating popcorn, drinking hot chocolate, and talking for hours on end.

Sometimes in the late afternoons, Daniel would come over to the greenhouse with his sister, Sarah Jane, who had taken over the job as schoolteacher right after Mary Ellen had gotten married. The three of them would repot plants, take cuttings off larger ones, or start flowers from seeds.

Rebekah and Daniel seemed to be drawing closer, and she had gotten to know Sarah Jane better, too. She was tempted to write something in her column for *The Budget* about the times she spent with Daniel, but she didn't feel it would be appropriate. The readers wanted to know about significant events such as births, deaths, and birthday celebrations, as well as community events, visitors from other states, hospitalizations, accidents, illnesses, and weather conditions.

One evening in late February, Daniel stopped by Rebekah's house for a visit. Everyone else in her family had already gone to bed, so he and Rebekah sat in the kitchen, looking through a stack of nursery catalogs that had recently come in the mail and discussing what she might order for her greenhouse in the months ahead.

After they'd been sitting there awhile, Rebekah looked up from her studies and saw Daniel looking intently at her. "What's wrong?" she asked. "You're looking so thoughtful all of a sudden."

"Nothing's wrong. I was just thinking how lucky I am to have you as *mei aldi*," he answered with a smile. "My girlfriend," he repeated. "You're so kind and sweet."

"Me, sweet?" She averted her gaze as heat flooded her face. "I never thought anyone would think of me as sweet."

Daniel reached out and took hold of her hand, sending a warm sensation traveling all the way up her arm. "Why not? You have a most generous spirit, and your expression is always so sincere. I find everything about you to my liking, Rebekah."

"Even my stiff, crippled legs?" She hated to spoil the moment by bringing up her disability, but she felt the question needed to be asked.

"Your legs only serve to remind me that you haven't

allowed your handicap to stop you from doin' good things with your life." Daniel stroked the back of her hand gently with his thumb. The light of the lantern hanging above the table lit his dark eyes. "I want to spend the rest of my days with you, Rebekah," he whispered. "I want you to be my wife."

Rebekah stared at the table, thinking she must have misunderstood what he'd said and wondering if he might have been joking.

Daniel lifted her chin, so she was looking directly at him. Such a serious expression she saw on his face. It let her know that she hadn't misunderstood, and she felt sure he wasn't joking. "Would ya be interested in marryin' me come fall?"

Rebekah felt like all the air had been squeezed out of her lungs—like when she was little and had taken a tumble from the hayloft. She had known she and Daniel were getting closer, but a proposal was the last thing she'd expected to hear tonight.

When she opened her mouth to reply, nothing came out but a little squeak.

"So what's your answer?" Daniel prompted. "Will you agree to be my wife?"

Tears sprang to Rebekah's eyes, clouding her vision and stinging her nose. She had never known such joy before Daniel came along. He made her feel whole and alive—so much so that she couldn't think clearly when he was looking at her in such a sweet way. Maybe that was the reason she was able to find her voice and didn't hesitate to answer, "Jah, Daniel, I would be honored to be your wife."

Daniel leaned his face close to hers until their lips nearly touched. Rebekah closed her eyes and waited expectantly for the kiss she felt was forthcoming. She had never been kissed by a man before. Not in the real sense of the word, anyway. Hugs and quick pecks on the cheeks didn't count, and those had only come from family and close friends.

The gentle kiss Daniel placed on her lips didn't last long, but it took Rebekah's breath away. When Daniel pulled back a few seconds later he was grinning from ear to ear. Rebekah suppressed a giggle, and without a word, she picked up the seed catalog they had been looking at. Except for the gentle hissing of the gas lantern above the table, all was quiet, and Rebekah felt more at peace than she'd ever thought possible.

CHAPTER 22

Winter melted into spring, and spring blossomed into summer. Everyone's life was busy as usual, and the new season was full of changes. Aunt Grace had given birth to a baby boy toward the end of March. About the same time, Mary Ellen announced that she, too, was expecting a baby, due in November.

Rebekah was happy for her cousin, but hearing the news put an ache in her heart for a child of her own. It also caused her to have second thoughts about whether marriage for her was such a good idea. What if she didn't make Daniel happy? What if she could never conceive? What if she got pregnant but couldn't take care of their baby? She determined to keep those nagging doubts hidden from Daniel, who seemed to be anxiously awaiting their wedding day set to occur on the third Thursday of November.

"How would you two young women like to drive over to Lewis and Grace's place with me later this morning?" Mom asked as Rebekah and Nadine helped to clean up the kitchen after breakfast.

"I'd like to go," Nadine said in an excited tone. "Last

Sunday after church was over, Uncle Lewis told me that one of his rabbits had given birth to ten little *haaslin*. It will give me a chance to see 'em."

Mom clicked her tongue. "We're not going over to see the baby bunnies, Nadine. We'll be making the trip to see Aunt Grace and Uncle Lewis's growing boppli." She smiled. "Wouldn't you like to spend some time holding your little second cousin?"

Nadine wrinkled her nose. "I'd much rather hold a *haasli*. At least they don't wet their *windles* and spit up all over the place."

Rebekah, who had been drying the dishes, spoke up for the first time. "Baby bunnies may not spit up on you, but since they don't have the protection of a diaper, they can sure make a mess."

"Jah, well," Nadine said, grabbing a broom from the closet, "I'll take my chances holding a haasli any old time."

As Rebekah sat in Grace's living room, with baby Timothy nestled in her arms, her eyes stung with tears. He was such a beautiful baby—dark hair, like his mother's, and a turned up nose like his father's.

If Daniel and I could have children, I wonder what they would look like. Would their hair be light brown like mine or dark like Daniel's? Would their eyes be blue, brown, or a mixture of the two?

"Would you like to hold the boppli for a while?" Aunt Grace asked, looking over at Nadine, who sat next to their mother on the sofa.

"I don't think so. He might spit up on me or somethin'."

"I have a burp cloth you can drape over your shoulder."

"He's a bundle of sweetness," Rebekah said, smiling down at the baby.

Nadine shook her head. "No, thanks." Then she looked over at Mom and said, "Can I go out to the barn to see the haaslin now?"

"I suppose if you don't get to hold one of those bunnies today, we'll have to hear about it all the way home."

"Danki, Mom." Nadine stood and rushed out the door.

Aunt Grace smiled at Rebekah. "How are things with you these days?"

Rebekah shifted the baby from her lap up to her shoulder. "Okay."

"Things are going well in Rebekah's greenhouse," Mom spoke up. "Word of mouth and a few newspaper ads have helped her business, and she's getting more customers all the time."

"That's good to hear."

"As I'm sure you know, she and Daniel will be getting married this fall, so Rebekah has a lot to do between now and then to get her dress made and do everything she wants done before the wedding."

"I can imagine how excited you must be, Rebekah," Aunt Grace said. "I remember when Lewis and I were betrothed—I was just counting the days until we got married."

Rebekah nodded as a rush of heat covered her face and neck. "I am excited," she admitted. "And a whole lot *naerfich*, too."

"There's no reason to be nervous," Aunt Grace said with a wave of her hand. "It'll all be over with sooner than you thought, and then you'll settle into the routine of being a hausfraa and probably a *mudder* soon after that."

"I'm not so sure about me being a mother," Rebekah mumbled. "The doctor said I may never be able to have any bopplin."

"Doctors have been known to be wrong," Mom interjected. "After they said you'd always be in a wheelchair and would probably never be able to stand on your legs, who'd have guessed that you could walk again?"

"Walk?" Rebekah looked down at her crippled legs and frowned. "What I'm able to do with those rigid leg braces and crutches isn't really walking, Mom."

"It's more than we could have hoped for, and it does get you out of that wheelchair for a time."

Rebekah shrugged. Walking with the leg braces was a chore, but rather than say anything, she thought it best to keep her opinion to herself. "Is it okay if I write something about little Timothy in my next article for *The Budget?*" she asked her aunt.

"Jah, sure. That'd be real nice."

The three women sat awhile. Mom and Aunt Grace sipped from their glasses of iced tea, and Rebekah snuggled the baby in her arms. The warmth of his soft skin and his sweet baby smell made her long all the more for a boppli of her own.

It was already mid-August, which left only three short months until the wedding, and Rebekah knew if she didn't do something about her doubts and apprehensions soon, she might not be able to go through with her marriage to Daniel. She still loved him—probably more with each passing day. However, fear of the unknown was paralyzing her soul, causing more discomfort than the partial paralysis of her lower body.

What's wrong with me? Rebekah silently moaned as she sat in her wheelchair, repotting a spider plant that had grown too large for its container. *I thought I had all this settled in my mind. I believed I could take the step of faith necessary for love and marriage. When I agreed to marry Daniel, I thought it was God's will. I'd decided that He had brought the two of us together, yet now I'm not so sure.*

She patted some fresh potting soil around the roots of the plant, feeling downright jittery inside. "I need to stay busy, that's all. If I keep my mind occupied, I won't have time for second thoughts."

Rebekah's self-talk was cut short when a customer rang the bell and entered the greenhouse. She wheeled herself out to the front section of the building and was greeted by Johnny Yoder. As a married man, he now sported a full beard, and for the first time since they had become adults, she thought he actually looked mature.

"Guder mariye," she said.

"Good morning, Rebekah." Johnny took off his straw hat and wiped his forehead with the back of his hand. "Ach, my! It's hot out there. Only ten o'clock and already it's over eighty degrees."

Rebekah nodded. "Another hot and humid summer, that's for sure."

"I think the only critters who like this kind of weather

are the lightning bugs," Johnny said with a deep chuckle.

Rebekah nodded and smiled. "So what brings you here today?"

"I thought I'd get a nice plant for Mary Ellen. It might make her feel better."

"She's still not feeling well?"

"It's that awful morning sickness. Doc Manney says it should go away soon, but she's already in her sixth month, and still she fights it." Johnny shook his head. "Her back hurts somethin' awful, too, and the poor thing can't stand or sit long, neither."

Rebekah clicked her tongue. "That must be hard. I'll try to get over and see her soon."

Johnny nodded "You're Mary Ellen's best friend, and I'm sure a visit would do her some good."

"What kind of plant did you have in mind?" Rebekah asked, bringing the subject back to the reason for Johnny's visit. "Something for the flower garden or an indoor plant?"

He scratched the back of his head and squinted. "I'm not sure. Maybe something for the porch. Mary Ellen spends a lot of time outdoors in the shade there, since it's been so hot inside."

Rebekah smiled. Johnny did seem to care about Mary Ellen's needs. She was glad he had made her cousin so happy. "Let's go on back to where my plants are kept. I think I have a nice pot of mixed pansies she might like."

Johnny followed as she rolled into the other room, and a short time later, he was at the cash register, paying for a large pot of yellow, white, and purple pansies. As he opened the front door, he nearly bumped into Daniel, who was just coming into the greenhouse.

"That's a beautiful bunch of pansies you've got there," Daniel said, as he hung his straw hat on one of the wooden wall pegs near the door.

"Jah, and they're for a beautiful wife!" Johnny waved and was gone before Daniel could open his mouth to respond.

"Marriage seems to agree with him," Daniel said, smiling at Rebekah. "I think he's excited about becoming a daed, too."

Rebekah nodded but made no comment.

Daniel knelt next to her wheelchair and reached out to take both of her hands. "Is something wrong? You look kind of down in the mouth this morning."

Rebekah was about to reply when the doorbell rang again. Two English couples entered the greenhouse. "I've got to wait on those people," she whispered to Daniel, then wheeled away.

"May I help you with something?" she asked the two young couples who stood looking around the room.

"We were wondering if you might sell anything cold to drink," one of the women said. "It's so hot out today, and we're all thirsty."

Rebekah shook her head. "I don't sell any beverages, but I do have some cold water in the back room." She looked over at Daniel. "Would you mind getting the pitcher, along with some paper cups?"

"Sure, I can do that," he responded with a nod.

The group of English looked grateful and offered their thanks when Daniel reappeared a few minutes later with a pitcher of water and some paper cups.

"What do you sell here?" one of the young men asked Rebekah.

"Plants, flowers, and all garden-related items." Rebekah had to wonder why these people didn't know what things were sold in a greenhouse. They were obviously city folk.

"You could probably triple your profits if you sold some food and beverages, especially during the hot summer months," the other man said.

"Maybe so."

The tourists finished their water, then turned to leave. They were about to exit the building when one of the women spotted a wooden whirligig shaped like a windmill. "Look at this, Bill. Isn't it cute? I'd like to have it for our backyard."

The man reached into his pants pocket and handed his wallet to her. "Here, help yourself." He grinned, then turned to Rebekah. "We're newlyweds, and I can't seem to say no."

Rebekah just rolled her wheelchair over to the cash register.

"This is so nice," the woman said. "You should offer more handmade items for sale. Almost anything made by you Amish would probably sell well."

Rebekah smiled and muttered her thanks.

As soon as the customers left, Daniel moved over to stand beside her. "Those English tourists might have a good point about you sellin' more things in here."

Rebekah wrinkled her nose. "It wouldn't be much of a greenhouse if I sold all sorts of trinkets and souvenirs just to please the tourists."

"It would still be a greenhouse, Rebekah. It would simply have a few added items for sale, is all." His brown eyes fairly sparkled. "I sure can't wait until we're married. Then we'll finally be business partners. Why, I have all sorts of new ideas I'd like to put into practice here."

Rebekah felt like a jolt of lightning had shot through her. Was that all Daniel wanted—a business partner? Had he proposed marriage so he could become part owner of Grandma's Place?

"And what if there is no partnership, Daniel?" she asked pointedly.

He squinted. "No partnership? What do you mean? Two heads are better than one, ya know."

"That may be true, but what if I change my mind, and we don't get married after all?" The words seemed to jump right off her tongue, but there was no taking them back now.

"You're teasin' me, aren't you?"

She shook her head. "Here of late, I've been having some serious doubts about marriage, and what you just said only confirms my thinking."

"What? You can't mean that." Daniel bent down and took hold of her shoulders. "Please say you don't mean it."

She swallowed past the lump in her throat. "I—I do mean it. I'm thinking maybe you only want me for this business. Could be that the greenhouse is the only reason you ever showed any interest in me at all."

"Jumpin' frogs, Rebekah, I never thought anything of the kind! I care about you. Surely you can see that."

She bit her bottom lip so hard she tasted blood. "I'm not sure what I see anymore, but I know one thing—I can't be a normal wife, and I'm pretty sure I can't have babies. I also know that—"

Daniel stopped her rush of words by placing his finger against her lips. "Please don't say those things. We've talked about this stuff before—all except me wanting to be your business partner more than your marriage partner. I do want to be your business partner; I won't deny that, Rebekah. I've wanted it for a long time, but—"

Rebekah jerked her wheelchair to one side, cutting him off in midsentence. "I've heard enough, so please don't say anything more. It's over between us, and it's best that you go home and forget you ever knew me."

Daniel's face was red as a cherry. "Can't I have my say on this?"

She shook her head vigorously. "There's already been too much said. I should have never let things go this far. My answer to your proposal should have been *no* from the beginning."

Daniel shuffled his feet a few times, then jerked his straw hat off the wall peg and marched out the door.

CHAPTER

23

"Nadine and I have to go into town today. Would you like to go along?" Mom asked Rebekah the following morning as they prepared breakfast. "We're going to eat out afterward, so that might help lift your spirits."

"I don't need anything in town right now, but I would appreciate a ride over to Mary Ellen's," Rebekah answered, making no reference to her spirits. She'd already broken the news to her family about Daniel and her not getting married, and it was bad enough just doing the telling. No use sulking about it or trying to make herself feel better with food from the Plain and Fancy or some other restaurant. Rebekah figured the best thing she could do was go calling on her friend. "Get your eyes off your own problem, and help someone else with theirs"—that's what Grandma Stoltzfus often used to say.

"Taking you by Mary Ellen's won't be a problem because we're only going into Bird-in-Hand today, and it's right on the way," Mom said, cutting into Rebekah's thoughts. "Are you sure you wouldn't rather go with us? You can always visit your cousin some other time."

Rebekah shook her head. "Mary Ellen's not feeling well. I think a visit with her is more important than shopping or going out to lunch."

"What's wrong with Mary Ellen?" Nadine asked when she entered the kitchen.

"She's still having some morning sickness, and Johnny said that her back's hurting, too," Rebekah answered.

Nadine wrinkled her nose. "I think bein' pregnant must be the worst thing any woman could ever go through. I'm not gonna have any children when I get married."

Mom smiled and gave Rebekah a knowing look. "When you do get married, Nadine, children will come in God's time, not yours. And God will give you the strength to get through it, too."

"Jah, well, maybe I won't get married, then." Nadine folded her arms and frowned.

Rebekah smiled, even though her heart ached like crazy over her breakup with Daniel. "You? My boy-crazy little sister, not ever get married? That's about as silly a notion as thinking the robins won't come back in the spring."

"Don't make fun of me," Nadine mumbled. "I don't like to be laughed at."

Rebekah sobered. "I'm sorry, sister. No one likes to be laughed at. I should know that better than anyone."

Nadine moved over to the table where Rebekah sat buttering a stack of toast. "I'd never laugh at you, Rebekah. I admire you too much."

Rebekah looked up at Nadine with tears obscuring her vision. "You do?" Things had been better between her and Nadine of late, but she'd never expected her sister to say something like that.

"Of course. You've done so much with your life. Running a business of your own is something to feel good about."

"Nadine's right," Mom put in from her place at the stove. "If anyone should ever laugh at you, then they truly don't know you at all."

Rebekah's mind pulled her back to that day at the market when the two English boys had taunted her. They'd laughed in her face and made fun of her, not caring in the least how she felt. Those fellows hadn't known her. She hadn't really known herself until she'd begun to search the scriptures for answers and had taken a huge leap of faith by opening the greenhouse.

Rebekah had never mentioned that incident at the market to her folks, nor was she willing to admit to them that breaking her engagement to Daniel had nearly broken her heart. Despite them encouraging her to reconsider, she was convinced that she had made the right decision. With God's help, she hoped to get through this horrible letdown and move on with her life—without Daniel.

She added another piece of toast to the plate she'd already started and said, "We'd better finish getting breakfast ready and call Dad and Simon in to eat. I'm anxious to see Mary Ellen."

"It's sure nice to have you back workin' full-time with the cows," Daniel's father said as the two of them mucked out the horses' stalls. "For a while there, I was afraid I'd lost you to Rebekah's greenhouse since that's where you seemed to be spending all of your free time."

Daniel grimaced. Just the mention of Rebekah's name sent a pang of regret coursing through his body. If only she hadn't broken their engagement. If only she'd let him explain how things were.

"You okay, son? You're lookin' kind of peevish today. Aren't ya feelin' to rights?"

"I'm okay, Pop. Just feelin' a bit down and wishin' some things could be different is all."

Pop stopped scooping and set his shovel aside. "What's the trouble?"

Daniel leaned against the wall with his arms folded and his shovel wedged between his knees. "I can't accept Rebekah's decision not to marry me. We've been so happy together these past few months, and it makes no sense that she would call off the wedding now and wouldn't even let me have my say on things."

Pop scrubbed a hand down the side of his bearded face and squinted. "Maybe it's for the best, Daniel."

"How can you say that?" Daniel felt his defenses rise. Didn't Pop care how much he was hurting? Didn't his daed realize how much he loved Rebekah?

"Think about it, now. Rebekah's pretty much stuck in that wheelchair of hers, and her handicap could make for a difficult marriage."

Daniel shook his head. "No way! I know Rebekah has limitations, but I'm willing to do more than my share of the work in the greenhouse and around our home, too."

"That may be true, but what about kinner? Do you even

know if Rebekah's able to have any bopplin?"

"Well, no, but—"

"And even if she could get pregnant, how would she care for a baby when she can barely take care of herself?"

Daniel stared at the floor as he contemplated his father's words. Maybe Pop was right. Maybe Rebekah couldn't have any kinner, and maybe it would be difficult for both of them if they were to get married. Still, the thought of spending the rest of his days without the woman he loved by his side left Daniel feeling as if life had no meaning at all.

"I don't have any answers, Pop," he finally said, "but I do know that I love Rebekah with all my heart, and if we were to get married, I would do everything in my power to make her happy."

Pop thumped him lightly on the back. "Well then, be a man, boy! If ya love the girl, you'd better go after her."

"It's not that easy," Daniel mumbled. "Rebekah's made up her mind that I only want to marry her so I can get my hands on her business. I don't think I can say anything to make her think otherwise, either."

"Hmm. . .guess you'd best be prayin' about the matter."

"I have been prayin', and I've decided that if God wants Rebekah and me to be together, then He'll have to pave the way." Determined to get his mind off Rebekah and the void she had left in his soul when she'd called off the wedding, Daniel grabbed the shovel from between his knees and resumed his work.

Mary Ellen and Johnny's home was set on the back side of

Uncle Amos and Aunt Mim's property. It had been built by both of their fathers and was a two-story house with white siding and a long porch wrapped halfway around the building. Johnny had hung a two-seater swing under the overhang of the porch, and it was there that Rebekah discovered Mary Ellen. She held a glass of iced tea in one hand and was swinging back and forth, with her head leaning against the wooden slats.

After helping Rebekah down from the buggy and making sure she was secure in her wheelchair, Mom climbed back into the driver's seat. "If you see Mim, tell her I'll be over for a visit one of these days soon," she called before pulling out of the driveway.

"Jah, okay." Rebekah waved and propelled herself up the wheelchair ramp.

Mary Ellen smiled. "What a nice surprise. I'm so glad to see you today."

"Johnny was by the greenhouse yesterday and said you were still feeling poorly. I thought maybe a little visit might do us both some good."

"Johnny and Pappy are out in his shop. Pappy's getting way more work than he can handle these days, and Henry's help just isn't enough." Mary Ellen motioned toward the blacksmith shop on the other side of their property. "So Johnny helps him when he's not busy farming with his daed."

"Ah, I see."

"Would you like me to call Mama Mim and see if she can help you into the swing?"

"That's not necessary." Rebekah eyed Mary Ellen's protruding stomach. "You're getting kind of big around the middle these days. I think maybe you might need the swing all to yourself."

Mary Ellen grimaced. "Do I look that big?"

"Jah, just like one of Dad's draft horses!" Rebekah giggled. "But you're still as pretty as ever. I think being in a family way becomes you. You look almost radiant, in fact."

"My radiance comes from being much too warm, I'm afraid," Mary Ellen said, as she held the glass up to her flushed cheeks. "This late summer weather's sure getting to me, and my back—oh, it hurts something awful!"

"Johnny said you're still fighting the morning sickness, too."

Mary Ellen nodded. "It comes and goes, but when it comes, it can get pretty bad."

"Are you drinking plenty of peppermint tea to help with the nausea?"

In response, Mary Ellen lifted her glass. "Several glasses a day."

"Then all you can do is pray that the sickness goes away soon."

Mary Ellen sighed. "I hope the boppli comes in plenty of time before your wedding. I wouldn't want to miss that big occasion."

Now it was Rebekah's turn to sigh. "There will be no wedding; I called the whole thing off."

"You what?" Mary Ellen's raised eyebrows showed her obvious disbelief, and her mouth hung slightly open.

"I told Daniel we weren't getting married." Rebekah's vision blurred with unshed tears, and she looked away, hoping Mary Ellen wouldn't notice.

"You didn't really say that, did you?"

"Jah, I did. I was beginning to have some doubts as to whether I could be a good wife to Daniel anyway."

"Because of your concerns about whether you can ever conceive?"

Rebekah nodded in reply.

"What does the doctor say?"

"He doesn't really know. He said that in some cases of spinal cord injury, a woman can never conceive, but—well, some have actually been able to get pregnant and carry the baby to term."

"You might be one of those women." Mary Ellen tapped her fingernails against the side of her glass, making a clicking sound. "That's surely no reason for calling off the wedding."

Rebekah's forehead knitted into a frown. "Oh, Mary Ellen, I do so want to be a wife and mother. God's already given me one miracle, so I don't know if I dare ask for yet another."

"Of course you can ask. The Bible tells us in Luke 11:9: 'Ask, and it shall be given you; seek, and ye shall find; knock, and it shall be opened unto you.' Our heavenly Father wants to give us good things."

Rebekah sniffed. "Sometimes I think I'm not deserving of the things God gives to others."

"You are so," Mary Ellen said in an earnest tone. "All God's children are deserving of His love. He doesn't always give us everything we ask for, but He does give us what He knows is best for us."

"My own capabilities aren't the only problem," Rebekah finally admitted.

Mary Ellen tipped her head. "What else is there?"

"It's Daniel."

"Daniel? How could Daniel be the problem? He's so much in love with you that it's downright sickening."

"I thought so, too—until yesterday."

"What happened yesterday?"

Rebekah quickly related her and Daniel's conversation about him wanting to be her business partner and the fact that she was certain it was the only reason he wanted to marry her.

"I hope he set you straight on that one," Mary Ellen said.

"He tried to deny it, but in the process, he admitted to wanting the greenhouse real bad. That fact alone is unsettling to me."

"Sometimes we draw the wrong conclusions because we want to."

"What are you saying? Do you actually think I want to believe such things about Daniel?" Rebekah's voice raised at least an octave, and her cheeks felt flushed.

Mary Ellen shifted on the swing as she held up her hand. "Please, don't get defensive on me. I only meant that since you were already having some doubts about being a wife, maybe Daniel's comment was misunderstood. Maybe you were looking for a way out of what you felt wouldn't work."

"Now, listen, Mary Ellen—"

"Wie geht's, Rebekah?" Aunt Mim asked as she stepped up to the porch.

"I-I'm fine, danki."

"It didn't sound to me as if you were all that fine. You sounded pretty upset about something a moment ago."

"Rebekah thinks Daniel only wants to marry her so he can become her partner at the greenhouse," Mary Ellen was quick to say.

Rebekah nodded. "It's true. He sweet-talked me for months just so he could get his hands on my business."

"Do you have time to hear another one of my little stories?" Aunt Mim asked, squeezing in beside Mary Ellen on the swing. "I think it might give you some insight on a few things concerning you and Daniel."

"I guess so. I'll be here until Mom picks me up later this afternoon." Rebekah moved her wheelchair closer to the swing, ready to hear her aunt's story, although she couldn't imagine what it would have to do with her and Daniel. "By the way, Mom says she'll drop over for a visit sometime soon."

Aunt Mim nodded, then began her story. "A long time ago, when Miriam Hilty was still Miriam Stoltzfus, she thought that a certain Amos Hilty wanted to marry her for reasons other than love."

"Really? I never knew that, Mama Mim," Mary Ellen said with wide eyes. "What other reasons might Pappy have had?"

Aunt Mim patted Mary Ellen's hand. "Well, I thought your daed only wanted a mudder for his little girl." She shrugged. "I figured he probably wanted someone to do all his cooking and cleaning, too. It wasn't until well after our marriage that I finally woke up and realized that Amos cared deeply for me. What he really wanted all along was a companion and helpmate."

Aunt Mim motioned to Rebekah. "I've observed you and Daniel plenty of times, and I daresay he loves you very much. While it might be true that Daniel desires a partnership in your business, I'm convinced that he wants you as his wife even more."

Rebekah nibbled on her bottom lip. "I do appreciate your sharing another story with me. Only thing is, it doesn't change anything where Daniel and I are concerned."

"Why not? It seems a shame for you to give up on love and marriage, dear girl," Aunt Mim said, shaking her head.

"Daniel doesn't love me. He never even said he did, for pity's sake!"

Mary Ellen's eyebrows raised high on her forehead. "You're kidding, right?"

Rebekah shook her head. "Nope, and he only wants my business. I know it, sure as anything—and we're not getting married."

Chapter 24

Rebekah moved restlessly about the kitchen on her crutches. She felt so fretful and fidgety this morning. She stopped pacing a few moments, and when she glanced out the window, she spotted a sparrow eating from one of Daniel's handcrafted feeders. *Oh, Daniel, why'd you have to go and break my heart? Didn't you know how much I loved you? I was so hoping things would work out between us.*

It had been two weeks since their breakup, and the pain was no less hurtful now than it had been on that terrible day when she'd discovered that her intended had only been using her to acquire a business selling flowers. Seeing Daniel at the preaching service last week hadn't helped any, either.

Rebekah thought, maybe even hoped, that he might try to win her back. She squinted and then blinked a couple of times so the tears wouldn't give way. *Not that I'd ever consider taking him back.* No, she was through with men and all their sweet-talking, conniving ways. God had given her a business to run, and this summer it had done real well for her. If things kept going as they had been, she would be self-supporting in no time. That was the miracle she had been waiting for, wasn't it?

She trembled slightly as she thought about Daniel sitting across the room from her during church. He hadn't even looked her way, let alone said anything to her after the noon meal. It just proved what she had known as a fact—Daniel didn't love her now, and he never had.

Rebekah leaned her full weight against the windowsill. "God takes care of the little bitty birds, so He will most assuredly take care of you"—Grandma's words tumbled around in her mind like the clothes in Mom's old wringer washer on laundry day.

"I think what I need is a breath of fresh air," Rebekah said aloud, though no one was in the kitchen to hear but her. Mom had gone outside to hang some freshly laundered clothes, Nadine was in the barn playing with a batch of new kittens, and the menfolk were out working in the fields.

Rebekah thought about casting off her leg braces and taking the wheelchair outside, but it was such a job to get them unhooked. Besides, as Mom always said, "The exercise will do your whole body some good."

With the crutches fastened securely to her arms by leather straps, Rebekah grabbed a light shawl from a wall peg and headed out the back door.

Mom seemed to be struggling with a sheet the wind had caught in the clothesline, and she didn't notice when Rebekah plodded past her and down the path toward the creek.

A definite nip was in the air this morning, and Rebekah knew fall would be coming soon. Autumn. The time for most Amish weddings here in Lancaster County. Her own wedding was supposed to be in November. If only. . .

She shoved the familiar ache aside once again and attempted to pick up her speed just a bit. Walking stiff-legged was such a chore, and she was beginning to wonder if she had made a mistake by leaving the wheelchair parked in the kitchen. Already she was huffing and puffing, and she was only halfway there. At this rate, how was she ever going to make it all the way to the creek?

" 'I can do all things through Christ which strengtheneth me,' " she quoted from the scriptures. If she could just go another fifty yards or so, she would be at the water's edge and could hopefully find a log or something to sit on. Trips to the creek in the past had always been made in her wheelchair, which meant finding a place to sit and rest had never been a problem.

Rebekah lifted one foot, then the other, guiding herself along with the aid of her metal crutches. She could hear the water gurgling over the rocky creek bottom. The melodic sound soothed her nerves and gave her the added incentive to keep walking.

Soon, the rushing water came into view, meandering gracefully through a cluster of red maple and white birch trees. Rebekah scanned the banks, looking for something to use as a bench. She felt a spasm in her back, and the muscles in her arms had become tight. Even her legs, which normally had little feeling in them, felt kind of tingly and prickly-like.

With great relief, she spotted a fallen tree, its branches stretched partway across the water and the trunk lying on dry land. A few more determined steps, and she was there. Drawing in a deep breath for added strength, Rebekah lowered herself to the stump. The bumpy surface offered little comfort for her backside, but at least she was sitting and could finally catch her breath. Even her hands trembled, she noticed.

The trek from the house had nearly been too much. Oh, how she wished she had told someone where she was going. What if she couldn't make it back to the house on her own strength? The way she felt right now, she wasn't sure she could even stand up again.

"What a dunce I was for thinking I could be so independent and go traipsing on down here without my wheelchair," Rebekah chided herself. "It was just plain *kischblich* of me. I should know better than to be so silly." She wrapped her shawl tighter around her shoulders and shivered—not so much from the chilly morning, but from all her energy being used up.

The rustle of fallen leaves caught Rebekah's attention. She glanced to the right and saw Brownie, their mixed-breed farm dog, running for all he was worth. Out in front of him was something fuzzy and small. A white ball of fur, that's what it looked like.

Rebekah squinted, trying to get a better look. What in the world? Brownie was chasing one of those new baby kittens! Along the bank of the creek, the poor critter ran, with the old dog right on its tail.

"Run, kitty, run! Go quickly!" Rebekah cried. She knew the kitten couldn't understand what she was saying, so she turned her attention toward Brownie. "Bad dog! You come here and leave that poor cat alone!"

Brownie cocked his head as though he might actually be listening, but then he forged right ahead and kept on with the chase.

"Dumb dog," Rebekah mumbled. "You never did know when to hearken." She watched helplessly as the exhausted kitten began to lose ground. Brownie was about ready to pounce when the unthinkable happened.

Plop! Right into the cold water the poor kitty sailed. Rebekah gasped, and Brownie, apparently surprised, slammed on his brakes and nearly ran straight into a tree.

Rebekah stared in horror as the white ball of fur turned into a soggy little mass that resembled something akin to a roll of cotton when it had been drenched in alcohol. Tiny paws began to flail helplessly about, making trivial headway through the swirling waters holding it in its grip.

"It's not strong enough to swim yet," Rebekah moaned. "The poor little critter will drown sure as anything." She couldn't just sit there and watch it happen. She had to do something to save the kitten's life.

Rebekah grasped the crutches tightly and pulled herself up with a grunt. "Hang on, little one. I'm coming!"

Down the creek bank she went, inch-by-inch, step-by-step. At the water's edge, she let go of one crutch. Since it was strapped to her arm, it dangled precariously as she attempted to lean across the current in hopes of rescuing the perishing cat.

Brownie was at her heels now, swishing his tail from side to side and barking like crazy. It only seemed to frighten the pathetic little fur ball that much more. With eyes open wide and claws splashing against the water, it was swept farther downstream. Rebekah saw the poor critter take in a mouthful of water. Then down it went.

In a state of near panic, she took a few more steps. The creek water rose over the top of her sneakers. No doubt it was stinging cold, but her unfeeling legs knew no pain. Further into the creek she trudged, lifting first one foot, then the other. The swift-moving current made it more difficult to navigate, and soon she felt winded and emotionally spent.

"Help me, Lord," she prayed. "Allow me to reach the kitten in time." A few more steps, and she was almost there. A slight bend at the waist, a hand extended, and then. . . *splash!*

Facedown in the chilling water, Rebekah landed. She gurgled and gasped as her nose and mouth filled with unwanted fluid. She thrashed about with her arms and nearly smacked the side of her head with one of the crutches. All thoughts of the stranded kitten vanished from her mind. All she wanted to do was save herself. The more she flailed against the creek's rapid flow, the deeper her body seemed to be sucked under.

Rebekah had never learned how to swim, and even if she had, her crippled legs would have been useless. If her arms had been stronger, maybe she could have paddled her way to the grassy banks. But no, she had used all her strength just getting down to this silly creek. The panic she felt rising in her throat kept all clearheaded thinking away. She couldn't pray, she couldn't swim, and she couldn't think of any way to get back on her feet.

As Daniel cut through the fields bordering the Stoltzfus place, he wondered if it was such a good idea for him to try and see Rebekah today. His father had told him to be a man and go after her, but he didn't think he could deal with it if she rejected him again. Still, he had to at least try.

Normally Daniel drove his horse and buggy whenever he went to the greenhouse, but he'd decided that a good long walk might be what he needed, so he had headed out from his place on foot, walked up the road a ways, and then taken a shortcut through the cornfields near the Stoltzfus property.

"Sure hope Rebekah's willing to listen to what I have to say this time," he mumbled. "I need to make her understand the way things are and how I feel about her."

Daniel pulled an ear of corn from one of the drying stalks and peeled it back. The kernels were hard and dried up, just like his heart would be if he had to spend the rest of his days on earth without Rebekah.

He took a few more steps and halted when he heard a muffled scream. He tipped his head and listened. There it was again—a little louder this time. He dropped the corn and sprinted across the field toward the sound.

A few minutes later, the creek bordering the Stoltzfus property came into view.

"Help! Somebody, help me, please!"

Daniel's heart leapt in his chest when he saw Rebekah lying in the water, her arms splashing like crazy, and her head bobbing up and down as she gasped for air.

With only one thought on his mind, he sprinted down the slippery bank and dashed into the water. "Rebekah, I'm coming!" he hollered. "Here now, grab my hand!"

Rebekah turned her head to the right, taking in another murky mouthful of water in the process. She blinked rapidly, trying to clear her vision. Was she dreaming? Was there someone standing over her? No, it couldn't possibly be.

She opened her mouth to cry out, but nothing more than a pitiful squeak came from her cold lips.

"Rebekah, listen to me now," the deep voice said sternly. "Quit your floundering and take hold of my hand." Daniel's concerned-looking face was mere inches from hers, and she knew for certain that it wasn't an apparition after all.

She lifted one arm, but the weight of the crutch seemed to be working against her. Daniel's firm hand grasped hers, pulling with all the strength of an able-bodied man. Still, she couldn't seem to right herself, and instead of coming to her feet as she had hoped she would, Rebekah fell backwards, dragging Daniel into the water with her.

He came up spitting and sputtering, with a look of sheer bewilderment spread over his dripping wet face.

"Well, Rebekah Stoltzfus," he said, shaking his head and sending rivulets of water flying everywhere, "you had better have a mighty good reason for this."

Daniel swept Rebekah into his arms and carried her over his shoulder as if she were a sack of grain. He plodded through the murky, swirling waters until he reached dry land. Then he placed her in a sitting position on the grassy bank and dropped down beside her. "Are you okay, Rebekah? What were you doin' in that creek? How come you're all alone and without the wheelchair?" The questions seemed to pour out of him until Rebekah finally interrupted with a raised hand.

"Don't you think you should ask only one question at a time?" She coughed a few times and reached up to pull her soggy head-covering off. Her damp hair came loose from its usual bun, and long, thoroughly saturated hair tumbled down around her shoulders.

Daniel lifted his hand to her cheek and swiped at a splotch of mud. "You look like a drowned pup, you know that?"

Rebekah sniffed deeply and glared at him. "Jah, well, you don't look so good yourself."

Daniel's lips twitched. Then he burst into laughter. "No, I don't guess I do!" His face sobered after the laughter subsided. "So are you gonna tell me why you're down here all alone, and how you ended up in that water or not?"

"I w-went for a walk," she replied, her lips trembling like a leaf caught in the wind. Her whole body had begun to shake, and she wrapped her arms around her middle, trying to warm herself. "I was sitting on a fallen tree when I noticed our dog chasing one of Gretta's new kittens." She paused for a breath. "The helpless little critter couldn't outrun the mutt, so the poor thing ended up falling into the creek."

Rebekah and Daniel both turned their heads toward the swiftly moving water. "I–I can't believe it!" Rebekah pointed across the creek bank. On the other side, sitting in a patch of grass, was one waterlogged kitten, licking its tiny paws as if it didn't have a care in the world. The yapping dog that had caused all the trouble was nowhere to be found.

"Can you believe that?" Rebekah groaned. "I nearly drowned myself to save that silly creature, and there it is just fine and dandy."

"I'm so glad you didn't drown. I don't think I could stand it if something bad happened to you."

Rebekah jerked her head toward Daniel. "What are you doing here, anyway, and how'd you know I was in trouble?"

"I was out for a walk, and I heard a scream. When I ran through the fields and saw you splashing around in the creek, I thought my heart was gonna stop beating." Daniel grinned, looking kind of self-conscious. "To tell you the truth, I was on my way to the greenhouse to see you."

·She blinked several times, as she stared at him. "You– you were?"

He nodded. "I thought it was time we got things aired out between us. I. . .well, I've been actin' like a mad dog these last few weeks, and I'm sorry to say that a bit of hochmut got in my way or I would have come to see you sooner." He paused a few minutes, searching for the right words. "I just can't stand the idea of facing another tussle with you, Rebekah, so I hope you'll hear me out this time."

Rebekah dropped her gaze to the ground. "You hurt me bad, Daniel. I thought you cared for me, but then–"

"I'm sorry for hurting you and for letting you think things that weren't true." He lifted her chin so she was forced to look directly into his eyes. "I love you, Rebekah

Stoltzfus. I will always love you, now and forever."

Stinging tears flooded Rebekah's eyes, and she gulped back a sob. "Oh, Daniel, you've never said that to me before."

"Never said what? That I'm sorry?"

"No. That you loved me."

"I—I haven't?"

She shook her head.

He hung his head sheepishly. "I'm sorry about that. Guess I was a dumb old *kuh.*"

"You're not an old cow, Daniel. You just don't always know the right words to say."

"Jah, well, I kind of figured you knew how I felt."

"I—I didn't."

"Well, you do now I hope."

"Jah."

He took hold of her hand. "So is everything okay between us again?"

She shrugged. "But what about being partners? You did say you couldn't wait until you could help run the greenhouse, and—"

Daniel stopped her flow of words by planting a surprisingly warm kiss on her mouth, despite their encounter with the chilly creek water. When he released her, Rebekah felt as though she could barely catch her breath. Daniel had kissed her before, but never like that!

"If you would have just listened to me that day at the greenhouse instead of jumpin' to conclusions about my feelings and all, I would have told you that even though I wanted to run a greenhouse, that was never the reason for me wanting to marry you."

"It wasn't? But I thought—"

"I know what you thought. You thought I was just using you so I could get my hands on that business of yours, am I right?"

She nodded. "That is what I believed."

"Well, it just isn't so, Rebekah. I've been in love with you ever so long. Way back when we first started going to singings, and you would sit there in your wheelchair, so sweet and sincere." He touched his chest. "I felt a stirring deep in my heart. Why, it was all I could do to keep from rushing right up to you and declaring my love."

Rebekah stifled a giggle. She could hardly imagine Daniel announcing his love that way; he had seemed so shy back then.

Daniel pulled her into his arms and held her real close, as though his life depended on it. "Please say you believe me, Rebekah. I want you to be my wife, honest I do. It truly isn't for the business, neither." He patted her gently on the back. "If it will help anything, I'll even agree to let you run the greenhouse by yourself. I won't be co-owner of Grandma's Place at all. I'll just keep on workin' at the dairy farm with my daed and brothers. Jah, that's what I'll do."

Rebekah swallowed hard and nearly choked on a sob. "Oh, sweet Daniel, I couldn't ask you to do that. I know how much you love flowers. Your love for cows in no way compares to that."

"That's right, but my love for flowers is nothin' compared to what I feel for you. So don't send me away again, for I just couldn't bear it. Will you marry me, Rebekah, and love me forever?"

Daniel's eyes glistened with unshed tears, and it tore at Rebekah's tender heart to see him show his emotions like that. She stroked his clean-shaven face and sighed. "Oh, Daniel, I do love you so much. I'm sorry for doubting your intentions and not giving you the chance to explain."

"Does that mean you're willing to become my wife?"

She nodded. "I'd be honored."

CHAPTER
25

Rebekah was awakened by the sound of someone knocking on her bedroom door. "Who is it?" she called groggily into her pillow.

Mom opened the door a crack and poked her head inside. "You're still in bed? Such a sleepyhead. I thought you'd be up with the chickens on your wedding day."

Rebekah yawned and grabbed the sides of the bed in order to pull herself into a sitting position. "I was having such a nice dream, I guess I must have not wanted to wake up."

"That's good," Mom said with a smile. "All brides should have pleasant dreams." She entered the room and poured fresh water into the basin on Rebekah's dresser. "It's time to rise and shine, though. Breakfast is waiting, and it won't be long before the first of our guests begin to arrive."

"But Mary Ellen probably won't be one of them."

"Now you don't know that." Mom handed Rebekah a damp washcloth. "Mary Ellen still hasn't gone into labor, so why wouldn't she be here for your special day?"

Rebekah shrugged. "She might not feel up to coming. I can't speak firsthand, of course, but I hear that women are pretty miserable when they're this close to delivering."

Mom nodded. "That's true enough. At least it was for me. However, some women carry on as usual, right up to the beginning of their labor."

"Then I guess I can only hope Mary Ellen's one of them who can carry on as usual, because I'll be mighty disappointed if she isn't here today."

"Good morning, wife," Johnny said, as he stepped into the kitchen.

Mary Ellen had been standing at the counter, cracking eggs into a bowl, and she turned around to face him, forcing a smile. "Morning, husband."

"Did you sleep all right last night?" he asked, moving over to stand beside her.

"Oh, so-so."

"You were actin' kind of restless for a while there, shifting back and forth from one side to the other and scrunching up your pillow like you couldn't find a comfortable position."

Mary Ellen gave her protruding stomach a little thump and smiled. "You try carrying this weight around for a while and see how comfortable you are."

Johnny chuckled and leaned down to kiss her on the cheek. "Did you finally get some good sleep then?"

Her only reply was a brief shrug.

"Are you feelin' okay? You're lookin' kind of done in this morning." He tipped his head and stared at her with a look of obvious concern. "Maybe you ought to stay home from the wedding and rest all day."

She shook her head. "I'm fine, and I won't miss Rebekah's wedding."

"I'm sure she would understand."

"Well, I wouldn't. Rebekah was there for our wedding, and I'm going to be there for hers."

He gave her shoulder a gentle squeeze. "All right then, if you're sure you're up to going."

"I'll be okay. Just feeling a bit tired, is all." The truth was Mary Ellen had been having a few pangs through her middle ever since she'd gotten out of bed, but she was certain they were nothing to be concerned about. Probably just a little indigestion. Jah, that's all they were. She'd feel right as rain once they got to the wedding and she saw how pretty and happy Rebekah was on her special day.

Rebekah sat straight and tall on a wooden bench directly across from her groom. She had chosen to wear her leg braces today so she could stand for her wedding vows, rather than sit in the confining wheelchair. She wore traditional Amish bridal clothes—a plain blue cotton dress draped with a white cape and matching apron, and a white kapp on her head. Daniel was dressed in a white shirt, black trousers, black jacket, and a matching vest.

Rebekah glanced over her shoulder and smiled at Mary Ellen, who sat two rows behind. She knew from the expression on her friend's face that she was probably not feeling her best, but she cared enough to be here, and that meant a lot.

At eighty thirty sharp, the service began with singing from the *Ausbund*. A lengthy sermon from Bishop Benner followed, covering all aspects of the Christian marriage. Then he read several scripture passages, including one from Colossians that said, " 'And whatsoever ye do in word or deed, do all in the name of the Lord Jesus, giving thanks to God and the Father by him.' "

In a booming voice and with a most serious expression, he quoted from yet another passage. " 'Wives, submit yourselves unto your own husbands, as it is fit in the Lord. Husbands, love your wives, and be not bitter against them.' "

Rebekah looked at Daniel and smiled, feeling kind of shy all of a sudden. He nodded and graced her with a heart-melting smile of his own. His serious brown eyes, filled with obvious adoration, told her all she needed to know. He loved her with all his heart, and if her disability didn't matter to him, then she wouldn't worry about it, either. Her life was in God's hands, and He would see that her needs were met. She would just keep trusting Him.

When the Bible reading was done, two of the ministers spoke awhile. Rebekah fidgeted nervously, wondering if they would ever finish. Finally, Daniel and Rebekah were ushered into Grandma Stoltzfus's old room for counseling from the bishop. Rebekah's attendants, Nadine and Sarah Jane, Daniel's sister, waited in the other room with the guests, along with Daniel's two brothers, Harold and Abner, who were his attendants.

The counseling session consisted of several more scripture references and a long dissertation from Bishop Benner on the importance of good communication, trust, and respect in all areas of marriage. He reminded the couple that divorce was not an acceptable option among those of their faith, and he emphasized the need to always work through their problems.

When they finally emerged from the bedroom, Rebekah released an audible sigh. Even though she had been allowed to sit during the counseling session, she felt all done in and a bit shaky.

Returning to the main room, Rebekah and Daniel sat on their original benches while the bishop gave a rather lengthy prayer. At long last, he motioned them to step forward and stand in front of him.

Rebekah's heart pounded like one of Dad's hammers when he'd worked on the new barn. It seemed as if this had been the moment she'd been waiting for her whole life. She was about to repeat her wedding vows before family and friends, and most importantly, before her heavenly Father.

Daniel gave a reassuring smile, and she steadied herself with the crutches strapped to her arms, waiting for Bishop Benner to begin.

Finally the bishop turned to Daniel and asked, "Can you confess, brother, that you accept this, our sister, as your wife, and that you will not leave her until death separates you?"

Without any hesitation, Daniel answered in a clear voice. "Jah, I do."

"And do you believe that this is from the Lord and that you have come thus far by your faith and prayers?"

"Jah."

Then it was Rebekah's turn. Her quiet voice quavered as she answered each of the bishop's questions, taking the meaning fully to heart.

A rustling noise on the women's side of the room drew Rebekah's attention. Out of the corner of her eye, she caught sight of Mary Ellen leaving the room, assisted by Aunt Mim and Aunt Crystal. *Maybe she's tired from sitting so long,* Rebekah reasoned. *Or could be it's too warm in here. There are nearly two hundred people crammed into our house today. Maybe this is a bad sign. Maybe. . .*

"Because you have confessed, brother, that you want to take this our sister for your wife, do you promise to be loyal to her and care for her if she may have adversity, infirmities that are among poor mankind—as is appropriate for a Christian, God-fearing husband?"

Rebekah jerked her thoughts back to the present as Daniel answered affirmatively to Bishop Benner's last question. Then, when the elderly bishop asked the same question of Rebekah, she answered, "Jah."

Placing Rebekah's hand in Daniel's, the bishop pronounced the blessing. "The God of Abraham, Isaac, and of Jacob be with you both and give you His rich blessings for a good beginning, a steadfast middle, and may you hold out until a blessed end. In the name of Jesus Christ. Amen."

Rebekah and Daniel returned to their respective benches as husband and wife.

As soon as the closing prayer was said, everyone who wasn't helping with the cooking or serving went outside to wait for the wedding meal. Tables were quickly set up in the living room and adjoining room, and the benches that had been used during the ceremony were placed at the tables.

"We need to take our place at the eck soon," Daniel whispered to Rebekah.

She nodded. "I know, but I want to check on Mary Ellen first. She left the room during our vows, and I think something might be amiss."

"All right then. We'll meet at the corner table as soon as you come back." Daniel gave Rebekah's arm a gentle squeeze, and she hobbled out to the kitchen. She found Mom and several other women there, scurrying about to get all the food dished up.

"Frieda, do you think these children of ours can keep house?" Mom asked Rebekah's new mother-in-law.

"Well, if you raised Rebekah as well as I raised Daniel, I believe it will go," Frieda replied with a laugh.

"Do you know where Mary Ellen is?" Rebekah asked Mom, as she stepped between the two women. "She left during the ceremony, and I'm a bit worried."

"Mary Ellen's water broke," Mom explained. "I hear tell she's been in labor for several hours already. They've taken her upstairs because there's no time to get to the hospital now."

Rebekah's mouth dropped open. "Why did she come to the wedding, then? She should have insisted that Johnny take her to the hospital right away when her labor first started."

"Mim said Mary Ellen didn't want to miss your wedding. She thought, this being her first baby and all, that the labor would be a long one."

Tears welled in Rebekah's eyes, and she blinked a couple of times. "Oh, Mom, if anything happens to Mary Ellen or the baby, I'll never forgive myself."

Mom draped an arm around Rebekah's shoulders and led her to a chair at the kitchen table. "Don't go talking such foolishness, now. You can't take the blame for something like this. Mary Ellen had a choice to make. You didn't force her to come to the wedding today."

"I know, but she knew how much I wanted her to be here," Rebekah argued. "If only she would have had that boppli on schedule. She's over two weeks late, and—"

"Hush, now," Mom said, interrupting Rebekah's rush of words by placing a finger against her lips. "Nothing we say or do will change the fact that the baby was late or that Mary Ellen's here now. The best thing would be to carry on with the wedding meal so our guests don't go hungry. Women have been having babies for thousands of years, and we just need to pray that everything will be all right in the birthing room upstairs." Mom nodded toward the steps. "I'm sure Mim and Crystal are capable of helping with the delivery, but Johnny's ridden into town to get Doc Manney, in case any problems should occur."

Rebekah's hand trembled as she wiped a stray hair from her face. She bowed her head and silently petitioned the Lord for both Mary Ellen and the baby.

The wedding meal consisted of roasted chicken, mashed potatoes, bread filling, creamed celery, coleslaw, applesauce, fruit salad, bread, butter, jelly, and coffee.

Rebekah sat at the corner table with Daniel while they ate and visited with their guests, but she kept thinking about the new life that was about to be brought into the world. This was Daniel's and her special day. She should be laughing and enjoying all the jokes and stories people were telling.

She ought to be savoring the delicious foods and the love she could feel radiating from her new groom. Instead, she worried and prayed, until Mom finally came into the room and announced, "Mary Ellen's just given birth to a baby girl. Dr. Manney is with her right now, and the report is that both mother and daughter are doing well."

A cheer went up around the room, and Rebekah choked back a sob. With tears in her eyes, she turned to Daniel. "Would you mind if I slipped out for a moment so I can see the new boppli and her mamm?"

Daniel shook his head. "Of course not. You need to find out all the details so you can include them in your next *Budget* column." He squeezed her hand. "Would you like me to come along? Someone will have to carry you up the stairs."

"Why don't you stay and enjoy our guests? I'll ask Dad to take me up."

Daniel smiled and shrugged. "Okay then, do as you like."

With the aid of her crutches, Rebekah made her way out of the crowded room. Soon Dad carried her upstairs, and she found Mary Ellen lying on the bed in Nadine's room. In her arms, she cradled a small bundle of pure, sweet baby.

Mary Ellen's cheeks were flushed, and her voice filled with emotion as she whispered, "I'm sorry I missed the end of your wedding."

Rebekah hobbled over to the bed, then leaned over to give her friend a kiss on the forehead. "You had a pretty good excuse, I'm thinking."

"Why don't you say hello to your cousin Martha Rose?" Mary Ellen murmured.

Rebekah's eyes clouded with tears, and she stroked the baby's downy head. "It's soft as a kitten's nose." A small sigh escaped her lips, as she blinked back tears. "Today's been such a perfect day. I'm married to a wunderbaar man, and now I'm looking on a true miracle from God."

"Jah," Mary Ellen agreed. "God has surely blessed us with this sweet baby girl."

Rebekah nodded. "God is truly the God of miracles."

Epilogue

Rebekah closed the drawer of the cash register as an English man and his two small children left the greenhouse, carrying a pot of petunias. It had been a good year for her and Daniel's business and for them as a married couple, as well.

Their home, built by Rebekah's and Daniel's fathers, was connected to her parents' house. It gave them a place of their own, yet they were near enough to family to have help available should it be needed.

Rebekah smiled to herself. She and Daniel had been married a little over a year now, and their love seemed to grow stronger with each passing day.

Daniel no longer helped his father in the dairy business. He was too busy helping out at the greenhouse or building wooden gadgets to sell. He had added weather vanes, wind chimes, and lawn furniture to the other items he sold in the store. Rebekah had also begun selling wicker baskets and plant stands for her flowers and plants.

In the summertime, they sold bottles of Dad's quick homemade root beer and some of the tasty shoofly pies

Mom often baked. In the wintertime, they offered coffee and hot chocolate and several kinds of cookies.

They were making enough money to live comfortably. Their meat and milk were supplied by Daniel's father in exchange for fresh vegetables from the garden Daniel tended in the summer months. Mom saw that they had plenty of fresh eggs and chicken meat whenever they needed it, too. Setting her pride aside, Rebekah had learned to accept help from all available sources. She'd proven to herself that she could be financially self-sufficient, but it was no longer so important. What truly mattered was the love of family and friends, and especially, God's love.

Rebekah was jolted by the shrill sound of a baby crying. She left the cash register and wheeled quickly into the back room. Next to Rebekah's cot sat a wooden cradle, hand-made with love by the little one's father.

Reaching into the cradle, Rebekah picked up her month-old baby daughter. "Little Anna, are you hungry?" she crooned. The baby nestled against her mamm's breast and began to nurse hungrily. "If your namesake, Grandma Anna Stoltzfus, could only have seen you," Rebekah whispered, "I'm sure she would have loved you as much as we all do." She stroked the soft, downy hair on top of her baby's small head and closed her eyes.

"She's sure a miracle, sent straight from God, jah?"

Rebekah's eyes flew open, and she stared up at her tall, bearded husband. Blinking away the tears of joy that had crept into her eyes, she said, "She certainly is. I never dreamed God would be so good as to give us a child of our own. Someday I hope little Anna and her cousin Martha

Rose will have a special friendship like Mary Ellen and I have had for so many years."

Daniel bent down and touched his warm lips to Rebekah's mouth, causing little shivers to spiral up her arms. She never got tired of his kisses, nor of the look of love that so often crossed his face.

"Your faith has become strong, and God has given our girl a blessed gift having you as a mudder." Daniel kissed Rebekah again. "I thank God for baby Anna and for the love we share."

Rebekah wiped more tears from her eyes and murmured, "I thank God for all of His miracles."

Recipe for Andrew's Quick Homemade Root Beer

Ingredients:
2 cups white sugar
1 gal. lukewarm water
3 tsp. root beer extract
1 tsp. dry yeast

Mix all ingredients well and pour into jars. Cover and set in the sun for 4 hours. Chill before serving the next day.